of them you'd like to see win. Richly drawn characters, a crackerjack plot, and a setting that is equal parts glamorous and deadly make *The Last Twelve Miles* a must-read for 2024."

—Deborah Goodrich Royce, national
bestselling author of *Reef Road*

"*The Last Twelve Miles* is the thrilling story of two extraordinary women on opposite sides of the law but with more in common than they think. Based on a true story, Elizebeth, a meticulous government codebreaker, hunts down Marie, the flamboyant rumrunner who makes and loses fortunes on the waters off the Florida Keys during Prohibition. Both the G-woman and the mobster are also wives and mothers struggling to thrive in men's domains. A breezy and brutal glimpse into the world of Jazz Age gangsters from a fresh angle. Really enjoyable!"

—Anika Scott, international bestselling
author of *Sinners of Starlight City*

PRAISE FOR ERIKA ROBUCK

"What a fun and riveting ride! Erika Robuck has unearthed two real-life Prohibition-Era heroines—one a savvy rumrunner, the other an ambitious codebreaker—and vividly recreated their adventures, including a tension-packed cat-and-mouse game that threatens to destroy them both. *The Last Twelve Miles* so immersed me in the wild and raucous world of the Roaring Twenties that I never wanted it to end—even as I furiously turned the pages to see what would happen next."

—Karen Abbott, *New York Times* bestselling author of *The Ghosts of Eden Park*

"*The Last Twelve Miles* is a richly detailed portrait of two compelling women on opposite sides of the law. Set against the backdrop of the Prohibition Rum Wars, Robuck has brought two real-life figures to the page with heartfelt intimacy and crackling suspense. A fascinating read!"

—Chanel Cleeton, *New York Times* and *USA Today* bestselling author of *The Cuban Heiress*

"Action heroes have nothing on real life cryptologist Elizebeth Smith Friedman. *The Last Twelve Miles* is a nonstop historical thriller that poises two brilliant women against each other in a deadly game of rumrunning, codebreaking, and murder. Erika Robuck brings this real American hero and real criminal mastermind to vivid life. Knock back a shot and prepare to have this novel knock your socks off. Dazzling!"

—Pamela Klinger-Horn, event coordinator,
Valley Bookseller

"In this gripping and devilishly exciting Prohibition-Era novel, *The Last Twelve Miles* effortlessly tells the story of two real and brilliant women, one running illegal booze between Miami, the Bahamas, and Cuba, and the other, a master codebreaker, hot on her trail. Robuck's meticulous research and impeccable characterization shine through in this fierce, feminist, and unforgettable novel."

—Nicola Harrison, author of *Hotel Laguna*

"Two women, a coast guard special agent and a bootlegger, face off against each other in this Prohibition-Era novel. Their journeys of marriage, motherhood, and career intertwine in this fascinating story based on true events."

—Rae Ann Parker, bookseller at Parnassus Books

"Move over Al Capone and Eliot Ness! It's time to make space for Elizebeth Friedman and Marie Waite—a captivating pair of badass women on opposite sides of prohibition law. In her terrific new historical fiction, *The Last Twelve Miles*, Erika Robuck brings you Elizebeth, the brilliant cryptanalyst who breaks code for the U.S. Coast Guard, and Marie, the equally brilliant rumrunner who plies the waters off the coast of Florida. Never has there been a more fascinating set of rivals, and you will find yourself torn over which

HISTORICAL FICTION
BY ERIKA ROBUCK

Receive Me Falling

Hemingway's Girl

Call Me Zelda

Fallen Beauty

The House of Hawthorne

The Invisible Woman

Sisters of Night and Fog

THE LAST TWELVE MILES

A NOVEL

ERIKA ROBUCK

Copyright © 2024 by Erika Robuck
Cover and internal design © 2024 by Sourcebooks
Cover design by Chelsea McGuckin
Cover photographs © Laura Ranftler/Arcangel (fence, woman), Maryanne
Gobble/Stocksy (beach), andreev-studio.ru/Shutterstock (palm fronds)

Sourcebooks and the colophon are registered trademarks of Sourcebooks.

Published by Sourcebooks Landmark, an imprint of Sourcebooks
P.O. Box 4410, Naperville, Illinois 60567-4410
(630) 961-3900
sourcebooks.com

Cataloging-in-Publication Data is on file with the Library of Congress.

Printed and bound in the United States of America.
MA 10 9 8 7 6 5 4 3 2 1

For Robert Shephard, my father, the absolute best.

"If I may capture a goodly number of your messages, even though I have never seen your codebook, I may read your thoughts."

—Elizebeth Smith Friedman, cryptanalyst

Dear Reader,

*While on book tours for my novels featuring the true stories of women in intelligence and resistance in World War II—*The Invisible Woman *and* Sisters of Night and Fog—*three separate people at three separate places told me I had to write a novel about American codebreaker Elizebeth Smith Friedman. I take those kinds of signs seriously.*

Through research, I soon became enthralled with the stories of Elizebeth and her husband, William, whose careers spanned both world wars and beyond and helped lay a foundation for modern intelligence, particularly in the fields of cryptanalysis and signals intelligence (SIGINT). However, I wanted an emotional break from writing about WWII, and I needed a little fun. So, it was Elizebeth and her role in Prohibition, fighting the Rum War, that began to consume me, especially in some of the settings that have captured my imagination in the past, like Key West.

I started following leads and connecting dots to read about the rumrunners Elizebeth helped capture but none of the "bad guys" fascinated me. I sat up in my chair when I read about a female Axis spy Elizebeth helped snag during WWII, but I didn't want to write about that time. I began to search for a female rumrunner—a woman of wits and daring, and maybe even a sociopath, for extra flair.

Reader, I found her.

After the joy of discovering my antagonist came another struggle. Though I am not a biographer, I try to be as faithful to history as possible, but because of the nature of the work of both women, the rumrunner, wisely, did not leave much of a paper trail, and not only are there some of Elizebeth's files that will never be declassified, but there also are conflicting timelines in limited sources for both women. Rumors about the rumrunner range from small squabbles over whether her eyes are brown or blue to large differences in parental ancestry—from France, to Belgium, to Spain. The only thing one can be sure about is she enjoyed the speculation and attention. I do not typically enjoy working from speculation, but in spite of my frustration, I knew I had to start writing.

The words came fast. I began to feel the women urging me to have fun, to remember I write historical fiction. Elizebeth had majored in English, loved Shakespeare, and always wanted to write a book. The rumrunner loved notoriety, performance, and theater. I felt the permission from each woman to use what I knew and to run with what I didn't. So that's what I did.

One note for cryptanalysts or aficionados of the science: I often use the term codebreaking *to cover all manner of decipherment, decoding, and associated problem-solving. I realize this is not always technically correct, but I chose to do so not only because my intellect does not allow me to grasp the intricacies of the nuances of cryptanalysis, but also for simplicity of language and story.*

When you finish reading, I hope you'll do your own research to decide if you agree with the ways I found to fill in the missing spaces of plot and character for these women. If I misread the feeling of their blessings, I apologize. Either way, I thank these two forces of nature for the use of their good names in real and possibly fictional ways to tell this story of desire, envy, the need for control, and the incredible strength and power of women that, when misused, can cause a fair amount of chaos.

Cheers,

Erika Robuck

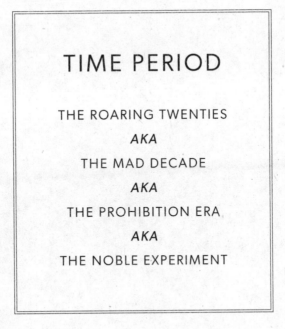

TIME PERIOD

THE ROARING TWENTIES

AKA

THE MAD DECADE

AKA

THE PROHIBITION ERA

AKA

THE NOBLE EXPERIMENT

ONE

MARQUESAS KEYS

Elizebeth

No matter how many jokes Elizebeth cracks, she can't make the coastguardsmen on patrol relax. Especially now that they've got the suspect's three-masted schooner in their sights.

"Special Agent Friedman, I beg you to go belowdecks," says Commander Jack Wilson. "This could get dangerous."

Jack is a gentle giant of a man, who's probably not much older than Elizebeth's thirty-four years but weathered far beyond. They're both a decade older than any of the crew onboard this brand-new seventy-five-foot patrol boat—*CG-249*—and Elizebeth is the only female in sight, a reality that she lives daily in her profession. Jack has been fretting all morning about the fact that he's responsible for her safety, especially since their first stop involved the empty, blood-splattered boat they found adrift and are now towing.

Jack would have a stroke if he knew it wasn't only me that he had to worry about, she thinks, touching her stomach.

"If anything happens," she says, "I promise you won't be held accountable. I signed a waiver. Besides, they wouldn't dare shoot a lady. Well, probably not, with so many witnesses."

The commander and his crew look at Elizebeth with unmasked horror. Until she arrived at base at sunrise, the coastguardsmen of Sector Key West hadn't known Special Agent Friedman—the one who solved a two-year backlog of intercepted messages in just three months, bringing an increase in the coast guard budget, allowing for shiny new boats like the one they're on—was a *she*. Her husband, William, would have laughed aloud to have seen their faces. Their bulging eyes and gaping mouths made them appear like a school of grouper on ice.

In addition to the shock of her womanhood, Elizebeth also showed up wearing linen trousers and a sleeveless white top, an outfit a Key West shop owner assured her was all the rage in women's nautical fashion. It has proven to be an unfortunate distraction. The coastguardsmen look from her bare arms to her trousers to each other in wonderment—as if she's a rare new marine species—when they think she's not paying attention.

I always pay attention, Elizebeth thinks.

"The rummy in charge could very well *be* a lady," says Jack, "and let me assure you, if it's one of the so-called ladies who run these operations, she has no conscience about whom she shoots."

Elizebeth motions to Boatswain Harvey Parry—the lanky fellow with big lips, whom the others call "Two-Gun"—for his field glasses. She lifts them to her eyes, and when she sees the vessel's name, passes back the glasses.

"This schooner does not have a lady onboard," Elizebeth says.

"It's the *Betty*, captained by Robert Peltz, a so-called gentleman rumrunner. Based in Nassau, he has no record of violence, only extreme craftiness. It will be interesting to see why he's chosen to anchor within American waters, but no doubt he'll have a good explanation, and if we're in luck, the cargo that will land him in prison. I have good intelligence that his live well doesn't hold only bait."

Jack's great shoulders slump. Beaten, he commands the helmsman to steer closer and a boatswain to raise the pendant and the ensign.

Elizabeth inhales a deep breath of briny air. She can't believe this is her life.

The youngest child of nine, she endured half a lifetime of midwestern winters, lost her beloved mother too young, and had to work jobs she hated to pay back her father's loan for her college tuition at six percent interest because he didn't think women had any business in higher learning. Years ago, if she was asked if she could ever imagine she and her husband would be among the most highly sought-after minds of American military intelligence, traveling on work trips to places like this, Elizebeth would have laughed.

I have it all, she thinks.

Elizebeth is too busy to examine the reasons why her stomach constantly rumbles, why her sleep is so fitful, and why she often finds herself holding her breath. The perpetual shadow of unease is only quelled when she's codebreaking. At work, when she immerses herself in the letters and numbers, her mind takes an elevator that lifts her above her daily cares. Coming down from that headspace into wifehood and motherhood, however, is another story. It isn't a gradual ride, but a drop, like the plunge of a coast guard patrol boat on rough waves.

A flare shoots high, drawing her out of her mind. The crew watches, tense, but no one can be seen onboard the *Betty*. They increase their speed, and as the patrol boat slips in the crosscurrents, Elizebeth loses her footing and grasps the railing for balance. An easterly wind picks up, blowing strands of her hair in her eyes. If only she remembered to buy new sunglasses. Her two-year-old daughter, Barbara, snapped Elizebeth's while she was packing for the trip. Elizebeth leans forward, scanning the scene before her, straining to catch a glimpse of Peltz.

Robert Peltz came on Elizebeth's radar last month. A coast guard patrol intercepted a group of messages in alphabetic codes from Nassau via radio. The coastguardsmen at Sector Key West and Base Six, in Fort Lauderdale, couldn't make heads or tails of them, so the messages were sent to Elizebeth, in Washington, DC. At first run, the letter groupings didn't point to any known codebooks, like *Bentley's*, so Elizebeth thought they might represent a book cipher, where a common text was agreed upon between supplier and runner.

Working the marks methodically, hour after hour, pencil on graph paper, Elizebeth found the telltale letter pairings that gradually revealed words, including *Nassau* and *Friday,* which, while possibly referring to a day of the week, also—because of her English degree—called to mind Robinson Crusoe and his man Friday. Further, she intuited this meant a smuggler had a Black man as a mate, likely Bahamian. Searching *Robinson Crusoe* as the codebook quickly brought success. As she broke the code to find the pages, lines, and positions of words, more started to come.

Peltz, Betty, Turtles.

Elizebeth's knowledge of the patrol region and fluency in the Spanish language brought to mind the translation of turtles—*tortugas*—which indicated the Dry Tortugas, which were close by. The other word of note was *Lunar*, but since it didn't come with any comment on the phase of the moon, she would consider it extraneous information until it wasn't. A call to the American Consul in Nassau revealed the date the *Betty* was registered at harbor and when she left. The ship manifest listed fish—canned and fresh—but omitted what was likely *under* the fish and the ice.

There can be no high like codebreaking, Elizebeth thinks.

This kind of high lasts and requires no loss of self and no inebriation. It's better than all the whisky they're about to confiscate. Better than the opium on the West Coast freighters she's intercepted. It's the thrill of hunting, of catching one's prey—of power—and she will never tire of it.

Something winks in the sun. A hastily thrown sailcloth fails to fully conceal the submachine gun bolted to the bow of the *Betty*. Elizebeth nudges Jack and motions with her head. At his word, Harvey "Two-Gun" and the portside crew point their weapons at the schooner. Elizebeth swallows. She longs for a glass of water, but now's not the time to ask.

"Fire a shot across the stern," says Jack to Harvey, "but do *not* hit the vessel."

Harvey's frown reveals his disappointment, but he obeys. The blast causes hysteria among the gulls bobbing on the surface of the water, and Elizebeth feels it in every cell of her body. A moment later, there's another sound, like the prolongation of a gull's cry. Hearing it causes the hair on Elizebeth's neck to rise, and her hand to move to her stomach.

"Is that...?" she asks.

The *Betty* comes to life. There's a stirring from inside the cabin, and a man dressed in white, from his hat to his boat shoes, strides out and throws up his arms. His shouts, alternating with what is now clearly a baby's cry, reach them on the wind gusts.

Jack's shirt is soaked through. His Adam's apple bobs as he swallows and tells his men to stand down.

Though the coast guard, and all who enforce Prohibition, are technically the "good guys," public opinion in the Rum War runs against them. Eleven million gallons of illegal liquor a year have created a booming smuggling economy, and the majority of Americans resent the liquor laws and sympathize with the rumrunners over the feds. The press feeds the division, characterizing smugglers as Robin Hood figures.

If they only understood the depths of the depravity of the illegal booze industry, Elizebeth often thinks, *they'd think twice about their contributions to it.*

As someone who's always been able to take or leave alcohol, Elizebeth doesn't find the country going dry to be a trial. She believes in the rule of law, believes that criminals should not profit at the country's loss, and has an insider's view into the horrors of the culture of violence that dominates smuggling. Women and children—particularly the poor—suffer the worst from it. Those who scoff at the law for a night of fun refuse to allow themselves to see the dark underbelly of the industry, and the papers don't want to run those stories, especially when it comes to mobsters, who think nothing of offing journalists.

Popular or not, Elizebeth and the agencies fighting the Rum War have pledged to uphold the law, but that doesn't make bad publicity easy to stomach. If the newspapers get wind of coastguardsmen firing on a schooner with a baby onboard, there will be no end to the trouble.

Elizebeth grips the railing. The metallic smell of her sweating hands on the steel bar puts an unpleasant tang in the air, and she wonders if the sudden rise of nausea is more from pregnancy, seasickness, or shame. She was so sure of herself about the boat and its function, and so intent on showing these men that she was capable. If she's wrong about the purpose of the schooner, she will not only embarrass herself, but also feed the inherent prejudice against her, as a woman in a field populated almost exclusively by men. Not to mention putting a baby—or *two*, she thinks—in harm's way.

No. Baby or not, she's certain: Peltz is a criminal. He might also be a father, but that doesn't change the fact that he's breaking the law. She'll be angry with herself if she missed a detail that should have alerted her to a baby onboard, but until then, she'll only be angry with Peltz.

A Black man emerges from the *Betty*'s cabin, tips his wide-brimmed straw hat at them, and hurries to raise a white flag. Once Peltz sees the lowered guns, he dips down and picks up the squalling infant, who has crawled out of the cabin door. He lifts her and plants a kiss on her fat cheek. Her halo of blonde ringlets is the same color as little Barbara's, and the girl wears only a tiny pair of pink gingham breeches, dirty at the knees. When she points at the cannons, Peltz says, "Boom! Boom!" until she giggles. The laugh triggers a physical ache in Elizabeth to hold Barbara, followed by an impulse to slap this man who's raising his baby like a pirate.

"*Betty*, ahoy!" calls Jack.

A boatswain throws Peltz's mate a line, and he catches it and pulls them in with ease, slipping bumpers between the boats so they don't smash against each other in the currents.

When the tanned, tall Peltz notices Elizebeth, she can see his surprise and pleasure. He flashes a white-toothed grin that she's mortified to realize draws forth a blush, though he could never tell. Her skin was already flaming red from the sun.

"Look, Betty," Peltz says. "A lady, on a coast guard patrol boat. What a novelty."

Betty, Elizebeth thinks. *A boat name and a baby name.*

"See, daughter," Peltz continues. "You can do anything you set your mind to."

Peltz's sentiment and his good looks are an irresistible package but Elizabeth can't allow herself to be charmed.

"Permission to come aboard, Captain?" she asks.

Jack whips his head around to look at Elizebeth as if she's gone mad.

"Only if you promise to leave your weapons behind," says Peltz, with a wink.

My only weapon is my brain, and that's coming with me, she thinks.

To Peltz's amusement, and the coastguardsmen's continued astonishment, Elizebeth makes a show of emptying the pockets of her trousers. A moment later, Peltz passes Betty to his mate and holds out his hand as if expecting Elizebeth to climb over, like a capuchin monkey, from one railing to another.

"I can't advise this," says Jack, intercepting. "It's not protocol."

Elizebeth can see that Jack is flailing and feels as if he has lost control of his ship. She doesn't want to undermine his authority in front of his subordinates.

Lord knows, I've felt the sting of that, she thinks.

"I agree," says Elizebeth. "But I want to get my hands on that sweet baby, and I can't do it from over here."

She looks up at Jack and widens her eyes, hoping to convey to him she can help them gather intelligence, which is, after all, why she's along for the ride. When he sighs, she knows he's going to let her. He's not a fighter. She can see that Jack went into the coast guard to rescue people, not enforce smuggling laws.

Though that enforcement, in many cases, she thinks, *is arguably a kind of rescue.*

"At least board safely," Jack says.

Elizebeth acquiesces, allowing him to escort her to the stern, where a side door opens that allows her to step down onto the *Betty*, rather than scamper from one railing to another. Peltz is there, hand out, and she takes it, noting his hand is even sweatier than hers, and that his blue eyes shift away when she looks up into them at close range. He's a head taller than she is, and so ripe she has to hold her breath. Her eyes sweep the decks, noting an empty crate on its side, a line of fishing poles with rusty reels, and a tangle of dry-rotted lines. There's a border of grime on the boat's edge, and several empty sardine tins in a bucket, revealing this ship is not shipshape.

Concern for the child's welfare rises, but when Elizebeth sees Betty's easy attachment to both her father and the mate, and how they soften and smile when the sunbeams of her attention hit them, Elizebeth is reassured. Though in need of a bath, the baby is clearly happy and well fed, and her skin is tanned, but not burned.

Peltz takes Betty from his mate, and she gazes at Elizebeth with frank curiosity. Elizebeth smiles and holds out her arms, which Betty looks at for a moment before turning to her father with a question in her eyes. When he nods, Betty consents, and Elizebeth's arms are filled with the very heavy infant.

"How old is Betty?" asks Elizebeth.

"Eleven months, but she's about to outweigh me," Peltz says.

"She looks wonderful."

"It's a good life on the sea," he says. "Are you a mother?"

Elizebeth doesn't answer. She tries never to give personal information. Increasingly, Elizebeth needs a security detail when appearing as an expert at trials. There are many criminals who would love to "take her for a ride."

"Pardon my curiosity," she says, "but is Betty's mother onboard?"

Elizabeth notes the tightening of Peltz's jaw.

"No, she prefers dry land," he says. "Thousands of miles away."

Elizabeth burns to ask more, but senses that subject is closed. Instead, she walks the baby around the deck, pointing at objects and seeing if Betty can name them. The child parrots Elizabeth and soon points out things on her own for Elizabeth to mimic. The baby is so heavy that Elizabeth has to put her down and hold her hands to walk her.

"Po'," the baby says, passing a fishing pole.

"Pole," says Elizabeth. She steers the baby toward the live well, while pretending to allow her to lead.

"Wa wa," the baby says, stomping in the puddle by the well's hatch.

"Water," says Elizabeth.

Suddenly, looking in the well, Elizebeth hopes there's no illegal contraband on this boat. It will bring her no joy to see a father hauled into jail. She no longer feels like a happy hunter, no longer cares about proving herself to these coastguardsmen. She realizes that going in the field makes her targets human, which—while valuable from an intelligence-gathering standpoint—makes them sympathetic.

"Eith," says Betty, with a lisp.

"Ice," says Elizebeth.

"Sish," says Betty as they look down at fish covered in ice.

"Fish," says Elizebeth, her heartbeat quickening.

Peltz walks over and scoops up Betty, taking her to the railing.
He's trying to divert me.

"Pelicans," he says, pointing at the flock bobbing in the current.

"Pecansth," says Betty.

They laugh at her pronunciation, releasing the tension.

From the patrol boat, Jack has been moving parallel to Elizebeth the entire time, and now clears his throat.

"As you are within the twelve-mile zone," Jack says. "We are within our rights to board and search. We prefer to do so peacefully."

The United States has signed treaties with dozens of countries recognizing their authority over an increased area in offshore waters from three to twelve miles. This has made it harder for rumrunners to race the last twelve miles of their journeys from the islands and the floating offshore liquor warehouses—known as Rum Row—to the coasts. However, the change has also made it harder for the coast guard, whose patrol area has expanded exponentially.

"A squall put us off course," says Peltz. "We thought we'd camp here before we got back to fishing. You're welcome onboard. If you want to waste your time."

Jack nods at Harvey, who leads the crew as they climb onboard. Because of Peltz's cooperation, the coastguardsmen must search more cleanly than if they had been opposed, allowing the mate to open doors and hatches instead of breaking them down themselves. Elizebeth can see Harvey's unrestrained disappointment. Stiff and shifty-eyed, he looks like a coil about to pop. Jack, however, looks more at ease, glad not to have a contentious captain or a battle on their hands, only an interesting story to take home to the bars of Key West.

So far.

"Ba ba," says Betty, pointing to an empty bottle.

"Bottle," says Elizebeth.

She leans down to pick up the empty, label-free bottle. Making eye contact with Peltz, she brings the bottle to her nose and inhales at the opening. It smells only of the sea.

"You must be a reporter," Peltz says.

Elizebeth passes the bottle to him. He sits baby Betty down and gives her the bottle, where she proceeds to spin it around on the wooden decking.

"She keeps us honest," says Peltz. "No curse words when Betty's onboard. Which is always."

He gives Elizebeth a pointed look before turning his attention to the coastguardsmen, who inspect the live well.

Please, don't let there be any booze in there, she thinks.

Elizebeth moves away from Peltz, continuing to scan the ship, ending up at the helm. There's a radio in the dash, and a map is laid out on the stand behind the steering wheel. Her eyes dart left and right, up and down. She can feel the words on the map of the Marquesas Keys impressing themselves in her mind, sliding into one of the endless file cabinets contained there.

Mangrove, Mooney, Gull, Key, Harbor, Shoal.

She gets a thrill when she sees the spine of a book peeking out from under a map.

Robinson Crusoe.

Feeling Peltz's eyes on her, she walks over to the starboard side, which faces the uninhabited island, and notes the lowered straps, grazing the waves, where a dory is meant to hang. She realizes there have to be more than two people onboard to man a schooner this size. As if conjured, the small craft emerges from the mangroves, six onboard, on course for the *Betty.* The coastguardsmen haven't noticed. They're questioning the mate about the submachine gun.

Is the dory dropping off or picking up? she thinks.

Peltz joins her at the railing.

"I'm all Betty's got," he says.

Elizebeth continues to watch the dory, trying to make out its cargo, and opens the Peltz file in her brain. There has not yet been any tie between Peltz and a larger crime syndicate, so he's likely operating alone, both in his business and in his family. He has indicated that Betty's mother has abandoned them both.

Betty crawls over to Peltz. He lifts her, pressing his nose into the baby's cheek.

Elizebeth looks back at Harvey and the men, who still haven't noticed the dory. Peltz's crew, however, has noticed them and works to row back into the mangroves. They're lucky the wind, waves, and gulls are so lively. The noise hides the splashing sounds of their oars on the sea. They're soon swallowed by the vegetation. Peltz exhales.

"Thank you," he says.

For a moment, Elizebeth doesn't respond. She doesn't feel good about what she's done. Or rather, not done. She thinks she shouldn't have come out on patrol. It made the waters too murky, too gray. She prefers black and white. Pencil and paper. She can't wait to get back to her desk in her home library, and back to her husband and baby.

"I'm trying to be a better father," Peltz says. "Every day. For Betty."

The coastguardsmen complete their search and return to their patrol boat. Jack whistles and motions for Elizebeth to join them. Before she goes, she turns to Peltz.

"I hope so," she says. "Next time, we won't turn a blind eye."

"We?" he asks. "I thought you were a reporter."

"You said that. I didn't."

TWO

BAHAMAS

Marie

Watching the long, lithe Cleo Lythgoe, "The Bahama Queen," at her post at the bar of the Lucerne Hotel, in Nassau, Marie straightens her posture. The Lucerne is just blocks from where Marie and Charlie Waite's shabby, unnamed boat—crusty with the salt of the Atlantic and filthy with pigeon feathers—bobs among grander rummy vessels. In this dolled-up and illustrious company, Marie feels as if she and Charlie are an extension of the boat.

Not for long, Marie thinks.

It's Cleo's retirement party, and all night there's been a revolving door of some of the most notorious smugglers of the lower Atlantic. Cleo called a truce among the usual competitors for the night, in the spirit of passing her torch and bucking the feds. "The enemy of my enemy is my friend," and all that. For this reason, however, Marie can't relax. She keeps an eye on the door at all times in case of a raid. It's not just the feds who worry Marie. In fact, Marie thinks it would be more likely in Nassau—the Wild West of the Bahamas—for this all to be a ruse. For Cleo not to be retiring but bringing her peers together for an ambush.

Cleo's earrings are lines of diamonds leading down to onyx balls the size of canary eggs that swing and bounce off her long, tanned neck. Matching the grenadine-colored nail polish on her talons, Cleo's lipstick is a Cupid's bow that never wears off in spite of the fact that she's on her third scotch. Through the turquoise curtain of her silk dress, when Cleo crosses and uncrosses her legs, one gets glimpses of the garter that holds the revolver on her thigh, the one she's known for brandishing at the slightest provocation. Marie looks down at her own faded floral frock and worn purse with disgust. At least, fixing her wardrobe will be easy once they make some dough.

"I waited 'til Jimmy Alderman was lathered up," Cleo says, "leaning back in the barber's chair, a hot towel covering his eyes, his scrawny white neck exposed."

Cleo pays no mind to the women at the bar. Her focus is on capturing the attention of the men, and she's got every one of them leaning forward, hanging on her every word. All night, she's been regaling Red Shannon, "King of the Rumrunners," and his minions, including Marie's husband, Charlie, with tall tales of exploits on the high seas. Marie notes that Cleo puts on an affect that makes her sound as if she could be from Alabama, Scotland, or even Australia. Rumors about her origins abound. Depending upon who's talking, People call her a gypsy, a Frenchwoman, a Cherokee, a Scot, a Russian, or an Egyptian. She never confirms or denies a thing.

"I slipped the barber a hundred," says Cleo, "took his razor, and pressed it in Jimmy's neck, just hard enough to make him suck in his breath."

Charlie looks with unconcealed desire at Cleo. He's either forgotten Marie's here or he doesn't care. Likely the former, based on the amount of alcohol he's consumed. Marie knows, from her own experience, Charlie is easily distracted. Marie was once his "other woman," after all, and that means she knows the potential is always there for another.

With the carrier pigeon on his shoulder, Charlie is an embarrassment to Marie. He has trained his birds to return to his brother Theo's place in Miami, once the boat is Florida bound with booze. While rumrunner boat-to-shore communication grows sophisticated around them, Charlie is content to use methods of the last century and doesn't notice or care that bird droppings and feathers are ever present on his clothes.

"I leaned in close to Jimmy's ear," Cleo continues, "and I said, 'I heard you've been telling people I cut my whisky with water. Is that true?' While he started blubbering, I pressed hard enough with the razor to draw blood from his neck."

Marie sees Red Shannon reach for his handkerchief and dab the sweat from his own neck before signaling to the bartender.

Is this story a warning for Red? thinks Marie.

It's probably a warning for all of them. Jimmy Alderman is known to be the most soulless, most dangerous rummy among them, but Red Shannon's a close second. The infamous Bill McCoy kept submachine guns on his boats, and it wasn't to fight the coast guard. Rumrunners' peers are more of a threat than the feds, who are obliged to obey the rules of engagement.

A breeze sends napkins fluttering to the sticky wooden floor. In spite of the piano player pounding away, one can hear the noise of Market Street—the clopping of horse hooves, the thunderous rolling of barrels, the shouts of locals high on the thought of the abundance of fast cash they'll earn all because the United States government made selling and distributing alcohol illegal. Such foolishness can't last forever, so everyone from Great War veterans to ministers abandoning their congregations—banking on the Lord's mercy after they make a quick fortune—are getting in on the profits while there are profits to be had. Marie and Charlie are no exception.

Over the last few months, however, Marie has had to admit to herself that Charlie is at best a fool, at worst a liar. She's long had suspicions about discrepancies between cargo forecasts and what Charlie actually brings home, so she insisted on accompanying him on this run. They'll load up in the Bahamas and motor the rum the 160 nautical miles to Miami. The cargo is legal for 148 of those miles, but once they hit the last twelve miles and the cargo becomes contraband, the game of cat and mouse with the coast guard begins.

Working with Charlie, Marie has grown frustrated by his overindulgence in the product, the animal level of his responses to passions—from bar fights to women—and, for Marie, the conflagration that brought her and Charlie together has been doused. The luster is off the penny. Far from this depressing her, however, Marie sees opportunity. Though he doesn't know it, Marie thinks of Charlie as a shield for her and her children. Marie and Charlie grew up poor as dirt, and she's tired of poverty. Smuggling will give them the life she has always dreamed of, the one she knows she and her children deserve. Marie will do anything to make sure it's possible, and she won't let anyone stand in her way.

Not even her husband.

"Suffice it to say," says Cleo, "I've not had a problem with Jimmy Alderman since."

There's nervous laughter, but Cleo takes the edge off with her announcement.

"Next round's on me!"

Now would be a perfect time for an ambush, thinks Marie. But it doesn't happen.

Marie knows her mind is dark. It always has been. She doesn't know why or how she was born without much of a conscience. She thinks it's probably because of her cold mother and their miserable poverty, but Marie knows her edge gives her an advantage. She's only at odds with herself when bad consequences result from a tendency to impulsive behavior, but even then, she's self-forgiving.

When you have only yourself to trust, you must be your own ally.

While cheering rises, Marie sees Cleo slip a hand into her brassiere, pull out a bill, and lay it on the bar. It's a U.S. thousand—the greenback featuring an eagle and its talons and many zeros. Though a British island, the Bahamas takes American currency. Since Prohibition began, there are more dollars circulating here than pound notes. Marie has only heard of the highly coveted thousand-dollar bills the rummies love to brag about, but now she sees one with her own eyes. Marie's fingertips tingle and her skin warms at the thought of such a small powerful piece of paper. That could get her and Charlie well on their way to purchasing another boat, one worthy of a name. In this den of thieves, however, the bartender makes the money disappear as quickly as it is placed.

While the men press toward the bar for their drinks, Marie sees Cleo slip to the stairway that leads up to her office. Marie is as aroused by Cleo as the men are, but for a different reason. Marie wants to *be* Cleo. The queen's retirement has left an opening, and Marie intends to fill it. Just before Cleo disappears, she pauses, looks at Marie, and nods upstairs.

Eyes at half-mast, Charlie doesn't notice Marie slip through the crowd and climb the staircase. The second floor is dark—Cleo's office door is locked—but a breeze beckons from another staircase at the end of the hallway. Marie proceeds and climbs to a rooftop that looks all the way to the harbor. Under a vast ceiling of stars, palms hiss and wafts of vanilla burst from the golden trumpets of the elderflower tree climbing over the railing, its leaves and stems coiled like slender snakes. Cleo pulls out a dagger from the garter on the non-gun leg and slices off a fragrant bunch, holding it out to Marie.

"*Por toi, ma chère,*" says Cleo.

"*Merci,*" says Marie.

She slides the yellow flowers into her black glossy hair, letting her hand rest for a moment on her chignon, while eyeing Cleo's sleek dark bob.

Cleo stands a head taller than Marie's five feet two inches. What Marie lacks in height, however, she knows how to make up for with feistiness.

"When I was last in Provence," says Cleo, "I had a perfume made from yellow elderflower. I'll send you a bottle."

"No, thank you," says Marie. "I prefer a signature fragrance. Not another woman's."

Cleo grins.

"I won't offer you a drink," Cleo says. "Because I see you don't indulge."

"Not when I'm working," says Marie.

"Neither do I."

Marie gives Cleo a look with a question.

"I let them think I'm drinking whisky," says Cleo. "But my bartender knows, only iced tea for me. Doing business in the Spanish Main, my aim better be straight."

"*Inteligente.*"

"So, what do you want to know?" asks Cleo. "Now that I'm retired, I should share some wisdom. I'd rather it be with a fellow wench than with one of the bandits downstairs."

"Pardon?"

"You've been studying me all night."

Marie doesn't deny it.

"Your husband is part of Red Shannon's rumrunner court,"

says Cleo. "I probably don't have to tell you, no good comes from associating with men like Red and Jimmy Alderman, men who'll stab you quite literally in the back and dump you overboard as shark bait without a second thought. But your husband doesn't appear to be the brightest star in the constellation."

Marie clenches her fists and feels her temperature rise. Charlie is hers, so only she can make such judgments.

"I didn't say that to insult you," says Cleo. "If anything, it's to elevate you. I thought we were on the same page."

Marie's rage abates.

"In this line of work," says Cleo, "I would never recommend marrying. But you have, so you should use the tools at your disposal."

"There are some who say you eloped with Bill McCoy."

Cleo sighs and looks at the horizon. It's the first time the woman has softened all night. Her voice gets quiet, so Marie strains to hear.

"If I were to marry, it would be Bill," Cleo says. "But I value my independence more than any man. Besides, the logistics make it impossible."

"Why?"

"He's in jail."

Marie blanches. If the feds have caught "The Real McCoy," that doesn't bode well for any of them.

"They got me, too," says Cleo. "There's a new man in the government. Something has changed. He knows where we'll be before we're there. It's uncanny."

Marie files this information in her mind. They'll have to outsmart the guy.

"It's why I'm getting out of the business now," says Cleo. "I think I have a jinx."

"But you're not in jail."

"I sacrificed a scapegoat. I had misgivings about my partner. He was a fool, and I was sick of cleaning up his messes, so I stopped. That's what you have do. Have the discipline to quit while you're ahead. Be willing to sacrifice any of them for the work. You can't afford to be soft in this business. If you have any conscience about it, even the smallest tug, you should abandon ship immediately."

Marie narrows her eyes, making them hard and black as Cleo's onyx earrings.

"I have none," says Marie. "I'm resolved. Besides, with the retirement of the queen, there's a vacancy."

"You're not deterred?"

"No."

Cleo nods and pulls out a silver cigarette case. She offers a cigarette to Marie—who declines—and lights up while appraising her protégée.

"You have an exotic look about you," says Cleo. "A perfect French accent. Perfect Spanish accent. Your English is also perfect. Where are you from? No, don't answer that. Never answer that. I'm thinking one of your parents must be from Cuba. Belize. No, Spain. What's your name? You can tell me that."

"Marie."

"Marie, Maria, Marianna, Mariella," says Cleo, trying on different names, drawing them out with a Spanish accent, shaking her head at each. Then her eyes open wide, and she lights up. "Spanish Marie."

Marie feels a ripple of pleasure.

"Her father's a Spaniard," says Cleo, looking in the distance, gesturing as if she's on a stage, speaking to a vast audience. "Her mother, Swedish."

Not quite, thinks Marie.

"Spanish Marie has merciless eyes like cold glittering sapphires," Cleo continues.

"My eyes are light brown. Like golden beryl."

"Are they? I've seen them turn from black to gold, then flare to red, cool to indigo, and return to black, and that's only over the last ten minutes."

Marie likes this. She likes the attention, the spinning of the lore.

"Spanish Marie has a temper like a volcano," Cleo continues. "And she's quick on the draw."

Cleo slides the revolver out of her garter and passes it to Marie.

"I couldn't," says Marie, the gun warm from the other woman's skin. "I won't leave you vulnerable."

"Me? Please, *chérie.* You think that's the only gun I carry? You think there isn't someone watching you right now?"

Startled, Marie looks over her shoulder and sees the outline of a man at the door to the stairs. Inwardly cursing herself for letting down her guard, Marie takes the gun and slips it into her purse, between the stacks of tens. Seeing the money, having Cleo's ear, Marie asks the blunt question.

"How much can I expect to make?"

Cleo's quiet for a moment, taking a long draw from her cigarette. Marie knows it's impolite to ask another's income, but this is not polite society, and Cleo told her to ask anything. Cleo exhales.

"Nine," she says.

Marie feels a wave of disappointment. Then she realizes Cleo must have thought Marie meant on a single run, to start.

"I mean over the course of my career," says Marie.

"Not nine thousand. Think bigger."

Marie's eyes widen.

"Nine...teen?" she asks.

Cleo shakes her head.

"Nine *hundred* thousand?" Marie asks.

The corner of Cleo's mouth rises, and she nods, almost imperceptibly.

That's more than Marie has imagined. At once, she sees a film flash before her eyes, a parade of boats, of cars, of fine clothes. A beautiful house in a good neighborhood. A sturdy house, to survive hurricanes. A live-in nanny, so Marie won't have to rely on her parents for babysitting. A good school for the kids. A Catholic school. Trips. Swanky hotels. A dance academy, one of her own.

Independence. Power.

Marie almost can't catch her breath. She feels ravenous.

"How long will it take?" Marie asks.

"It depends how hard you work. How smart you work. Innovation. Associates. Luck."

"How long?" Marie asks, more urgent.

"It took me five years."

I'll do it in half the time, Marie thinks.

She feels a need to get busy.

"Thank you for this," Marie says. "I'd best be getting back. Is there a way for me to contact you if questions arise?"

Cleo stubs out her cigarette.

"Carrier pigeon."

THREE

KEY WEST

Elizebeth

As a wife and a mother, leaving one's family is harder than being gone.

Feeling the gentle breeze coming off the Gulf of Mexico, Elizebeth walks with Commander Jack along the waterfront at Mallory Square. Her mind returns to the scene in her home when she left. Her toddler clung to her; her husband consoled her. Crypto—their Airedale terrier—bounded circles around them, barking. In spite of the fact that William had only encouragement for Elizebeth's trip, parting from her family unleashed a dam from her eyes.

"Tears?" William asked. "From you? Unprecedented!"

Elizebeth laughed. She had longed to tell him about the pregnancy, but then she thought he would worry about the trip, and worry tended to set off the episodes of anxiety he's suffered since returning from his army service in the Great War.

"I should cancel the trip," she said. "How could I think this was a good idea?"

"Because it is a good idea. They need you."

"So do you. And Baby B."

"Nonsense," William said, extracting Barbara from Elizebeth's arms. "We're already planning all the bedtimes we'll break, and the pop we'll drink, and the cat we'll buy."

"No cats," Elizebeth said. "We have our hands full enough."

"And your sister will be here tomorrow to help," he said. "Believe me, one sight of those tropical waters, a kiss from the sun, and you'll never want to come home."

True to what William had said, it only took until the train crossed into North Carolina, and the sunny skies opened before her, that Elizebeth was able to shed her cold winter feelings. By the time she hit Florida's perpetual summer, she was fully at ease. Since arriving in Key West, she feels as if she's died and gone to heaven. Because there won't be work trips after the new baby for a long time, Elizebeth is determined to enjoy every moment of this one.

Elizebeth and Jack soon arrive at the Custom House—a four-story, redbrick, red-roofed, Richardsonian Romanesque structure—where the offices of the coastguardsmen of the Seventh District are housed. They climb the entrance stairs, walk under the arches into the recessed door and then up three floors, receiving the greetings and salutes of many young men in uniform as they pass.

When Jack opens the door to his office and turns on the light, he gasps, nearly jumping out of his boots. Elizebeth looks around him to see what's caused all the fuss. Staring back at her—from every table, shelf, and cabinet—are dozens of pairs of shiny, lifeless eyeballs from an army of Mama dolls.

"Oh my," she says. "I wouldn't have taken you for a collector."

Sniggers reach her ears from the room behind her, where the coastguardsmen scatter like water bugs.

"Hilarious," Jack calls over his shoulder. "Now, about-face, and clear these out."

The men pivot and file in, collecting the dolls, their mumbled apologies mixing with an unsettling, high-pitched chorus of "Mama." After the decks are clear, Elizebeth takes the seat across from Jack's desk, while he sits in his own chair. A cracking sound, followed by a muffled "Mama," indicate one doll was left behind. Jack leans to one side, removes the doll from under his bottom with as much dignity as he can muster, and places it on the desktop.

"Dare I ask?" says Elizebeth.

Jack shoves the broken doll toward her.

"Lift up her skirt," he says.

Elizebeth obeys. The area between the doll's legs has a large hole, and some of the stuffing has been removed from the body, making a well-cushioned sack.

"Who would have guessed a Mama doll's body perfectly holds one bottle of Spanish wine?" says Jack. "We confiscated hundreds of these on a raid last week, and now the men think it's funny to place them in dark rooms for unsuspecting targets."

"Ha," she says, inspecting the doll. "Rummies are creative. You have to give them that. Just think how the world would improve if criminals put their powers to good use."

"Criminals and coastguardsmen," he says. "There's often overlap."

"You sound paranoid, like Hoover," she says.

J. Edgar Hoover, an unpopular DC lawyer, has recently been named the director of the Bureau of Investigation by President Coolidge. Because the coast guard and the Prohibition Bureau are stretched so thin, the Bureau of Investigation has been called in to assist with law enforcement. Elizebeth has only crossed Hoover's path a few times, but he immediately lost her when she learned he'd fired every woman working for the Bureau and said no more could be hired. Now his chief focus is finding double agents within law enforcement organizations, rather than criminals.

"Like all law enforcement," says Jack, "we do have many who've come from a bad past, who've matured. They're mostly assets. They know how the criminal mind works. They just have to be careful not to be tempted to return to old ways."

"I see," she says.

Jack turns his attention to the file folder on his desk and slides it toward her.

"Are these the new intercepts?" she asks, eyes brightening, tapping her fingertips together.

"None other," says Jack. "But if you want some time to rest or explore before your meeting with the assistant DA, you can leave these for another time."

"Absolutely not. That's what I'm here for. Besides, you'll make me feel better about earning my pay if I sit at a desk for a few hours, instead of riding along on adventures on the high seas. I can hardly call that work."

"Then I'll leave you to it," he says, with a smile.

Jack picks up the broken doll and is pushing back from his desk when a knock calls their attention to the doorway.

"Sir, we have an ID on the boat," says Harvey "Two-Gun." "The empty one we brought in, with the blood."

"That was fast. Good work. Whose is it?"

"Cockeye Billy's. Bought just weeks ago. I'm gonna start asking around town if anyone's seen him."

"Hold it, sailor," says Jack. "Get the police on that. You know that's not our jurisdiction."

Harvey frowns, but salutes and leaves.

Elizebeth exchanges a glance with Jack.

"You have your hands full with that one," she says.

"Yes."

"Tell me about this Cockeye Billy," she says. "I'd remember that name if I saw it somewhere."

"He's from Miami, operates there and here, and has a lazy eye. He used to be a fairly harmless small-timer, but recent rumors suggest he's started carrying dope out of Cuba."

Most of Elizebeth's work with the West Coast involves the narcotic trade—opium, morphine, and the like. Those cases often feel heavier, drawing more violent and aggressive smugglers than the boozers on the East Coast, though drug smuggling has been on the rise here, too. Worse, those networks almost always have parallel lines of sexual slavery running alongside them.

"It takes a dark turn when go they go that route, doesn't it?" she asks.

"It does. And based on the blood in the boat and the absence of cargo, Cockeye Billy might have gotten in over his head."

Elizebeth widens her eyes.

"It was more fun when we were talking toys and pranks," she says.

"If you want to talk pranks, or at least tricks, Billy has some," says Jack. "We've tried to nab him a few times, but he just jumps overboard and disappears. He can hold his breath forever and swims like a dolphin. Maybe he'll turn up soon at a speakeasy with some wild tale."

"I hope so," she says.

Jack nods and continues toward the doorway, until she calls to him.

"It's strange when we start rooting for the bad guys, isn't it?" she says.

"The bad guys?" he asks. "Sometimes, I can't tell who they are."

FOUR

MIAMI

Marie

In the reflection on the small spotted mirror, Marie stares at the blades of the garment shears on the dresser. Wearing only a black slip and a garter to hold her new gun, Marie lifts her long hair off her neck and fans herself with a green sheet from the Pompano horse racing track. Charlie lost a fortune in bad bets tonight. For every fathom she takes them forward, he takes them back five.

Marie spots a feather on her slip and flicks it off in disgust. From their filthy cages on the floor, every time carrier pigeons ruffle and fluff, they send tiny explosions of shit-covered down all over the room. In Charlie's brief brush with military service during the Great War—that never even took him out of Georgia—he was put in charge of the pigeons. He likes to tell Marie that some pigeons were decorated with service medals. He's an evangelist for the birds the way some men are for Jesus.

"They can fly a mile a minute," Charlie likes to say. "They are fearless. Loyal."

Charlie says these things while raising his eyebrows with emphasis, as if to compare Marie to birds, as if to say she's the one who comes up short. He talks to them. He dotes on them. Marie thinks it's a sign of low intelligence for a grown man to give his best to animals, to attribute human characteristics to them, to be kinder and gentler to them than to people.

Marie hates feeling jealousy over birds. She knows it's beneath her. She hates sharing a bedroom with them. They smell, and they stare, and they keep her up when she tries to sleep. She would love to break their necks, but if she did, Charlie would break hers.

As Charlie stumbles in the room, Marie releases her tresses and glares at him in disgust.

"Why're you drunk?" she asks. "You know we have a run tonight."

On run nights, Marie's children from her first marriage—Josephine and Joseph—stay at her parents' house. Marie lies that she and Charlie are going on dates. Her father pretends to believe her. Her mother loves the control and the meddling. Marie hates relying on her parents, especially her mother, but beggars can't be choosers.

On their last trip, without asking, Marie's mother, a Belgian, gave her childhood doll—a blankly blue-eyed, blonde-headed, white-dressed horror—to Josephine. Marie's mother had tried to give it to Marie when she was young, but Marie had rejected the doll that looked nothing like her. Josephine—Marie's doppelgänger—was more polite. She thanked her grandmother and now carries the doll with her everywhere, a fact that aggravates Marie while bringing a triumphant sneer to her mother's face.

One day, I'll be able to afford a nanny, Marie vows. *So there'll be no more silent mother-daughter wars fought with weapons like toys.*

"We're not leaving 'til midnight," Charlie says. "I'll sleep it off."

Charlie wears only a sleeveless white undershirt, pants, and suspenders to hold up his pants. In spite of his condition, seeing his lean, muscular biceps and lusty blue eyes never fails to ignite Marie's desire. The bruise on his left cheek also stirs her in ways she tries to deny. He got it in a scuffle at the racetrack with a man who whistled when Marie sauntered by him. She likes Charlie's jealousy because it shows he's still interested. It almost makes up for the leering he was doing at a group of young dames while he thought Marie was in the lavatory. The memory of those stupid, silly girls fluttering their eyelashes up at Charlie, and the way he softened under their attention and leaned over them, kindle Marie's fury. Be it desire or temper, everything about Charlie ignites her.

"How do you expect to get anywhere?" Marie asks. She feels her heart race faster, knowing how dangerous it is to lash out at Charlie when he's drunk, but helpless to stop her tongue. "Tight now, and a fool earlier with those whores at the track. And this filthy cage of an apartment. There's nothing respectable about you."

Charlie covers the space between them with a stride, grabs her by the hair, and yanks it back. He glares at her a moment before his eyes travel down to her neck, which he kisses hard enough to pull her anger back to desire. She revels in the feeling for a moment but then pushes him. He stumbles to the bed and sits heavily.

"I'm doing the best I can," he says.

"How about starting easy, like not betting everything we have? Like getting rid of these filthy squabs."

"These *pigeons* help us make our landing spots. Help us make money."

If we make money, it's when I pull the strings, Marie thinks.

She again looks at her reflection in the mirror. Before deliberating any longer, she picks up the shears with one hand, gathers her hair in the other fist, pulls it taut, and cuts it off, bobbing it as short as Cleo's. Charlie jumps to his feet and again looms over her.

"What the hell are you doing?"

Heart racing, Marie slams the shears on the dresser, slips the revolver out of her garter, and pushes it into Charlie's chest. She enjoys the animal flash of fear in his eyes, the involuntary movement of his hand to the knife scar on the back of his neck, which his first wife gave him the night she caught him cheating on her.

With Marie.

He takes a step back and raises his hands.

"I surrender," he says. He walks backward until he hits the bed and drops. "What'll you do to me?"

She keeps the gun pointed at him, still enjoying the range of

emotions flickering over his face. When he leans back, she can resist
him no more. She throws the revolver on the bed and takes him.

In the small hours of the night, the closer the boat gets to Fort
Jefferson, the greater the towers of the abandoned Civil War
Union prison grow. Marie's at the helm while Charlie is passed
out in the stern. She likes it this way. She loves the silence and
the control.

Situated in the Dry Tortugas, Fort Jefferson looks like a
medieval fortress dropped in a tropical paradise. It even has a
moat, complete with a fat crocodile that must have been blown
here in a squall. Though it's federal land, the only people who
dare to make the trip through dangerous waters to this lonely
outpost are the occasional naturalist, fishermen, and rummies.
No one stays long. Island fever sets in fast.

Marie is here on her first rendezvous—brokered through
middlemen in Nassau—with supplier Robert Peltz. Then she'll
run the rum to Key West to fill an order from Joe Russell at his
speakeasy, the Blind Pig. Seventy miles from Key West, Fort
Jefferson's a haul, but Peltz has a reputation for fair deals and
quality liquor, so he's worth their time. He alternates between the
Tortugas and the Mooney Key drop site, but talk is, "the moon"
might be blown. The area has been crawling with coastguardsmen. Between this and the tinder box of the Bahamas, Marie
senses they must shift their importing routes elsewhere, but
Charlie hates change. He hates progress. He has no imagination.

Marie spots the red light on the *Betty* and moves toward the dock. There's only one other boat, thankfully, and she knows it. It's the *ForEva*, the skiff of Key West small-timer, Hal Bennet. He's an old friend of Charlie's family. Hal's wife, Eva, is a devout Catholic with a temper as bad as Marie's. Eva can't like that Hal is here, which must be why he snuck in a night run.

On the final approach, Marie groans. She can't see the piling. Frustrated by how short she is, she looks down and thinks she'll have Charlie's brother Benny build her a step, one that can be removed and secured, depending upon whether she or Charlie drives. She should wake Charlie, but she wants to dock the boat herself. She hates relying on him, or anyone, for anything. She slows, takes the boat hook in hand, and uses it to pole her way into the slip before jumping out to tie up to the pilings. The wood on the pier is so worn from the weathering that a splinter the size of a toothpick stabs her. She curses, tears it out, and puts her finger to her lips, tasting the metal in her blood.

"What?" says Charlie, shooting up, disoriented.

"Go back to sleep," she says.

Charlie lies back down and, within moments, snores. Marie envies him. Even in the best circumstances, Marie always has a hard time sleeping.

It will be a while before the sun breaks the horizon, so Marie settles into the bow and cracks open a Coca-Cola. Peltz doesn't allow night transactions because of his baby, who's apparently a rabbit's foot for the guy. Many rummies won't agree to day transactions, preferring to travel under the cloak of night, but

Marie finds daylight travel easier. A woman on a boat in the sunshine is not high on the coast guard's suspect list. Besides, she'll do what she can to get in with Peltz. He's a high-quality dealer. With Charlie's reputation for fighting, she's lucky Peltz agreed to do business with her and thinks Cleo had something to do with that.

The wind picks up, howling through the halls of the behemoth. The fort is said to be haunted by dead Confederates, including Samuel Mudd, the doctor imprisoned here who tended John Wilkes Booth, President Lincoln's assassin. Marie doesn't believe in ghosts, but she's uneasy. The atmosphere at the fort is oppressive. For all its strange beauty, there's a darkness in the air. For all its loneliness, it feels like there are watchers around every corner. To busy her mind, she calculates.

I'll pay ten grand for this run. I'll charge enough to make eighteen. We'll go to Nassau, direct, for the next. Pay twelve for the next, charge twenty. I'll use it and our old boat to put a down payment on a bigger motorboat, one that can hold double the amount of liquor sacks. Then I'll be able to net thirty grand a run. I'll use it to put a down payment on the building where I'll put my dance hall. Then we won't have to pay Charlie's brother Theo for storage at his restaurant, and we'll be able to launder the profits until we're in the black. All income will be aboveboard. We'll finally be respectable.

In the darkness, imagining her future gives Marie a pleasure that almost reaches a level she'd call contentment, but at daybreak her peace is shattered. The birds at the point that juts out into the water come alive. They become one relentlessly screaming organism. Charlie will love to see this staggering display of nature, but Marie's fearful level of mistrust of birds is growing to a phobia. The only birds she likes are the victims of the crocodile, dead pelican bodies with broken necks and bloody feathers strewn about the fort like war victims. She's still in no hurry for Charlie to awaken. He's always salty when they run to and from Key West because his pigeons aren't trained on that route. He only wants to run between the Bahamas and Miami. The fool doesn't realize that routine allows for traps.

Marie's distraction has cost her. She curses, seeing Hal made it to Peltz's boat first and is now scrambling back and forth with Peltz's mate, loading sacks of booze onto the *ForEva*. Luckily, the boat is so small and his fish locker so shallow that Hal can't take much. He passes Peltz the money and is out of his slip at an impressive clip, making no eye contact with Marie. As Hal passes, he baits his fishing lines. He'll trawl on the way to Key West, hoping to catch enough fish to cover the contraband. Marie has no such need. Benny built enough false decks and lockers to hide the goods without any smelly coverage. If Benny could stay away from the drink long enough, he could make a swell carpenter. He has no head for business, however, and no discipline, except when Marie imposes it.

Marie opens her travel compact. She combs the wind from her hair and ties on a white scarf as a headband. She applies Tangee rouge to her lips, watching the color—which goes on orange—change miraculously until it complements her honey-colored skin, becoming red as the torch flowers that line the paths at Miami Beach's Flamingo Hotel.

If Marie learned anything from her theater days, it was the power of makeup and costume. The late play director at Marie's secondary school encouraged Marie's acting. After graduation, much to her mother's disapproval, Marie worked at playhouses all through Florida and has missed it every day since she left to raise babies. If there were any money in it, she'd go back in a heartbeat.

Marie unbuttons her black trench, exposing her new white wide-legged jumpsuit underneath. She slips the revolver from her garter and exchanges it for the bundle of cash in the panel under the helm. As much as she now hates to be unarmed, Peltz has been known to pat down those who board his boat, which she'll enjoy. She hears he's quite a dish.

Marie slips the money in her purse, passes Charlie sleeping, and climbs with ease out of the boat. Peltz smokes at the stern of the *Betty*, tracking Marie the whole way. She knows the light is behind her, and what a fine figure she must cut in its frame. The sun is on his face, his blue eyes lit like tanzanite, like the endless ocean around them.

"*Buenos días*," Marie says.

Peltz runs his eyes from her shoes up to her face, his smile rising like the sun.

"Are you the one I've heard about? Spanish Marie?"

"In the flesh," she says, not hiding her pleasure.

"But I was told you were a fearsome, gunslinging wench. You look like a film star."

"Cross me and find out, *querido*."

Peltz laughs, low and quiet, stubs out his cigarette, and rises to meet her. He holds out his hand and she takes it, stopping on the riser above the deck so they're eye to eye.

"I'll have to frisk you," he says. "Baby onboard."

Marie holds out her arms. He puts his hands on her, grazing just below her breasts, and he slides them down to her waist, her hips, and her thighs.

"You'd better hurry, sailor," she says. "As much as I'm enjoying this, my husband's waking up, and he's a live wire."

Peltz pulls his hands back as if he's been stung by a jellyfish.

"I've heard."

Marie leans down, slowly lifts the wide leg of her pants, and removes the money bundles from her garter. Peltz swallows and it appears to take him real work to leave her to count it. Once he's satisfied, he nods to his mate, who starts moving hams— sacks of six bottles, wrapped in burlap—from the fish locker to the dock. Marie returns to her boat to wake Charlie. She's not here for manual labor. After Charlie splashes water on his face and combs his hair, he heads over to the *Betty*.

While Charlie and the mate work, from their respective helms, Marie and Peltz watch each other. Peltz looks away first when a cry from the baby in the cabin reaches them. Before he does, and while Charlie isn't looking, he winks at Marie. Soon he's back on deck with a plump infant. Seeing the child sobers

Marie. The screaming of the birds has grown louder, and it feels like the flocks are nearer.

I have to get the hell out of here, she thinks.

After the last ham is loaded on her boat, and Marie pulls off the lines, Charlie takes the helm. As they pass Peltz, she nods and they set their course for Key West, the birds screaming in their wake.

═══

Marie curses when she sees the crowd at Key West's Seaport Marina.

On the way back, their weak sixty-horsepower motor was no match for the wind and the tide coming at them, and now it's almost lunchtime, a busy time at the docks. Against Charlie's wishes, Marie made him put on a button-down shirt and sunglasses and drive them right past the coast guard base, while she did her best to look like a pinup girl at the bow. She even waved at the guys on the deck of a patrol boat, a gaggle of Boy Scout types whose leader looked like a big sunburned teddy bear.

Yes, she thought. *We're just a nice couple, out for a pleasure cruise, who wouldn't dare get so close to law enforcement if we had anything illegal on our boat.*

When they passed, the teddy-bear commander tipped his hat at her. She wondered if he was buyable, like so many others. She'd put out her feelers to see.

Marie's smile fell, however, the moment she saw the dock teeming. Smugglers know about the hidden pier in the shadows of a fishing warehouse, where only those in the know can get slips without any questions asked. Now, there's a crowd, and it's because of that damned fool, Hal Bennet.

Charlie curses, pointing at the seven foot bull shark Hal has strung up.

A young girl of about nine—maybe one of Hal's daughters—catches Marie's eye. At ease among the weathered, crusty local men around her, the girl stands watching, hands on her hips, admiring Hal's catch. Flashbulbs go off as Hal poses with the shark. Marie wonders if he's already unloaded his booze. He must have, to be bringing all this attention. She doesn't appreciate it.

Marie feels eyes on her and scans the crowd until her gaze arrives back on the face of the young girl. Those eyes don't miss a thing. Marie feels a strange allegiance with the child, who reminds Marie of herself and of her own daughter. Joe Russell has also spotted Marie and moves between the girl and Marie's boat. He hits the arm of a large Black man—his bartender, Skinner—and they make their way through the crowd.

"How much are you charging?" Joe asks.

"Are we doing this out in the open?" she asks.

"I've bought everyone in this town who'd give you trouble."

They negotiate, each satisfied, and Marie takes the cash. While she counts—heart quickening with a joy like falling in love as the tally gets higher—Skinner, Charlie, and Joe get to work filling a cart. Joe dumps a basket of sea sponges to cover the sacks in each load and has Skinner pull the cart to the waiting car in the shadows of the fishing shed. Marie doesn't release her breath until the last sack is out of the last load.

A cheer goes up from the crowd, calling Marie's attention back to the shark. As Hal slices open its belly, a clotted tide of blood and bile gushes forth, carrying fish of all sizes. They splat and spill over the deck, along with what, at first glance, appears to be an eel.

"What the?" says Hal.

He picks it up before cursing and throwing it on the deck, recoiling. He moves in front of the girl, trying to block her view, but the child stares out from around his back. Marie slips to the front of the crowd, stopping short when she sees it.

It's a human arm.

FIVE

KEY WEST

Elizebeth

From Trumbo Point, at the Naval Air Station, Elizebeth watches the seaplane come in for a landing. Miami's new Assistant District Attorney, L. Russell—whose office has recently started working closely with all South Florida Prohibition enforcement agencies—heard Elizebeth would be in the area and wanted to set up a meeting about a partnership. A newly licensed pilot, Russell insisted on flying into Key West to meet Elizebeth.

As the seaplane teeters in the crosswinds, growing ever closer to the blue-green choppy water, Elizebeth finds she's holding her breath. She doesn't release it until the aircraft comes to a splash landing and bobs forward, motoring toward the dock.

"Astonishing," she says.

"I can never get used to it," says Jack. "The marvel of flying machines."

The men on dock help tie the lines, and the pilot climbs out, giving everyone in sight a shock. She removes her goggles, shakes out her wavy blonde bob, and grins while she walks over to meet Elizebeth, clearly enjoying the stir she's created. She wears the linen-trousers-and-sleeveless-top look Elizebeth donned on patrol. In her prim kelly-green A-line dress with a Peter Pan collar, Elizebeth feels frumpy. Further, she inwardly chastises herself for assuming Assistant DA L. Russell was a man. The assistant attorney general of the whole country—Mabel Walker Willebrandt—is a woman, after all.

I should know better, Elizebeth thinks.

Taking a deep breath, she extends her hand.

"Assistant DA Russell," says Elizebeth. "You know how to make an entrance."

"Call me Leila," she says, returning Elizebeth's firm grip.

"Elizebeth."

Whenever she introduces herself, Elizebeth thinks of her late mother. Mother insisted on spelling Elizebeth's name with an *e* in the middle so it would never be shortened to Eliza or any other conventional nickname. Mother wanted her girl to do great things and thought the full name had the dignity of a queen.

"Yes, I know," says Leila. "It's why I had to meet you. Women must stick together."

Elizebeth feels further deflated. Leila has done her homework. Elizebeth, for once, has not.

"I'm Commander Jack Wilson," Jack says, standing to his full height and reaching for Leila's hand.

"Attorney Russell," she says, giving him a swift shake before turning back to Elizebeth.

"Do you need an escort to Building 57?" Jack asks.

"Please, Wilson," says Leila. "Do either of us look like we need an escort?"

"N-no," he stammers.

Elizebeth gives Jack a small smile when she sees his sunburned cheeks have turned even redder.

This Leila is a firecracker.

Leila loops her arm through Elizebeth's and leads her toward the three enormous radio towers.

"Is your husband with you?" Leila asks. "You two have quite the reputation."

In military circles, Elizebeth and William Friedman are known as America's First Cryptographic Couple. Together, they are pioneers in the field that started at the Illinois think tank Riverbank, where they met and fell in love. It was there they ended up training most of the codebreakers sent into Europe during the Great War, before William enlisted in the U.S. Army Signal Corps and was deployed to France. Now Elizebeth and William are headquartered in Washington, DC, within intelligence units of the coast guard and army, respectively.

Elizebeth glances over her shoulder to see if Jack or any of the men are close enough to hear. Mercifully, they are not.

"I never talk about my personal life at work," says Elizebeth. "One can't be too careful in this line."

"Oh, true, true. I understand. Especially with the characters you're going to help me nab. I've heard you and your husband—pardon, won't bring him up again—have appeared as expert witnesses for the prosecution in various trials. Can I count on you for that?"

That depends on my due date, Elizebeth thinks.

"It depends on my work calendar and commitments," she says. "But whenever possible, yes."

"Good."

The women arrive at the small concrete block under the radio towers. Leila points up at them.

"This is my first visit to this transmitting building," she says. "The capacity of interception has increased dramatically over the years, as I'm sure your husband has told you—sorry, won't mention him again—so that's why our guys can listen in on everything just about everywhere. But that's also why the volume of messages has increased so much. I hope you have a team working. The traffic doubles by the day."

If only... Elizebeth thinks.

The women enter, Elizebeth flashing her badge at the men wearing headphones. Leila nods at them and spots an empty room ahead. After leading Elizebeth there, Leila closes the door behind them, leans against the windowsill, and folds her arms across her chest. The blue sky and radio towers behind her silhouette make her look like a starlet on a femme-fatale film poster.

"Your time is precious," Leila says, "so I'll be quick. Miami, and points surrounding, has become an epicenter of illegal booze activity, and it's starting to feel like a forest fire, growing out of hand. Alongside the alcohol channels, drug and human trafficking routes are starting, including sex slavery, as I'm sure you've heard."

Elizebeth's stomach roils. She can't help but think about her child—or anyone's—getting swept up in such a deadly current.

"I have," she says.

"In addition to savvy smugglers and growing organized crime," says Leila, "I have good reason to believe Miami-area law enforcement is being bribed to turn a blind eye. I need someone with muscle in DC to have undercover agents sent to South Florida pronto. Do you have the muscle and the connections?"

"I do," says Elizebeth.

Leila beams. "This is why I love having a woman in my corner. I know I can trust you'll go home and get right to work. Now, what can I do for you?"

Elizebeth feels her shoulders relax. While she finds Leila abrupt, Elizebeth is glad to have such a straight shooter and to be able to request a reciprocal offer of assistance.

"Constant communication," says Elizebeth. "Telephone. Telegraph. Letter. Message in a bottle. Carrier pigeon. I want it all. Every time you have the tiniest lead—the tiniest thread— send it to me. It's often extraneous, personal details that allow codes and ciphers to be cracked."

"I promise. I'll send you a bundle a week, including the local papers. Lots of the big personalities we hunt can't resist publicity."

"Perfect."

Leila produces a card from her pocket and passes it to Elizebeth. "My office number, should you need it," Leila says. "My secretary is the most loyal, competent woman in the world. But if you'd rather have me, just say so. I'll tell her I'll always pick up the phone for you."

"While my position, and that of my husband—sorry, won't bring him up again," Elizebeth says with a wink, "make it impossible for me to provide my number, I'm grateful for this line of communication. I'll be in your ear often."

"I look forward to it."

A stir outside calls the women's attention to the window. They look together at the car that has arrived. Harvey "Two-Gun" jumps out, carrying a trash bag toward the lab building and wearing an expression that can only be described as triumphant horror. Elizebeth and Leila look at each other, silently agree to investigate, and leave the transmitting building to enter the lab.

Commander Jack meets them and holds up his hands.

"Harvey phoned," he says. "This is not a sight for a lady."

"If you wanted to get rid of us," says Leila, "that was not the thing to say."

Elizebeth can't suppress a smile. She's growing to like this Leila more by the second.

Beaten again, Jack sighs and proceeds inside with them. A coastguardsman in a lab coat stands at a metal table, waiting for Harvey to empty the bag, which he does, with relish.

Elizebeth smells it before she sees it. She steps closer for a better look and immediately regrets it. A severed, decaying human arm lies on the table.

Elizebeth only just makes it outside before she vomits.

SIX

KEY WEST

Marie

The house on Whitehead Street is a crumbling Spanish-style beauty of two stories, wrapped in porches. Marie feels drawn to it every time she visits Key West and wonders if she's destined to own it.

Though the ornate railings are rusted and half the shutters on the arched windows are missing or broken, Marie can see the bones of the house are sturdy and made of rock. Looking inside at the empty rooms, she sees water-spotted floors and walls creeping with vines that have found cracks and crawled in with their tendrilled fingers. Around back, there's even a cellar, an oddity for a Florida home but a perfect place to store liquor.

Marie imagines herself and the children living here. Josephine and Joey playing hide-and-seek in a lush garden, picking and arranging flowers—as Josephine loves to do, a servant fanning Marie while she sips a cocktail. Maybe Marie will even allow the children to have a cat if it lives outside.

A rooster's crow causes Marie to jump, and she swats at it, shooing it away.

A cat or two, Marie thinks, cursing the bird.

She returns to the front yard and sits on the side of the dry circular fountain there, looking up at the balconies and sagging wraparound porches. The house has clearly faced many storms yet has remained standing. She can relate.

A thump calls her attention to the ground by her foot, where a small green fruit, like an apple, has fallen. She leans down to pick it up but—when she sees the leaves on the cluster from which it has dropped—she jumps up and takes several steps back.

The fruit of the manchineel tree is known as *la manzanilla de la muerte*, the little apple of death. The fruit, the sap, the leaves—every bit of it is toxic—and it's growing coiled around the fountain. She's lucky her skin didn't encounter any part of it.

"I knew I'd find you here," says Charlie.

Her heart still racing, Marie turns to her husband, who has been visiting with his mother. Marie never joins him. Charlie's mother hates Marie. Marie feels as if her mother-in-law, like her own mother, can see right through her and into her dark mind. Marie must interact with her own mother, for now, but she has no reason to cross paths with her mother-in-law. Charlie doesn't force the issue. The women clash like storm fronts, with him stuck in the middle.

Marie joins Charlie on the sidewalk and the two proceed toward Duval Street.

"I can see us here, one day," she lies. Charlie is never in that fantasy.

"I'm surprised you'd want to live so close to my mother."

She won't live forever, Marie thinks.

"It's close to Cuba," she says.

"Why do you want to be close to Cuba?"

"To grow our empire."

Charlie laughs. "Our empire. We have a two-bedroom apartment and a boat with almost no power."

"Yes, but luckily, you have me," she says, coiling her arm through his. "And I have big dreams."

On the way back to the marina, the radio towers of the Naval Air Station draw Marie's attention.

Though their boat doesn't have the capability, Peltz and a rising number of more sophisticated rumrunners have started using radio to communicate. They send coded messages to other boats and pirate radio stations onshore to discuss drop points, coast guard sightings, and warnings about feds. That kind of up-to-the-minute communication could change the game for them. It would turn the tables, keeping the rumrunners one step ahead.

Cleo clearly didn't want to keep up with the times. Charlie, with his damned pigeons, would balk at the suggestion, so Marie keeps the idea quiet, for now. She knows that if they truly want to grow an empire, they must keep up with progress and be innovators.

With an hour to kill before their departure for home when the tides change, she and Charlie stop into the Florence Club at 1117 Duval Street. The charming Conch-style house turned speakeasy is unobtrusive. The only signs of underground activity are the bottle shapes cut into the gingerbread railings. Inside, the air is smoky and sweet from Cuban cigars. The proprietor, Raul Vasquez, is there and welcomes them with kisses on both cheeks. Raul is nearing forty but looks older, with deep wrinkles around his eyes and mouth from cigars and from smiling. He's the kind of man whose good nature is contagious, even if only while in his company.

Charlie and Marie take a seat at the marble bar slab on the bench Raul's bartender says he "borrowed" from a streetcar stop.

"What have you got?" asks Marie.

"An overload is what I've got," Raul says.

"What do you mean?"

"There was a Shriners' convention here last weekend, and they didn't drink as much as I'd hoped. I have sixty cases of Cuban rum left over."

Marie's eyes light up.

"We're running to Miami in an hour," she says. "We'll take it off your hands."

"Fifty-fifty split?" Raul asks.

"It's still broad daylight," says Charlie.

"You know I like running in the daytime," says Marie. "The coasties think no one would be so brazen. And with me, a woman, there, the fools will never suspect."

"No, I'm not up for it," says Charlie. "We made out with our haul for Joe Russell. I just want to relax."

"I know you do," says Marie. "You always want to relax. That's why we can never get ahead."

Raul tries to move away, to let them duke it out, but Marie shoots out her arm and grabs Raul's.

"Seventy-thirty," she says.

"I don't know," Raul says, scratching his neck. "I ran all that myself, from Cuba. In no easy seas, mind you."

"Sixty-forty, then," she says.

"Deal," says Raul.

Charlie groans and puts his face in his hands.

Raul pours Charlie a shot of rum.

"On the house," Raul says.

———

While Charlie drinks, Marie oversees the transaction. Raul has his bartender load up his car and drive it to the marina, where he can stock Marie and Charlie's boat without any interference. Like Joe Russell, Raul has the local lawmen paid off, and besides, they love him too much to stop him. Once the bartender is back, Marie and Charlie will head out.

Charlie has entered a card game and has an ugly losing hand. Marie's stomach roils. The unease makes her feel helpless, the way she did growing up when her parents would fight about money. She'd watch her mother berate her father, lamenting that she should have listened to her parents and not married such a humble man. Marie's mother would rail in disgust that she'd have to take jobs in service to make ends meet, and how beneath her it was.

Never, young Marie would think. *I'll never live like this.*

Yet, here she is, living like this, depending upon a man, and not even a kind man like her father. Charlie is a weak, mercurial man. His addictions are like the Devil's Triangle in the Atlantic, swallowing vessels without a trace. She feels the constant undertow.

I will not let him drown me, she thinks.

Marie closes her eyes and wills her unease to transform into anger, from passivity to activity, defense to offense. Anger lights a fire in her, giving her the fuel that allows her to take what control she can. While Charlie walks the plank to his inevitable demise, Marie pulls Raul aside.

"What do you think about me starting a route between here and Cuba?"

"I'd caution against it. Since signing the Rum Treaty, Uncle Sam's undercover booze cops are working with local enforcers in Havana."

"If you can navigate that, I can. Besides, my brothers can help me. One lives there."

Raul sighs.

"If you're thinking of doing a Cuba run, you'll need more power in your boat," he says. "The Straits of Florida are rough and crawling with coasties. And, unlike the land lawmen, the coasties here can't be bought."

"That's too bad," she says, mentally crossing off the idea of approaching the big teddy-bear commander with a bribe. "Second, do you know anyone who might have a pirate radio station here in Key West? For us rumrunners to use?"

Raul laughs, the wrinkles at the corners of his eyes deepening.

"*Us* rumrunners? I can barely manage a telephone," he says. "Your ambition is admirable."

"We have to move with the times, Raul."

"That's for young people like you. I just want to make a little more for my family so I can retire and have time for collecting shells with my grandbabies."

Raul is a good-hearted man, a simple man, she thinks. *We have little in common.*

"Well, keep your ears open, will you?" she asks.

"Of course," he says.

Marie turns to collect her husband, but now it's Raul's hand that reaches to stop her.

"I heard you've armed yourself," he says.

"News travels fast," she says, cognizant of the weight of the gun at her garter.

"Be careful there. It's better to keep things simple."

"Like I said, we must keep up with the times. Northern mobsters are coming in and changing the game."

"Which is why we have to know when to duck out."

Marie shakes her head, again thinking how little they have in common, how Raul and even Cleo are relics. Marie is no relic.

"Let me ask, are you tithing?" says Raul.

"Tithing?" asks Marie. "You mean, to the church?"

"Yes. At least ten percent. I do twenty. Ill-gotten gains require more cleansing."

"That sounds like superstition. I'm a lapsed Catholic, but I'm pretty sure God can't be bribed."

Raul shrugs. "Maybe. But I'd rather hedge my bets on the mercy of God than on guns."

SEVEN

KEY WEST

Elizebeth

The Blind Pig is a crusty speakeasy with an ice-covered floor, populated largely with local fisherman, navy airmen, and the daughters of local fishermen hoping to snag navy airmen. It's the kind of place, Elizebeth thinks, a woman can walk into alone and not cause a stir, which could never happen in Washington, DC. At DC's Cosmos Club, women aren't even allowed membership. They can only come occasionally as dinner guests of their husband-members.

On a whim, for her last night in Key West, Elizebeth decides to pop into the Blind Pig and tells herself it's only to gather intelligence. Deep down, however, she acknowledges there's a thrill one gets sitting in a bar where people are thumbing their noses at the law. Because of her government position, she resolves not to partake. Though after seeing and smelling the severed arm earlier, she thinks she could use a drink.

"Orange juice," she says to the large Black man working the bar.

He pauses, pours, and passes it to her, a wary expression on his face.

Darn, she thinks. *I've raised his hackles.*

Word will ripple like an undercurrent through the bar to be on guard.

"On the house," he says.

"Thank you."

She moves to a seat alone, near the end of the bar, where she can watch its patrons in the mirror behind it. She perks up her ears, imagining raising antenna, hoping to snare someone talking about suppliers.

Maybe I'll even hear something about Cockeye Billy, she thinks.

"This used to be a morgue," says an old salt to a group of young airmen at a high-top behind her. "Hand to God. The attached icehouse was the only place on the island to keep dead bodies."

While the airmen laugh, the girls hanging off their shoulders wrinkle their noses.

"See that?" the fisherman continues, pointing to the large tree growing right up through the middle of the bar built around it. "Hangman's tree. The place is haunted by Elvira Edmunds. In the old days, she and her husband were playing cards with two sailors. A fight broke out. She stabbed every one of 'em. Must have been a witch 'cause legend says it took her a week to die."

Gasps emerge from the girls' mouths.

"Eighteen people were hung on that tree. Including a pirate or two."

At the word *pirate,* a cheer goes up. Elizebeth smiles into her drink. When she looks up, however, her smile disappears. The barman whispers in the ear of a leathery man with bad teeth who's staring her way. She shifts and tries to arrange her face blandly. Seeing the reflection of her prim green dress with the Peter Pan collar for the second time today, she realizes this outfit was a mistake. In a place like this, she should have worn trousers. She should have ordered a beer.

The man saunters over to her and places his hands on the bar.

"The Victoria Restaurant," he says.

"Pardon?"

"I think you meant to go to the Victoria Restaurant. Leave, turn right, and it's there on the corner of Duval and Greene Streets."

She stares at him a long moment, then finishes her orange juice.

"I thought I might have taken a wrong turn," she says, standing.

"Mind the ice," he says. "People fall all the time."

There's a warning in his words.

"Thanks for the tip," she says.

The whole way out, while Elizebeth picks her way over the wet floor, she feels the weight of his stare. William would be mortified to know she put herself in danger several times during this trip, and he doesn't even know about the baby. She resolves to play it safe from here on out. Once outside, she nearly runs into Commander Jack.

"Special Agent Friedman," he says. "We meet again."

The large teddy bear appears far more relaxed than he did earlier. He's accompanied by his sidekick, Harvey "Two-Gun." They look from her to the Blind Pig with a question in their eyes.

"Caught red-handed," Elizebeth says. "I wish I could say I

imbibed something more exciting than orange juice before being carted off to the brig."

"We can't arrest you here," says Jack. "Our jurisdiction ends onshore."

"That's a relief."

"We were just walking to dinner. I like to spend time with each of my men, one on one. But since you're here, we'd love if you joined us."

Elizebeth hides her disappointment with a smile. For a wife and mother of a young child, losing the chance to be afforded the luxury of a dinner alone—without having to prepare, feed, serve, talk to, or clean up after another person—is a small tragedy. She knows, however, that having a good relationship with these men in the field will be better for the work, so she nods.

"Happy to," she says, her smile not reaching her eyes. "The proprietor of the Blind Pig insisted I go to the Victoria Restaurant. Is that a better fit for someone like me?"

"Yes, ma'am," says Harvey.

The group strolls toward Duval Street, discussing the enchantment of the night air, the laughter and music, and the gentle breezes bringing the rich aroma of Cuban cigars. Though most of the buildings in Key West are dilapidated old fishing shacks converted to watering holes and eating kitchens of one kind or another, the decor of string lights and lanterns, fishing buoys, and conch shells give the town a certain charm.

"As it turns out," says Elizebeth. "I learned I would be a terrible undercover agent."

"How so?" asks Jack.

"First, I don't look the part in a dress like this. Second, when undercover, one should order what the patrons order, not orange juice. I put a target right on myself."

"At least you have a new appreciation for those doing the spy work."

"I do. And for all of you. You put your lives in danger every day to keep order for a public who curses you for it."

"Very nice of you to say," says Jack with a bashful smile. "Thank you."

Their short walk takes them to the Victoria Restaurant. Though recently built, it has an old-world beauty. On the outside, it's constructed of stucco with arched redbrick doorways. Inside, it has high ceilings, a piano, and clothed tables bathed in candlelight. The host greets them with a smile and leads them to a table located near an open window, where they can watch both their fellow diners and the steady parade of foot traffic on the street. Their waiter soon arrives. He looks like he's in his twenties, has black hair smoothed with pomade, and has a dimple when he smiles.

"Welcome to the finest restaurant in Key West," he says, his Spanish accent dressing up the words. "Our special tonight is snapper, caught hours ago, prepared simply, perfectly, in a lemon butter sauce. It's served over rice, with a side of grilled plantains. To drink, I have fresh-squeezed lemonade, orange or grapefruit juice, and Coca-Cola."

Elizebeth's mouth waters. She isn't feeling nauseous tonight and has heightened senses, especially taste. She orders grapefruit juice, and the men order Coca-Colas. The waiter brings them out quickly, and the bottles sweat in the warm air. For dinner, Elizebeth and Jack order the snapper, and Harvey orders paella, and they clink their drinks together and share the bread on the table—freshly baked *mollete*, with olive oil.

If only William was here, Elizebeth thinks. *He would love this place.*

She resolves they'll come back together some day.

"The owner is Spanish," says Jack. "He's made a very special place that combines his background with an American seaside flair. All the most important men and women on the island eat here."

"At nine o'clock," says Harvey, "they clear the tables, and a live band comes in for dancing."

"Oh, to be young at a dance in a tropical paradise," says Elizebeth. "Will you stay?"

Harvey frowns. "The wife—and my commander—won't let me."

"Yes," says Jack. "I took Harvey out tonight to remind him how coastguardsmen must always behave."

Harvey doesn't smile. Elizebeth knows why. Harvey was caught taking pictures of the arm.

"How about you?" she asks.

"Not tonight," says Jack. "Like Harvey's wife, mine's at home with our baby, and our men have an early morning patrol."

"You'll be relieved to know I won't be onboard," says Elizebeth. "My train home leaves at eight sharp. You're almost rid of me."

Both men sigh.

"You could at least pretend to be sad," she says.

"I'm sorry," says Jack.

"You know, we consider a woman a 'Jonah' onboard a boat," says Harvey.

"A silly superstition," she says. "Good thing I didn't tell you I had a banana in my handbag."

And a baby in my belly, she thinks.

Elizebeth enjoys their gasps. It was at base, where there was a sign hanging with a banana crossed out, that she learned of seamen's irrational fear of bananas on boats. When she probed them about why, there were mixed stories about fast-fermenting fruits causing fires, and bananas being all that's left floating above old Caribbean wrecks, but mostly they didn't know.

"In all seriousness," says Jack. "I was worried about having you on patrol. We've lost men in gun battles, you know. And—sorry to bring up a foul subject at dinner—but we fingerprinted that arm. You'll never believe who it belonged to."

"Who?"

"Cockeye Billy."

Elizebeth gasps.

"The sheriff had Billy's prints on file because he's been arrested a number of times," says Jack.

"I can't believe it," says Elizebeth.

"I know," says Jack. "Our guess: another rummy pirated him, likely made a small fortune, and got away with murder."

Elizebeth shudders.

"Well," she says, "scary as that is, call it intuition, but I somehow knew the *Betty* wouldn't strike. Though I was shocked about what we found."

"I know," says Jack. "Never saw a thing like a baby onboard a rummy's boat. She looked happy and healthy."

"Peltz said her mother abandoned them both," says Elizebeth.

"How sad," says Jack. "I saw the baby playing with a bottle, but we didn't find any booze."

Elizebeth raises her eyebrows.

"You think we missed something onboard?" asks Jack.

"Not onboard."

Harvey curses. Jack smacks Harvey's arm. Then gives Elizebeth a long look and follows it with a nod, understanding.

At the table next to them, the voices of the couple sitting with their two daughters reach Elizebeth's ears.

"I was trying to do something special for you," the man says. "It's never enough."

The man looks like a local. The woman—a beauty, likely Cuban—has long thick black hair, pinned up at the sides. The older of the two daughters, who looks to be about nine, squirms in her white lace dress. She has a sharp jawline and short hair, with a small barrette keeping the bangs out of her piercing eyes, which never leave her parents. The younger daughter—maybe three years old—has her long hair plaited. She's softer and sweeter-looking than her older sister and is consumed only with shoving food from her plate into her mouth.

"Devil's money," the woman hisses.

"You're impossible, Eva," he says, throwing his napkin over what's left on his plate.

The mother directs her gaze at the younger daughter.

"Slow down," Eva says. "You'll get sick."

The younger child stops eating and stares her lap. The mother turns her attention back to her older daughter.

"And you, Mariella, I don't want you at the dock anymore. Disgusting men. Terrible sights. An arm? Repulsive!"

This must be the fisherman who caught the shark, thinks Elizebeth. *Key West is a very small town.*

The child glares at her mother. Elizebeth can't imagine Barbara ever giving Elizebeth a look like that. The mother is unglued. Her hands are trembling. She's a woman at her breaking point.

Jack touches Elizebeth's arm, calling her attention to the photograph from his wallet. He and Harvey clearly didn't overhear the couple. Elizebeth admires the picture of the sweet-faced, plump young Mrs. Wilson holding an even more sweet-faced and plump baby, all while keeping an ear on the nearby table's conversation.

"Show her yours," Jack says to Harvey.

"No pictures of mine on me," says Harvey. "How about you? Married?"

He points at Elizebeth's ring.

"My college signet ring," she says, running her finger over the sapphire, blocking the lettering, and deftly averting personal questions. Next time, she'll leave the ring at home. Even with the good guys she must be careful. There are double agents, and something about Harvey's nickname and his jackal-on-the-hunt look make him appear untrustworthy. Further, she wouldn't think to disclose that she's a wife and mother. It could not only bring judgment from men who might frown upon a career woman but also lead mobsters to her door.

Elizebeth suddenly feels exhausted. She longs for William and Barbara. She has only been away from them a week, but it feels much longer. Now that she's here, she doesn't feel guilty being away from her family. Mostly. She agreed to do contract work for the coast guard because they let her work from home. Once a week, she takes the trolley into headquarters, meets with her boss, Commander Charles Root, gives him the intercepts she's solved, and retrieves a new envelope. She spends her other days alternating caring for Barbara, and codebreaking and keeping house while the baby naps. Elizebeth doesn't need much sleep, thank goodness, and she couldn't get it if she wanted it. There simply aren't enough hours in the day. Not to mention, the episodes William has had since the war often plague him at night. She has to be there to shepherd him through.

Their food arrives, fragrant, steaming, and delicious. In the quiet that settles at their table, the woman's whisper can be heard.

"I don't want you to have anything to do with that couple anymore," she hisses.

"If I hadn't met them, you wouldn't have a roof over your head."

The waiter appears with the check. Once he clears their plates, the woman continues.

"They're evil. A mother and a father, using their baby like a prop. Putting Betty in danger."

Elizebeth, Jack, and Harvey stop chewing and look up at one another from their plates.

"People do what they have to do to survive," the man says.

"Stop," says the older daughter.

Both of her parents look from the child to their plates, then slowly at each other.

"Sorry," the father says. After a few moments, he reaches for his wife's hand. "No more trips to the Tortugas. Or the moon."

At the word *moon*, Elizebeth's mind is on high alert.

"Gracias," says Eva. "We'll find another way, Hal. God will help us."

He brings her hand to his lips.

When the family leaves, Elizebeth leans in close to her companions.

"I thought a speakeasy would be the best place to gather intelligence," Elizebeth says. "Wrong again."

"So Peltz lied about the wife," Jack says, shaking his head. "She's not only in the picture, but apparently recruiting smugglers to shuttle their wares."

"And to use baby Betty as a decoy," says Elizebeth.

"Smart," says Harvey.

"Unconscionable," says Elizebeth.

"What do you think he meant by saying, 'No more trips to the moon'?" asks Jack.

Elizebeth thinks back to the map onboard the *Betty*, and

the intercepted message that set this morning's course to the Tortugas, only to become distracted at the Marquesas.

"Lunar," she says. "Moon. Mooney Key."

The men's eyes open wide, and they break into grins.

"When you go back, take along a dory to navigate the mangroves," says Elizebeth. "If you get there before the pirates do, I bet you'll find their treasure."

Lunar. Something else sparks in Elizebeth's mind. The word wasn't just in Peltz's messages. Her mental files open, close, shift, and shuffle.

"Now that I think of it," says Elizebeth, "Peltz isn't the only one who says *Lunar.* It's been on other intercepts. It must be a drop-off point for booze. I think I've seen it on Red Shannon's."

"Red Shannon," says Jack. "Getting the King of the Rumrunners would be a coup. It would knock out a whole ring."

"Or make room for the next king," says Elizebeth. "After all, *horror vacui.*"

"What's that?"

"Latin."

"For?"

"'Nature abhors a vacuum.'"

EIGHT

MIAMI

Marie

Charlie wears a pink linen suit and a white hat. Marie wears a pink satin dress and white gloves. His hand shakes when he signs the paperwork for their first home. Her hand does not when she snatches the key from the bank man's hand.

As she gazes up at 2901 Southwest Seventh Street, Marie's children stand on either side of her. The house is two stories of white stucco, with a red roof. Compared to the apartment they've come from—from all the hovels in which Marie has spent twenty-three hard years of life—it could be a palace. It has a driveway, where she hopes they'll soon put a new car, and a vacant lot on one side that she hopes to buy for future expansion.

"Children," she says. "We're home."

Josephine, at her right, is six. Joseph, at her left, is four. Charlie stands just behind them. He's not their father. That one is long gone. They have Charlie's last name, though. When they married, Marie allowed Charlie to adopt the children because he wanted them to be a respectable family, and she wanted to erase all trace of their real father. As the years have passed, however, she has grown to regret this. Charlie isn't proving to be much better than Marie's ex.

Charlie's brothers, Theo and Benny, wait at the old truck that holds the family's meager furnishings, topped off by those wretched pigeon cages. She'd rather the hangers-on not be there for this moment, but—even with the bonus cash from Raul's surplus—they couldn't afford movers.

"Respectable," Marie says.

"Cleaned us out," says Charlie.

She doesn't tell Charlie about the provenance of the house they've just bought at auction. Cockeye Billy had it built, but he turned up missing, and Red Shannon is the prime suspect. The gossip that has reached her ear is that the arm in the shark belonged to Billy. If Charlie spent more time sober and listening, and less time drunk and talking, he would also know such things.

"Only for the day," she says. "After tomorrow, we'll be able to buy new furniture. The day after that, another boat. Then, a new car, so we each have one."

Charlie looks at her with a mixture of skepticism and awe and, since she bobbed her hair and started carrying a gun, wariness. She has him right where she wants him.

Leading the family, she forces herself to walk slowly, with dignity, toward the wooden arched door. Matching arches on the rooflines of the first and second floor above the door draw the eye up to the peak, where a decorative medallion that looks like a doubloon is affixed. It's a house fit for a king and queen.

That will be us soon, she thinks.

Marie enjoys the sound of the key in the lock, the solid turn of the brass door handle, and the smell of new construction inside the home. There are walls to paint, lights to be installed, and furnishings to add. It will all be done in good time. Marie is not patient, but she doesn't have to be now that she's involved so deeply in the business.

Josephine charges ahead, her new patent leather shoes squeaking up the stairs, the blonde doll dangling from her hand staring back at Marie.

"I found my room!" Josephine calls.

Marie follows and is pleased to see that Josephine has chosen the largest of the three bedrooms. She likes her daughter's ambition, but the child must understand her place.

"You forget, I'm the queen," says Marie. "You're just a princess. And Joey is a prince, so you must come to an agreement with him about which of the smaller rooms is whose."

Josephine scampers out, knowing well not to argue, not to cross her mother who can turn as quickly as the Florida weather.

"I want to be with Mama," Joey says, joining her, clutching her leg.

Charlie follows, scowling from the doorway. He hates how clingy the boy is. Aside from the whining, Marie doesn't mind. She does everything she can to stifle the masculine aggression out of her son.

"All right," Marie says. "We'll put Charlie in the closet."

While Joey tries to hide his smile, Charlie's scowl deepens.

The small room off the master bedroom was likely intended to be a nursery, but Marie is having Benny hang shelves and bars to transform it into a massive closet. In addition to the costumes, she's lifted over the years—dresses, wigs, shoes, accessories, and a skull she stole from a production of *Hamlet*—Marie intends to fill the closet with an entirely new wardrobe of beautiful, expensive clothes. Charlie argued the pigeons should go there, but Marie refused, promising him a dovecote for the yard once finances allow.

Marie shoos Joey away and decides to be diplomatic with her husband. She wants peace within these walls and knows it largely depends on her acting. She comes up behind Charlie, where he stands at the window, and slides her arms through his, wrapping them around him from behind. He feels stiff in her embrace.

"It's too much, too fast," Charlie says.

"Too fast?" Marie says. "Not fast enough. Only a few more runs and we're set. This is all for the family."

"And then we can add some of our own?"

Forgetting the unkempt, half-starved tribes of waifs from which he and Marie rose, Charlie thinks large families are respectable. He thinks they reflect on his virility. He is preoccupied with respectability and virility. He has been hoping for a child between them. She doesn't tell him about the sponge she uses to make sure that doesn't happen.

"Of course," she lies. It's easy to lie to a liar. "This place, a new school for the children."

"They have a school."

"Gesú *Catholic* School," says Marie.

Charlie groans. He was raised Presbyterian but is now as far from any faith as one can be. His father drank himself to death, leaving his mother with eight mouths to feed and a deep prejudice against drinking. She was one of the supporters of the women's temperance movement that pushed Prohibition to a vote. Marie and her siblings were raised Catholic, a faith which historically had a higher tolerance for alcohol consumption. Churches, synagogues, and pharmacies have special permission to have wine and other spirits, and there are even rumors that a priest in Nassau is a supplier.

Charlie tries to pull away, but Marie squeezes him tighter, pressing her thigh with the revolver into the back of his leg. The feel of his unease empowers her. She knows she's taking on the burden of providing, but that doesn't scare her. It makes her feel triumphant. It gives her a feeling of control.

"The socials," she says. "The society pages. Once we have enough, we can start the academy."

An excellent dancer, it's Marie's ambition to run a dance hall and school. It will be as far away as possible from the hell of the lunch counter in the shabbiest part of town, dealing in illegal hooch and run by Charlie's brother Theo, which employs all of them. Charlie thinks he wants to be a race-car driver.

"It'll never be enough for you," he says.

Maybe, she thinks.

She doesn't like how dark Charlie's mood is. He's harder to control when he's in a temper.

"You won't complain when we build you a dovecote," she says. "You can even add more pigeons."

At that, he relaxes.

The children come into view in the yard. Josephine races to a patch of hibiscus flowers growing along the fence, Joey trailing her. She walks along the patch, finding the prettiest blooms, picking them, and making Joey hold them while she selects more. Once Josephine is satisfied, she snatches the bouquet from Joey's hands, and they scamper back toward the house.

"We'd have the space," Charlie says. "There, in the corner of the yard. I can train them to come home, here, instead of Theo's place."

Over my dead body, Marie thinks.

Theo and Benny interrupt, grunting their way into the room, struggling to carry the dresser, followed by the old mirror, which now has a crack like a diagonal lightning bolt running through it.

Charlie disentangles himself from Marie's grasp, crosses the room, and slaps Benny in the head. Benny is a big oaf without a big brain and takes a lot of abuse from his younger brothers. At forty, he's the oldest of the siblings, while Charlie, at twenty-nine is the youngest. A shoulder injury sidelined Benny's baseball career with the minor league team, the Miami Magicians, leaving him with the only option any of them can see: rumrunning. Since Theo and Benny don't know how to drive the boat, they're onshore bootleggers, a fact that frustrates Charlie—a skilled driver of anything that moves—to no end. He's too impatient to teach either of them, however, so he must suffer the consequences.

"You'll give us all bad luck, you moron," says Charlie.

"Sorry," says Benny. "It slipped."

"Superstition is for fools," says Marie. "The wise make their own luck."

Charlie and Theo leave the room to get more furniture.

Marie follows, poking her head out the door and calling after them, "Don't think of bringing the squabs inside. Take them to the shed."

Charlie curses.

Marie turns back to Benny.

"Don't worry about the mirror," Marie says. "I wanted to replace the ugly thing anyway. After this weekend, I'll be able to buy a big new gilded mirror, one that shows my whole body. I'll buy you one, too."

He blushes and looks at his boots.

"Get your ass down here, and back to work," yells Theo.

Benny scurries away, leaving Marie with only her reflection in the broken mirror. The diagonal crack gives her two images of herself: one high and one low. The high is tilted toward the window, and lit. The low is tilted away, in shadows.

That's right, she thinks. *There have always been two of me.*

Marie was barely in double digits when her family emigrated from Europe, looking for more opportunity than agriculture in a continent on the brink of war. Her mother—a temperamental blonde whose ancestors hailed from Belgium—passed the coloring down to her son Angel. Marie and the rest of her brothers have dark hair and eyes like her Franco-Spanish father. Growing up, Marie observed how beaten down her father got by the world and especially by Marie's mother, whose family had been one of some means, but which meant nothing here. Marie's mother had been forced into service—in everything from laundry to food—to help make ends meet, and she never could get used to what she considered the humiliation of waiting on others.

I will be better than both, Marie always vowed.

Marie worked in theaters from the moment she could and studied the performers—their accents, their affects, the way they carried themselves. Fluent in French, Spanish, and Dutch, Marie also learned to speak English more perfectly than someone born in America, absent any trace of dialect. This has always allowed her to blend into whatever company she keeps. She studies the players and adopts their identities.

Unfortunately, she fell for a fellow actor, Joe, with no real prospects to support her. She married him to get away from her mother—a woman whose criticism and perpetual dissatisfaction remain a poison to all of them—and was quickly pregnant, twice in a row. Marie was raising babies while Joe tomcatted with his fellow players. His betrayal annihilated Marie, and she nursed her wounds with alcohol. It was at speakeasies where she met Charlie.

Marie remembers the first night she and Charlie saw each other, in a dance pavilion by the sea. The heavens shimmered like her silver dress, like his blue eyes. The way she'd fit into his arms for the dance and the attention such a striking couple drew was more intoxicating to her than the whisky sours they drank. Marie hadn't known Charlie was married when she began her affair with him, but she couldn't stop once she started. She was addicted to him. Joe left Marie and the kids as soon as he found out about Charlie and hasn't been seen since. She's heard he's struggling on Broadway in New York.

Good riddance.

A slave to her passions, Marie knows she can be her own worst enemy. That's why she's so tired, so weighed down by the darkness. She longs for the day the two images of herself are joined into one, living fully in the light. She'll be a beacon to her children and a provider so they never have to live a double life in the shadows. Once she and Charlie do a few more runs, it will be enough, and she'll be able to leave rumrunning behind. She'll bow out the way Cleo and Raul have advised.

Soon, she thinks. *But not yet.*

NINE

FLORIDA KEYS

Elizebeth

E lizebeth can't take her eyes from the window of the overseas train that carries her through the Keys. The locomotive moves as if on the wings of a gull, gliding twenty feet above the blue-green waters of the Straits of Florida.

Elizebeth's gratitude for the time away in such a beautiful place, combined with the excitement of seeing her family, has her nearly too giddy to concentrate on her work. Once the train hits the mainland and travels north, and the passing scenery moves from endless summer to winter, from high color to black and white, she's able to focus on cracking the suitcase full of new intercepts and tips.

From her seat, alone, she decrypts. There are new and old words. New and old boats, names, stops, and hotels.

ForEva. Goose. Alderman. Lunar. Mooney Key.

Booze. Endless lists of booze. Enough booze to supply everyone on the planet, from Baby Betty Peltz to Zelda Fitzgerald.

Did people drink this much before they weren't allowed to do so?

When the words from different intercepts overlap, it's like

watching a string of lights illuminate. The process starts slowly and tediously, like the drip of water from a leaky faucet. Once the first letters come out of the spigot, however, the rest pour forth in a deluge. Her hand can't keep up with the messages exposing the senders, the receivers, and everyone in the pipeline.

By the time the train crosses into Virginia, Elizebeth has proven a link between Red Shannon and Peltz's Bahamian supply. She puts down her pencil and lifts her arms over her head, stretching them as high as they'll go. She massages her neck and shoulders, longing for William's hands to take over for her.

I should sleep, she thinks. *And eat.*

The nagging feeling that another connection is so close, however, is too enticing. If she can find the upcoming run that could allow the coast guard to catch Red Shannon, they could dethrone a violent king.

Just one more intercept.

As the miles pass, just one more becomes an entire folder. By the time Elizebeth pulls into DC's Union Station, twenty-four hours after starting her travels, she's half-delirious. Upon stopping, she grabs her luggage and nearly leaps from the train, searching the crowd for her beloved's faces, but they aren't there.

That's all right, she tells herself, brushing aside her disappointment. After all, she told William she'd just take the local trolley, and not to trouble with dressing and hauling Barbara to the station.

The thought of getting back on a train exhausts Elizebeth, but she can't walk several miles with luggage. On the local, the closer she gets to her stop, the more her nausea grows. She opens her compact mirror and pinches her cheeks to bring back some of the color, but she's pale as a marble statue, and her hands are trembling. Forgetting to eat would have been all right if she were only eating for one, but with the baby, it was a careless oversight. She feels a wave of guilt for again thinking she put the baby in danger, followed by the irrational fear that maybe something is wrong.

Maybe Barbara is sick, and that's why they couldn't meet her? Or maybe William isn't well? Without Elizebeth there to wrap her arms around him and assure him he was safe, what if his night terrors spilled over into the day? What if her sister had a travel delay, and William had to take off, when he couldn't take off because of his own top-secret work with the U.S. Army Signal Corps.

Elizebeth tries to stand before the train comes to the stop, but is hit with such dizziness, she has to sit back down in her seat until it passes. When the doors open, she stands again, flecks of light bursting in her vision, and struggles to manage her suitcase, the work suitcase, and her handbag. A man across the aisle tries to help, reaching for the work suitcase, which—knowing the classified material it contains—causes her to panic.

"No!" she says, more emphatically than she intended.

Scowling, he leaves her, and she's forced to manage the luggage alone, which is difficult, since her clothing suitcase is laden with gifts and oranges.

When she steps down onto the street, the bitter winter wind

is a shock to her sun-kissed skin. Low, heavy clouds press down, obscuring the last rays of sunset. In heels, she starts walking the five blocks home to 3932 Military Road.

A few houses away from hers, she vomits in the grass along the sidewalk and prays none of the neighbors sees. Crypto has. She can hear his barks.

When she gets to the front door, it's thrown open before she can knock, the familiar silhouette of her husband filling the view.

"Lizbeth!" he says, his joy quickly changing to alarm when he sees her state.

She collapses into his arms.

———

In the dream, Elizebeth is moving swiftly over the waters of the Keys. She thinks she's on a train, but realizes she's much closer to the waves, sprays kissing her face, the wind blowing in her hair, the sun warming her arms.

I'm all she's got.

She hears Peltz's words behind her, and in spite of knowing the words are lies, feels deep sadness for him. Looking back over her shoulder, toward the helm, she sees Peltz isn't steering. It's a woman, but the light behind her makes it hard to make out her features. Before Elizebeth can get a good look at the woman, she feels sticky hands touching her face and hears a tiny voice whispering.

"Mama."

Elizebeth opens her eyes. Baby Barbara kneels on the bed, her plump toddler hands cupping Elizebeth's cheeks.

"Mama!"

Though her head pounds, Elizebeth breaks into a smile.

"Baby Beeeeee," she says, pulling Barbara onto her chest and planting kisses all over her sweet curls and chubby cheeks. Barbara giggles and flops over Elizebeth's side, snuggling into her and sucking her thumb. William looks on, worried creases on his forehead. He sits down on the bed and touches his cold hand to her forehead.

"Let me guess," he says. "You were so engrossed in the work, you forgot to sleep."

"And eat, I'm afraid," she says.

"I have the answer to that," says Elizebeth's sister.

"Edna," says Elizebeth, another wave of joy hitting her.

Elizebeth's sister is only two years older, but was widowed young and is already graying at the temples. She has the gentle, careworn face of their mother. Edna comes toward the bed bearing a tray of hot roast beef and gravy over toast.

William disentangles Baby B from her mother, but the child protests so vehemently, he lets go. Elizebeth fixes a spot next to her on William's pillow and cuts the food to share with her daughter. William and Edna are pleased to see Elizebeth devour it, but almost as soon as she finishes, Elizebeth jumps up and runs to the bathroom to be sick. Horrified that she couldn't hide it, she takes a long moment washing her face, brushing her teeth and her hair. Once she's presentable, she steps out to the room, where her family waits. In spite of his worry, William beams, and his eyes mist over with tears.

"Lizbeth, do you think…?"

Elizebeth looks from her frowning sister, to her fussing toddler, to her fretting husband, to the suitcase next to the bed, and sighs. She touches her stomach and gives him a weak smile and a nod.

He crosses the room and wraps her in his arms.

———

After the busy blur of a weekend, after shipping Edna back to Indiana, after everyone's in bed, Elizebeth stares through the dark, at the ceiling, conversations echoing in her mind.

Since learning of the pregnancy, William's refrain has been, "You do too much. You need help." Edna joined the chorus. Elizebeth kept trying to refuse.

"Mother managed everything alone, with nine children," Elizebeth said.

"But she didn't work outside the home," William said.

"I don't either. I work *from* home. And I'm a private person. You are a private person. We have to be."

"My darling, please consider it. You can't do everything."

Elizebeth bristled and crossed her arms over her chest.

Registering her displeasure, William held up his hands in surrender.

"You know I didn't mean you weren't capable," he said. "You are the most capable, most brilliant woman I know. Only that you are in a position where you shouldn't have to do everything. If you had help with the house and the baby, you would have more time for concentration on the work. And all of it would help you have more energy for the things you want to do."

Edna interrupted.

"Goodness!" she said. "Get the help. As much as I loved my husband, he never would have argued for such a thing for me, God rest his soul. William, you are a prince. Elizebeth, you are a fool."

"How do you really feel?" asked Elizebeth.

"I won't lie to you," Edna said. "No one can have it all without suffering in some way, but you're doing so needlessly."

Edna's words continue to pierce Elizebeth because she knows, at some level, they're true. She has never had help, however. She has always managed best, and felt most satisfied, when she holds all the reins. She doesn't know how she'd relinquish any of her control.

Giving up on trying to sleep, Elizebeth slides out of bed and slips down the hallway. First, she walks across the soft rug in the nursery and looks down at her daughter, hair wild from sleep. Both dark-haired, Elizebeth and William marvel at their daughter's fairness. They marvel over her everything. Elizebeth keeps a meticulous record of Barbara's every utterance and milestone. William takes endless photographs. An excellent photographer, he has taken pictures of every stage of their courtship, their marriage, their travels, and now their growing family, and Elizebeth is grateful for it.

Knowing what a wonderful father William is, and how much joy Barbara brings to their household, Elizebeth smiles at the thought of another baby in the family. She wonders if it's a girl or a boy. She wonders if the siblings will be close—the way that she is with Edna—or more distant the way William is with his brother. William is Jewish, and his marriage to a Christian didn't go over well with his family. If he hadn't left the community, in Pittsburgh, where his parents emigrated to escape anti-Semitism in Russia, he says would have been cast out. Luckily, Elizabeth's in-laws have warmed to her, especially now that they have a granddaughter. While Elizabeth's late father was cold and aloof, Elizabeth's mother would have loved being a grandmother. It fills Elizabeth with sadness that it can never be so.

Of course, a new baby will mean more chores, Elizabeth thinks.

More diapers. More laundry. More feedings. What if this little one doesn't sleep well or is fussy? Though the pregnancy and delivery of Barbara were difficult, she has been a dream ever since. Will luck strike twice? Then there's the strange reality of being a wife and mother, where one feels each of her loved ones tethered to her, like birds on strings, always aware of their highs and lows, feeling their emotions as if they were her own. Now she's adding another child, tethering another bird. They're all so connected and even entangled that she doesn't know if it's always healthy, especially feeling the emotional fluctuations of her husband.

Elizabeth leaves the nursery and makes her way to the library. She tips back the plate on the phony light switch on the wall and slides the small box from the space. She spins the dials on the French combination lock William brought home from his war deployment and enters the code: *4188,* the simple coordinates of the latitude and longitude of Riverbank, the think tank from their past. From there, she removes the key and unlocks the door. Once inside, she closes it behind her, leans back, and inhales.

Seeing the glint of moonlight on the ax head hanging on the wall brings a smile to her face. She and William make their friends complete check-out cards when they want to borrow books, and inside each book is a plate with a Mayan warrior using his ax to smash a skull, along with a pictograph that, when translated, threatens thieves with death. While everyone finds it amusing, the message is clear.

The way some people love cathedrals, Elizebeth and William find the sacred in libraries. It's their shared faith, their common sanctuary. They started a collection on the tiny shelf of their first home—a Dutch windmill at Riverbank—where William, a trained geneticist, experimented with fruit flies, and Elizebeth worked in a group devoted to proving what ended up being the fallacy that Shakespeare was really Francis Bacon. That little shelf has matured into a room full of built-in bookshelves, lined with hundreds of tomes and artifacts she and William have collected over the years, including souvenirs William brought home from his service in France, like a small terrestrial globe and a pair of brass coasters.

Like an altar, a dual-person mahogany desk is central in the space and is where she and William work side by side, when possible, and where she does all the cryptanalysis for the coast guard on her own. Every evening after work, she tidies the space, placing her pencils and erasers in the top drawer, locking her files in the lower drawer, and straightening her stack of clean graph paper. She puts a fresh glass on a brass coaster and takes the water pitcher down to the kitchen to fill the next morning. A yellow-rose Tiffany floor lamp—gifted to them by the madman who owns Riverbank, George Fabyan—rests next to the desk. The click of the lamp's chain each morning and evening is Elizebeth's Pavlovian signal to start and stop work.

Elizebeth orbits the room, running her fingers along the well-worn spines, touching genetics books, codebooks, art and history books, the poetry of Tennyson, Bibles, Torahs, and their growing collection of Mayan art books. They have a shelf dedicated to Edgar Allan Poe's stories, including a green-covered miniature edition of Poe's cipher story, "The Gold Bug." Shakespeare has his own wall. He's what brought them together at Riverbank, after all. William photographed the letters from the folios and Elizebeth studied them. Through their partnership, the two of them realized, much to the vexation and denial of their employer, that there was no conspiracy of authors, only discrepancies of lettering and machine.

Elizebeth peruses the Shakespeare spines, settling on *Pericles, Prince of Tyre*. Much of the play is set at sea, including the supposed death of Thaisa during the birth of her daughter, Marina. Thaisa was not dead, however, only weak, and though the family was split apart for years, and a jealous woman tried to have Marina murdered, the family was brought back together by fate.

And pirates, Elizebeth thinks, with a smile.

A child born on the water reminds Elizebeth of Baby Betty. She thinks of murderous women, of runners dealing in human traffic. Of arms in sharks and of infants raised at sea. Of her own pregnancy. The words fall onto one another like dominoes, setting off a reaction.

Her gaze finds the desk and the suitcase under it. She slides *Pericles* back in its place and moves toward the desk, the pull of it magnetic. She knows she should return to bed, but the feel of the file opening in her mind is irresistible. It's a sunflower turning involuntarily toward the illuminating rays of the sun.

Just one, she thinks, as she takes her seat and pulls the chain on the Tiffany lamp.

As the minutes pass, the words take shape. Spanish words.

That's new.

Roja. Flamenco. Baile. Pescado.

Red. Flamingo. Dance. Fish.

The Flamenco? she thinks. *In Cuba? Miami Beach?*

Startled, she realizes, the note was *sent* to the coast guard, not intercepted. It's a tip.

The Flamingo Hotel, in Miami Beach, is owned by developer Carl Fisher. He's been greasing the wheels of local politicians, and maybe local law enforcement, for years, and he always manages to evade the law. Maybe not this time.

Roja.

Red.

Red Shannon.

A date.

A week from today!

At first light, Elizebeth dresses, scribbles a note to William, and hurries out the door to get to headquarters to tell her boss. They'll have to send a telegram to Commander Jack.

They're about to dethrone the King of the Rumrunners.

TEN

MIAMI BEACH

Marie

An inverted mirror image, blurred, reflects the lights of the Flamingo Hotel in the waters of Biscayne Bay. From the boardwalk along the hotel beach, Marie strains to see the entrance to the channel. Her eyes are fixed on Government Cut, gouged right through Miami Beach to join the Atlantic Ocean to the bay, to make an island oasis to satisfy the desire of a rich man. If one is wealthy enough, and one wants an island, it can be made.

The Flamingo—a pink glass-dome-topped monolith—was built by developer Carl Fisher. A conservative estimate of Fisher's worth is fifty million dollars. He's rumored to be working on a northern playground for the wealthy in Montauk, New York, to match his southern playground here. He and his wife, Jane, are prolific throwers of parties, and tonight's theme is Mardi Gras. Under glowing lanterns, the crowd in the Japanese garden is a sea of purple, green, and gold. The shimmer and the sound—the music of Blue Steele and His Orchestra—glide outward along coastal breezes in a heady cocktail of desire, women's perfume, and gin fumes propelled by quick pulses.

A lush garden of lushes, Marie thinks.

Fisher is a master of publicity, stunts, and pageantry. It's this Marie studies: the theater of it all. Flamingos wander about like stiff, paranoid children, their random squawks causing anyone within a ten-foot radius to startle. An elephant named Rosie carries a tray that serves champagne. Marie takes a glass, rationalizing that just one, nursed throughout the night, will help her relax while not scrambling her wits. She looks into the heavily lashed eyes of the elephant, wrinkling her nose at the smell, and senses judgment from the creature. Marie wonders if she's growing paranoid. She turns her back on Rosie and scans the crowd until she finds Charlie.

Marie's eyes narrow. For all Charlie's talk of respectability, he's managed to find notorious lowlife Jimmy Alderman and a few of his lackeys in the crowd. While Marie would never profess to be a saint, Alderman is of a different breed entirely. In addition to being wary of him from Cleo's warning, Marie knows Alderman has been trying to talk Charlie into running the kind of cargo that has made Alderman rich faster than rum ever could.

Human cargo.

In addition, rumor has it, Alderman's cargo doesn't always make it all the way to Florida shores. If caught, he and his crew would face the penalties for human trafficking, which are far steeper than those for booze. Charging immigrants at the docks in Cuba a hundred to set out, with the promise of a hundred on delivery, Alderman makes so much on the front end that he doesn't care about losing the rest on the back. Marie's shudders to think of the ends those desperate people meet in the Straits of Florida.

Clearly sensing he's being watched, Charlie looks around until he finds Marie. When he sees her glare, he makes his exit. Seeing Charlie in his new tuxedo, with his fresh haircut and cocky swagger, she can't help but feel a ripple of desire for him. He cleans up well. If only he could shed some of his darker nature like an old skin. If only they both could.

A newspaperman touches her arm for a picture. Marie puts down her glass and positions herself and Charlie with the hotel behind them. They stare, unsmiling, into the flash. After Marie gives the man their names, she walks along the boardwalk to the pier, with Charlie following. A gondola driver passes, tipping his hat at her. He paddles guests through the bay that, by day, hosts boat races. Farther in the distance, the gleaming white hull of Fisher's new one-hundred-sixty-foot yacht, *Shadow K*, winks in the moonlight. They say its engines can get the monster running up to twenty miles per hour.

An avid racer of anything that moves, Fisher worked on the Indianapolis Motor Speedway, ran the Dixie Highway, and has almost completed his brand-new Fulford Raceway in Miami Beach. The purse for the opening day race is thirty grand. Charlie hoped coming here meant he could rub elbows with Fisher. Marie was glad to hear of this ambition. Fisher hasn't made an appearance, however, so all Charlie has managed to do is his usual routine of getting drunk, leering at dames, and finding the lowest of the lowlifes. Marie is losing hope that Charlie has any capacity for improvement.

While she contemplates the power of the motors on the *Shadow K* and how to better their own, Charlie slips his arm around her waist. She pushes him off her.

"I told you to stay away from Alderman," Marie says. "I thought you wanted to be respectable."

"I do. But we could get there faster if we consider a change in cargo. I could get that race car I got my eye on and win Fulford. Jimmy said just one run with illegals could—"

"No. Don't even suggest it."

Marie turns back to the water, where the wind blows off the sea, bringing the smell of salt. She closes her eyes and imagines what it feels like to be the figurehead on a great ship. The siren's call reaches the salt and water of her body. Marie longs for open seas, for motion, to be borne through the indigo waters of the Spanish Main. Growing up, her father was a mate on a ferry in the Keys, and when school was out in the summer, he'd take her with him to work. She loved being on the water, feeling the motion of the waves and watching the wealthy women and men heading west for holidays. She studied their every move, mimicking how the women carried themselves, especially the ones who were in control of their men.

Marie is only twenty-three years old, but she feels ancient. She's not where she wants to be in life. After tonight, she'll be closer.

"What are you looking for?" Charlie asks.

What am I looking for? she thinks.

The question burrows much deeper into Marie's conscious-ness than he intended.

Is she looking for love? No. She doesn't believe men are capable unless it serves them. There has never been a man—not even her father—who has ever asked her, "What are you looking for?" in the deepest way, in a way that means, "I want to get it for you to make you happy." She tries to train her son, Joey, but she already sees how easily distractable he is, how drawn he is to what's right in front of him, what can meet his needs. It's as if it's written in his male blood.

What am I looking for?

Happiness? No. That feels flimsy. Marie can be entertained, aroused, and sometimes satisfied, but she's not capable of any traditional kind of happiness or contentment. It's independence she wants. She knows money is the quickest way to that so, vulgar though it is, she wants it. Marie wants a fortune. The kind of money that provides man-made islands, and wander-ing flamingos, and pachyderms serving good champagne from silver platters, with the music of Blue Steele and His Orchestra accompanying. But not the kind funded from human cargo. Even Marie has standards, and if not standards, a fear of ghosts, and of being haunted.

"What are any of us looking for?" Marie asks.

Charlie groans. He hates when she's philosophical. When she uses words that don't have to do with immediate objects in view. Words that don't have to do with booze, boats, banging, or Bentleys.

"I'm looking for the time," she finally says, exasperated.

Charlie raises his arm, the nine-karat rose gold of his new Rolex Oyster winking in the light of the Japanese lanterns strung out along the pier. Her eyes narrow every time she sees the watch. She wants expensive jewelry so much she can taste it, but she knows getting Charlie satiated has to be the first step. Like a child, he's more lenient and pliable when he's indulged.

"Almost seven," he says. "What, are there fireworks tonight?"

I certainly hope so, she thinks.

Marie grasps the pier railing tighter, and in seconds, right on schedule, she hears the buzz of the motors, growing louder by the moment. Her heart races faster the closer it gets. She can smell the fuel. What she was looking for is close enough to see.

"The *Goose*," says Charlie. "What the?"

The *Goose*, Red Shannon's thirty-five-foot motorboat, comes roaring through Government Cut trailed by a coast guard–converted rum vessel. Like conquering armies, it does something to the morale of the enemy to see their assets now in use against them. Psychological warfare is every bit as important as physical.

I'd burn my boats rather than allow them to be commandeered, thinks Marie.

She always thinks about what she would do in future scenarios. Thinking through the worst won't prevent it, but it will help her act quickly, if necessary.

While trying to steer, Red Shannon throws hams of illegal booze overboard.

Good thinking. Lighten the load. Lessen the charges.

The hams fall like bodies in a funeral at sea. The splashes draw the attention of the crowd, their gasps and sighs like mourners' dirges. They move from the garden to the beach next to the pier to get a closer look at the chase. On the lips of the spectators, Marie can hear their judgment of the enforcers and their hopes the liquor makes it ashore, where it can't be touched by the coast guard.

The *Goose* weaves in and out of the yachts at anchor, including the *Shadow K.* Sailboat halyards clang as the boats heave. Sound travels over water, and she hears the command of the coastguardsman—"Halt!"—followed by the blast of a gun. The orchestra abruptly stops. Marie can't tell if the shot was fired by the coasties or by Red. Gasps convey the growing shock and horror of the crowd, the women receding, the men surging closer. Jimmy Alderman is the exception. He has disappeared from the crowd altogether.

About a hundred yards out, the *Goose* turns toward the shore, barreling closer by the second.

Ninety yards. Eighty. Seventy.

"Let's go! Red's coming right at us!" shouts Charlie, trying to pull Marie back.

Another shot is fired, its source impossible to detect.

Ladies scream. The tide of men fully recedes.

Fifty yards. Forty.

"Marie! Get back!"

Charlie's voice is far behind her.

Coward.

Marie can see Red isn't heading for the pier. He's pointed at the shore, where he can beach his boat, jump off, and run. It's his best chance for escape.

At about thirty feet, a shot comes from the coast guard's boat, and the *Goose* halts, bobbing forward the final span until it runs aground at the shore of the Flamingo Hotel. Red stumbles to the starboard bow and heaves himself overboard. The coastguardsmen slow and slip their boat with precision along the dock where Marie stands. The large teddy bear of a commander she remembers from Key West jumps off first, doing a double take when he sees her. He's quickly followed by his crew, who pay her no mind. Their boots pound like war drums in the night. Charlie returns to her side.

Now that all danger has passed, she thinks, giving him the side-eye.

While well-dressed men and women boo and hiss at the coastguardsmen, they drag Red Shannon farther ashore. In the moonlight, Red's blood looks like ink on the sand. A man in a tuxedo rushes forward, cursing.

"Our hotel," he says. "How dare you bring this violence to our hotel! You could have killed one of our guests!"

"Sir," says the commander. "This rummy could have killed many of your guests. He was heading right for the crowd. He's one of the most violent—"

"I don't care who he is," the man says. "I am the manager, and I have called the police to haul you murderers to jail!"

"Murderers?" says the bemused coastguardsman.

As they argue over Red's shuddering body, sirens grow louder. Marie leads Charlie closer, stopping next to an empty party table strewn with half-eaten king cake, empty champagne flutes, plastic crowns, and beads. She can't take her eyes off Red. She feels a greediness, like hunger, watching him bleed. With this loss of blood, there's no way he can survive. He'll be dead before he gets to the hospital.

The police arrive shortly, led by Sheriff Paul Bryan, who resembles a walrus. The glares between Bryan's deputies and the coastguardsmen reveal whose side the local lawmen are on. Marie drifts close to the sheriff. It's a good relationship to cultivate.

"The commander fired into the crowd," she says quietly, deadpan, between the two of them, without an ounce of hysteria. "After the rummy had surrendered."

Sheriff Bryan places his hand on her back.

"Are you all right, ma'am?"

"I will be," she says, putting a tremble in her voice. "But Mr. Shannon's family won't. Such a shame. All those little mouths to feed."

The sheriff shakes his head, his mouth a grim line. He leaves Marie and slaps handcuffs on the big commander, who doesn't fight. The coasties look on with horror as their leader is carted off to the waiting cruiser.

Charlie shoots his gaze at Marie, all the color draining from his face.

It must have dawned on him what I've done, she thinks. *Maybe he's not as stupid as he appears.*

An ambulance arrives and Red Shannon is loaded onto a stretcher. Where he lay, a gruesome slick of blood makes a puddle in the sand. His eyes are glassed over, staring at the night sky. A trickle of blood slips down his cheek. After his body is carried past them, the crowd disperses, and angry words reach Marie's ears.

"Our night out, ruined!"

"The damned cure is worse than the disease."

"The King of the Rumrunners, dead."

The only music left is that of receding sirens.

Charlie doesn't move. He becomes transfixed by the stain in the sand, as if he's only just now realized the stakes of the game.

A plastic crown on the table winks in the moonlight. Marie picks it up. Her impulse is to place it on her own head, but she pauses. She regards the chessboard before her, taking time to think about her next move. After a few moments, she touches Charlie's face gently, moving it toward her. She conjures her most adoring smile.

"The king is dead," she says.

Marie lifts the crown and places it on Charlie's head. His unease transforms, and he beams at her, dumbly, while she curtsies.

"Long live the king."

ELEVEN

WASHINGTON, DC

Elizebeth

The secretary runs, heels clicking, toward Elizebeth.

"Got him," says Miss Anna Wolf, breathless.

Elizebeth turns from where she stands at the tall windows of her boss's office overlooking Pennsylvania Avenue and smiles at Anna. The interruption is welcome. Elizebeth has been contemplating how and when to tell Commander Charles Root about the baby, and how much time she'll need off after the birth, and hasn't yet come to a decision. Anna is barely out of high school, wears skirts to her ankles, has mouse-colored hair in a wound plait, and eyes magnified from her thick lenses. She is the anti-flapper, innocent and green. Elizebeth has no idea how Anna found herself in military intelligence, but Elizebeth hopes the world doesn't eat Anna up.

"Excellent," says Elizebeth.

Commander Root enters after the secretary, frown lines on his forehead.

"Dismissed, Miss Wolf," he says.

Anna's face falls, but she obeys, slipping from the room.

Elizebeth has admired her boss since the day he came calling at her front door, hoping to enlist her husband for coast guard intelligence, but happy to have her, his second choice. She admires Root because since that day, he has never made her feel like his second choice. While William would argue the opposite, Elizebeth thinks her husband is the better cryptanalyst, if only by a stride. Together, they are unstoppable. Unfortunately, their paths diverged during the war, but both hope to get back in the saddle as a team at some point. Elizebeth enjoys working for Root. He's become like a father figure to her, and a welcome one at that, her own father having been so difficult.

Root motions for Elizebeth to sit at the chair across his desk, and he takes his own. His eyes are dark. Elizebeth's smile falls, her face mirroring his.

"All didn't go as planned?" she asks.

He shakes his head.

"Did Red Shannon survive?"

"He did not," says Root. "But one of ours got snagged."

"Killed?"

"No, jailed. On murder charges."

Elizebeth shakes her head. "They can't win."

"No, I'm afraid not. Not in Miami Beach. Not when a witness claimed our man fired into the crowd, allegedly after Red Shannon had surrendered."

"I can't believe that."

"There's an investigation. They're gathering statements and evidence now."

Elizebeth pauses, thinking of the men from the Florida coast guard bases, the men with whom she dined, chatted, and joked. Unfortunately, she thinks there was one among them who might fit the bill. Harvey "Two-Gun" has a twitch in his trigger finger.

"Do I know him?" she asks.

Root opens the file and glances down the report. "Commander Jack Wilson."

"Oh no," she says, heart sinking. "I was with Jack most of my trip. There's no chance he breached protocol, especially doing something that would put civilians in danger. I would be happy to testify to his character."

Root makes a note. Then he looks back up at her, eyes heavy as a basset hound's.

"In our men's report," he says, "they note, Red headed straight for the party onshore at the Flamingo Hotel and fired upon the coast guard first. But the local police report is in conflict."

"No surprise. Sheriff Paul Bryan?"

"None other."

"Corrupt as they come. And Red knew exactly what he was doing. Tried to protect his own skin, while making our guys look bad."

Root nods.

"Put the new assistant DA, Leila Russell, on this," says Elizebeth. "She's good. I met with her when I was in Florida. She says Sheriff Bryan and his men take bribes. It's just a matter of finding hard evidence to convict them."

Without flinching or showing any surprise, Root notes "ADA Leila Russell" in the file. Elizebeth purses her lips. She still hasn't forgiven herself for assuming Russell was a man.

"Your work was flawless," says Root. "We've been tracking Red Shannon for a long time, with no success. If it weren't for you, he'd still be at large."

"Yes, but if it weren't for me, Commander Wilson wouldn't be in jail."

"That'll get sorted out."

"I didn't take you for an optimist."

"I'm not. But with your testimony, I have faith the rule of law will prevail."

"Thank you for your confidence. But, you know, I can't claim full ownership of my success in nabbing Red. I had a tip. I do wonder who the snitch is. It felt too direct and sophisticated for a neighborhood watcher. And it was anonymous. It has the feel of a competitor."

"Interesting. I can try to get more information about the source of the communication."

"That would help. In fact, I wonder if the snitch was a witness that night. If he might have been the one who fed the police false testimony."

"You're making me think I should send you back down to help with the investigation."

Elizebeth laughs. "I'm no good undercover. Believe me. And I'm afraid my husband would lose his mind. But keep me posted. I want to ferret this one out. It could lead us to more of the bad guys."

"Will do," says Root. "Anything else I should know, before you go?"

Elizebeth thinks for a moment but can't make herself say the words about her pregnancy. She'll stick to the work.

"Oh, yes," she says. "While I was at Sector Key West, I had the unpleasant experience of seeing a human arm a fisherman found when he cut open a shark's belly."

Nausea rises. She swallows and closes her eyes, willing it to pass.

"Appalling," says Root.

"I know," she says, grateful to have regained control of herself. "Our men had it fingerprinted. Lo and behold, the prints matched those of a small-time rummy: Cockeye Billy. The very smuggler whose boat we found abandoned, covered in blood, in the Straits of Florida. So, we can write his name next to the boat, cross him off the list of active runners, and add him to the *probable victims of other pirates* list."

"Well," Root says. "That is...something."

Elizebeth stands, approaches the display of wall maps and boats, and walks to the Florida section. After she finds the vessel, she makes a note of the change.

"I'm checking into the harbormaster's reports," says Elizebeth, turning back to Root. "I'll see if any of his peers took parallel journeys. A plain rummy is one thing, but a murderous rummy quite another. Hopefully it was Red Shannon who did in Cockeye Billy. Problem solved."

"Indeed."

"I know the coasties commandeered the victim's boat. Do you know what happened to Red's boat? The *Goose*?"

"I think it went up for auction."

"All right. Add that to the list of queries. If we know who bought it, we might know who gave us the tip."

"Will do."

Root stands, his chair scraping over the heavy wooden floor. He places his hand on the fat locked file bag on his desk.

"Are you up for the next batch?" he asks.

"Up for it?" she says. "I'm insulted you have to ask."

———

Elizebeth leans against the doorframe of the bathroom, arms crossed, admiring her husband's backside while he reaches over the tub's edge, washing Barbara. All Elizebeth has to do is look at William, and she's electrified. It's been that way since the first time she laid eyes on him. It's something she has in common with most women who look at William. His height, his dark, sharp features, and his polish are irresistible.

She remembers that first night she saw him like it was yesterday, instead of a decade ago. It was her first dinner at Riverbank, the day she'd taken the job. Perhaps the longest, strangest day of her life. That is, the longest, strangest day until last week in Key West, when she saw a woman land a plane and a human arm extracted from a shark's belly.

Before her job at Riverbank, Elizebeth was depressed. Her college love had broken her heart. Her mother had grown sickly.

Elizebeth hated working as a school principal, the position taken only to pay back the debt—including interest—she owed her father for her schooling. She made a meager salary at a place she despised, so on summer break she was determined to find something better in the big city of Chicago. She made a dress that she thought looked fancy but revealed itself as dowdy the moment she passed the windows of Marshall Field's. Still, she peddled her resume all day, but had no takers and felt the horror of knowing she'd failed. She'd have to go back to Indiana and confess to her father that she couldn't get work, and he'd tell her what a fool she was for wasting so much time and money.

Despondent, walking on Walton Street with only an hour before the evening train, Elizebeth tripped on a stair. When she looked up, the glorious facade of the Newberry Library rose before her. It felt like a godsend, one small oasis of joy in the midst of her misery. She walked slowly inside, as if entering a church, and inhaled the warm, ancient, wonderfully musty fragrance of books. She spun in a circle, looking at the ceiling, feeling a lightness she hadn't felt in months, when someone cleared her throat.

"May I help you?" asked a librarian.

"I hardly know," said Elizebeth. "I didn't plan on coming here, but the library stair stuck out its foot, tripping me, and here I am."

The librarian smiled. "It must have wanted you to come in."

"'Come,'" said Elizebeth. "'and take choice of all my library, And so beguile thy sorrow.'"

"*Titus Andronicus*," said the librarian.

"None other."

"You love Shakespeare."

"More than anything."

"Then you're in luck. Do you know, we have a First Folio here?"

Elizebeth drew in her breath. She had never in her life imagined she could see a rare first binding of Shakespeare's plays.

It was then that everything changed.

The librarian probed Elizebeth. She revealed she'd had no luck finding a job. The librarian's face grew strange, then thoughtful; then she left Elizebeth to make a phone call. An hour later, a huge man strode up to Elizebeth and offered her a job—and housing—at his think tank, studying Shakespeare texts to prove it was really Francis Bacon who had written them. Minutes after that, Elizebeth was in a limousine, then on a train, then at a grand estate. And that night, under the golden glow of sunset, she was introduced to the dapper young geneticist on staff—William Friedman—who would become her destiny.

As mercurial and domineering a boss as George Fabyan was, Riverbank was a wonderland. It was there, as if on the stage of a grand fantasy play—where the curiosities of the world were brought together in a rich man's collection in the middle west of the United States—that Elizebeth and William fell in love. Like a film in her mind, Elizebeth can see herself leading William on bicycle rides on the paths along the Fox River. She can feel the wind in her face as they passed the lighthouse, flashing its Morse code warning—*Skidoo*, keep out—and pedaled across the moon bridge to the Japanese garden, to the menagerie which kept a bear, ostriches, a kangaroo, and peacocks, among other exotic animals. She can feel the water of the Greco-Roman pool, where they swam—under the watch of white-eyed statues—beneath a dome of stars. She can smell the sweetness of hothouse flowers in the Villa, Fabyan's home that was remodeled by Frank Lloyd Wright, where all the furniture hung suspended from the ceilings, and where Fabyan's wife, Nellie, kept a chimpanzee she treated like the child she never had, and which screamed with jealousy when confined to its cage during dinner parties.

After Elizebeth and William married in 1917, they lived in the imported Dutch windmill on the property, where William did his genetics experiments with African violets and fruit flies. It really was a place like no other, but—like the animals in the menagerie—living there was being imprisoned. Permission was needed for everything. Scant wages were justified by being housed and fed. It was beautiful, yes. Stimulating, absolutely. But it was like being locked in a castle or encased in a snow globe. And when Fabyan's temper got the better of him, which was often, he'd give them all a hard shake.

The longer Elizebeth and William were there, the more they realized the Shakespeare investigation was a farce, and when they told Fabyan, he blew his top. It took many years to disentangle themselves from him, but they managed. And it was in their study of letters and words that Elizebeth and William were unknowingly training themselves, growing their capacities for concentration, for understanding patterns, for becoming codebreakers and, in William's case, codemakers. It was there they became cryptanalysts.

William looks over his shoulder.

"Are you staring at my behind?" he asks with an impish smile. "I feel so exposed. So vulnerable."

"Don't worry," she says. "You're safe with me."

"How disappointing. I was hoping to be taken advantage of the moment this squiggly octopus got penned."

Barbara sends a tidal wave over the edge of the tub, and William pretends to sputter and flail so wildly that Barbara's soon gasping in hysterical giggles that set them all off.

What did I do to get so lucky? thinks Elizebeth.

William is a rare man. Elizebeth cannot imagine her father ever giving a child a bath, changing a diaper, or playing, for that matter. She can't imagine any of their male friends doing so.

William lifts Barbara from the tub and swaddles her like an infant in a hooded pink towel. They wrestle the child into her yellow terry-cloth pajamas, and she soon quiets, allowing Elizebeth to comb her ringlets while William reads her the alphabet book Elizebeth wrote and illustrated.

"You should get this published," says William.

"It only goes to the letter *P*," says Elizebeth.

"When you finish it, I mean."

"I don't think my boss would be pleased to hear I'm setting aside the intercepts of violent criminals to complete a children's picture book."

"I'll help you finish," says William. "*P, Prohibition.*"

"A most *ig*noble experiment."

"*Q.* The most common letter in ciphers, and the least in life."

"That's not a word."

"Good point. *Q, Queen.* Illustration: Cleo Lythgoe, Queen of the Rumrunners."

Elizabeth smiles and shakes her head.

"Dethroned?" William asks.

Elizabeth nods.

"Brava," he says. "I know, Queen of the Codebreakers: Elizebeth Smith Friedman."

"Now you're talking."

Once Barbara is tucked in, William and Elizebeth retreat to their bedroom, turn outside the lights, and snuggle into each other, watching snow falling gently out the window. She says a silent prayer that William will be able to sleep the night through, to get to morning without nightmares or tremors. "Psychic giddiness," he calls it.

"Lizbeth, I don't tell you enough. I don't know what I'd do without you."

"Billy Boy, you tell me every day. Many times a day."

"But I think it even more than that. Much more than I say."

"I know your thoughts, darling. You don't have to say it."

He sighs.

"How did you fare while I was gone? Answer me truly," she asks.

His silence is answer enough.

"Have you given more thought to talking to someone?" she asks. "The psychoanalyst we met at the Cosmos Club dinner?"

"Dr. Graven?"

"Yes. He's a pioneer in the field. He's worked with many veterans of the war. He's an expert in shell shock."

"You know how foreign it is for me to share with others. It's practically been beaten out of me. You're the only one I care to do so with."

"Yes, but I'm not a doctor. He might have insights I don't."

"I find that very unlikely. You're the most brilliant person I know."

"Consider it."

He's silent. His stubbornness frustrates her.

"I'll consider it," he finally says. "If you consider getting help when the baby comes."

"Touché," she says, with a smile.

———

Elizebeth can't stop thinking about Commander Jack. And dead rumrunners. And corrupt police. And sharks. And arms in sharks. This business grows darker by the day.

She is desperate to connect with investigators, to talk to Leila Russell about how to free Jack, and to work on the new intercepts. Edna is long gone, however, and Barbara is getting her two-year molars and won't be put down. When Elizebeth finally gets through to Leila, the phone call is spent wrestling with Barbara for the phone cord and trying to hush the baby. By the time Elizebeth finally gets Barbara down for her nap, Elizebeth realizes William has no clean shirts left, so she has to get started washing immediately.

The cracked, bleeding skin on Elizebeth's knuckles stings in the borax. Once the shirts are hung, Elizebeth goes to her bathroom to moisturize her hands, but she can't get one more ounce from the empty bottle of Venetian Lille lotion. She throws the bottle in the waste bin with a clang, which wakes Barbara. Elizebeth groans and decides to leave Barbara crying, hoping she'll fall back asleep, but as if on cue, the doorbell rings, setting off Crypto.

"Rats!" Elizebeth says.

She can't recall any appointments in her daybook, so she'll ignore the doorbell, especially when she catches her reflection in the mirror. Her unkempt hair and pale skin are a fright, every kiss of the Florida sun vanished.

Barbara is showing no signs of slowing, and Crypto won't stop barking, so Elizebeth strides down the hallway to get the baby, but the phone rings the moment she passes the table where it rests.

"What?" she says.

"Lizbeth?" says William. "Are you all right?"

"Yes. It's just Barbara's a teething mess, and she won't sleep, and the doorbell's ringing."

"That's exactly why I called. I didn't get a chance to tell you. And I've only just been able to sneak away. You have an interview."

"Billy, what does that mean? I have a job."

"I know, dear. That's why I sent a woman to you. Cassandra. Her brother works at my building. We were talking about our families, and he said his older sister is a nanny. The child in her care has grown up and—having no husband or children of her own—Cassandra desperately wants a new family to work with. Her brother knows all about Baby B and says his sister is an angel and a phenomenal cook. She lives only a short train ride away from us."

The doorbell again rings. Barbara and Crypto are both at decibel ten.

"William. You must discuss these things with me first."

"You don't have to hire her if you don't like her. And there's something I'm working on here. Work that's consuming. I won't be able to take off the next time you have a trip, and with Edna living in Indiana—"

"I have to go," Elizebeth says, slamming the phone receiver into its holder.

Feeling hot with irritation, flustered by the chaos, and guilty because she hung up on William, Elizebeth hurries to rescue Barbara from herself. The child sweats and hiccups, and tucks herself into Elizebeth's side so sweetly that it dissipates her aggravation.

"I know," she says, rubbing Barbara's back.

Elizebeth heads downstairs and leads Crypto out back, while mentally preparing a kind but firm dismissal and apology for the trouble. But when Elizebeth throws open the door, the light is a halo around the tall Black woman with graying hair, and she has such a kind, motherly smile that Elizebeth has to hold herself back from collapsing in the woman's arms.

"Mrs. Friedman? I'm Cassie. Is this the famous Baby B?"

"It is," says Elizebeth.

Barbara lifts her head and beams at the woman at the door. Surprised by Barbara's immediate liking of a stranger, Elizebeth is even more dumbfounded to see Barbara reach out her arms toward the woman, who gladly takes her.

Elizebeth exhales. She hadn't realized she was holding her breath.

TWELVE

MIAMI

Marie

All morning, Charlie has been painting the thirty-five-foot motorboat on blocks in their yard, but his progress is slower than a manatee's. When she can stand it no longer, Marie takes the brush from Charlie's hand, plunges it in the bucket of white paint, and runs it over the word on the hull, covering it as if it never existed, forever blotting out the word *Goose*.

At her insistence, they bought Red Shannon's boat at auction. Charlie worried it had a jinx, but Marie convinced him that conquering armies absorb the power of those destroyed, not the opposite.

"If that's true, the coast guard has the gain," he said.

The coast guard only had it because of my tip, she thought.

"Your superstition is making you sound stupid," she said.

Rolex flashing in the sunlight, Charlie raised his arm as if he was going to backhand Marie, but she didn't flinch. He hadn't hit her since she'd started carrying a gun. Not only that, but

Benny also stepped toward Charlie, looming over him, which caused Charlie to lower his hand.

As Marie's involvement in rumrunning grows, Benny has fallen naturally into a protective role. He's sweet-tempered, but she has no doubt he'd snap anyone like a twig who crossed her, even Charlie.

From the first moment she saw Benny on the baseball field, and he gave her that big dopey grin, followed by a wave, she knew she had his loyalty. His heart is bigger than his brain, a rare and useful distribution of talents for a lackey. Charlie doesn't have a big brain or a big heart, but he's adventurous and sexy, and maybe even moldable, which for now is good enough for Marie.

Benny hums away at the stern, greasing the prop shafts of the motors. Josephine and Joey run about the boat deck, shooting each other with water from the liquid pistols Benny bought for them. Charlie is sober. The sky is Madonna blue. In the little garden, Benny helped Josephine plant blooms like jewels push up from the dirt.

Today is the first time in a long while Marie has felt something like contentment. She allows herself a moment to envision a future where they really are respectable. Where Charlie's gratitude for Marie's smarts increases his admiration for her. Where bills aren't piled up and unpaid, freeing them from the noose of poverty. Where they don't use drinking to escape, but to enhance. Where their names are in the society column of the *Miami Tribune* instead of on the crime pages.

Benny comes to stand with Marie, wiping his big mitts on a grease cloth.

"What'll you name her?" he asks.

"Josephine," says Marie.

"Yes?" asks her daughter.

"The boat's new name," Marie says.

Josephine beams.

"When do I get a boat?" asks Joey.

"Never," Marie says. "Boats are named for women. But I have my eye on another one that might come up for auction soon, and you can help me name it."

"Another one?" asks Charlie. "Marie, we don't need a damned armada."

"That's exactly what we need."

He groans.

"Did you hear?" asks Benny. "Red Shannon's wife is moving the kids in with her parents. He didn't have as much dough as everyone thought."

"Oh, dear, has she already moved?" asks Marie.

"I think so," says Benny. "Why?"

"I had Theo drop off a bougainvillea plant with a bow. Condolences."

Benny and Charlie look at each other and then at Marie. Without a word, they both get back to work. Marie watches for a moment before climbing the ladder to join the kids in the boat. Joey—soaked, liquid pistols empty on the floorboards—now pretends to fish from the starboard bow, leaning over the gunwale, struggling as if he has a marlin on the line. Josephine is in the cabin, at the helm, standing on the box Benny built to lift Marie.

Josephine's hair has come undone, so Marie rebraids it, ignoring her daughter's cries about how hard Marie pulls, while trying not to look at the doll on the ledge, staring at them. She just heard hundreds of dolls concealing wine had been nabbed by the coasties in Key West. She was envious of the doll idea, until the arrests. But she hates dolls almost as much as she hates birds, so good riddance. The moment Marie finishes braiding Josephine's hair, the child grabs the doll and scampers away, leaving Marie to contemplate how the boat could be improved.

The steering station is empty. Marie thinks the space could be altered to include a radio so they wouldn't have to use pigeons. The communication could be instant, up to the moment. She thinks Benny could wire it. They'd need only find someone who's willing to transmit onshore from a pirate station or two. She doesn't know the men who already operate stations. She'd want her own, but who would she trust to man such a place?

Joey's whining breaks Marie's concentration. Exasperated, she strides out to see what's wrong. Joey stares down at his wet, sailor buster short set, wiping at something he has smeared all over the front of it.

"What have you gotten into?" she says. "I told you not to wear the white one."

Marie kneels before her son, looking at his hands pawing at the brownish-red stain on his chest. Her eyes dart from the boy's sodden clothing to where he was leaning, and she sees it. In spite of the heat, she feels a sudden chill.

It's blood.

Inside the small washroom, she scrubs the white sailor suit until her skin is chafed.

Out, damned spot, she thinks.

Macbeth was the play where she met the kids' father. Joe played one of Macduff's murderers. Marie played Hecate, goddess of witchcraft. Marie hated the woman who played Lady Macbeth—a mere girl who had never washed anything in her life, who had never felt the desperation of loss or poverty. The girl's performance was flimsy as the shift she was wearing, especially in the famous sleepwalking scene that Marie knows she would have done perfectly. Marie would have hated the girl even more if she had known then that Joe was involved with both of them at the same time. If Marie saw the girl now, she'd feed her to the sharks.

Once the stain is gone, Marie drains the tub, rinsing it clear of Red Shannon's blood. She turns to leave, but trips over a pile of clothes on the floor, including Charlie's shirt from last night. He and his brothers went to the track to bet on the horse races, and the shirt reeks of cigarettes and some nondescript combination of colognes. Marie had approved the thousand Charlie used to bet and he won—tripling it—so she hadn't given him trouble for gambling. She resents every second of housework, however, and thinks about how she'll hire help soon. She notices a smudge on the collar that looks like blood, but when she picks it up to inspect it, it's clearly lipstick.

It feels as if something explodes inside Marie's head. Trembling with rage, she turns her attention to the window where she can see Charlie outside, painting the boat. On instinct, her hand goes to the revolver. She caresses it, allowing the full tidal wave of hatred to crash over her and surround her in its wake. Once she calms, she washes the lipstick while she plans.

Booze is the problem, Marie thinks.

Their bread and butter is their Achilles' heel. The more Charlie drinks, the more he drinks, and all the darker sides of his nature are unchained. Everything he restrains in his sober hours is unleashed when he's tight.

Why do I care about Charlie's dallying? I don't love him. Not anymore, anyway. Maybe I'll find my own fun. I can have any man I want.

That's what happened with her and Charlie's first marriages. But divorce is expensive and distasteful. Her mother never tires of reminding her of how ashamed she is of Marie. Marie was able to hide her first marriage from the public, but she and Charlie are growing in notoriety. They have even been listed in the *Miami News* society pages for the Flamingo Hotel party, though she refused to be quoted in the crime page article about the shooting of Red Shannon. Like it or not, she and Charlie are also business partners. They own property and goods together. Disentangling from Charlie will not be easy.

Cleo's words come back to Marie, as she watches him.

I sacrificed a scapegoat.

It won't be easy, but it will be possible.

That's what you have do.

THIRTEEN

WASHINGTON, DC

Elizebeth

E lizebeth massages her aching back and looks with exhaustion at the mountain of solved intercepts that she has to type by tomorrow morning. She hates wasting valuable codebreaking time transcribing, but there's no other way. No one can read her nearly illegible scribbles, and besides, the fewer people who know classified information, the better.

Since she connected with Leila Russell, Elizebeth's success has increased exponentially, but so has her work. Leila sends a bundle of newspapers, memos, and fliers every week, more and more to do with suspected police corruption. From top to bottom, from Sheriff Bryan to all seven of his deputies, rumors of bribery abound. With Bryan's arrest of Commander Jack for his so-called murder of Red Shannon, the work had taken a personal turn and kept Elizebeth up late nights more than ever. Disregarding lawbreakers was one thing. Cracking down on law upholders, quite another.

Elizebeth took Leila's request for T-Men—undercover Prohibition agents of the Treasury—to Root, who passed it along to the appropriate agency heads. Now, more than ten T-Men, posing as rumrunners and bootleggers, and as many coastguardsmen are on assignment in the greater Miami area. Using intelligence already gathered, and what they can garner on their own, they should be able to catch Bryan and his minions sooner rather than later, further disrupting the ever-growing ring of criminals whose epicenter is Miami.

Elizebeth takes a deep breath, checks the clock, and resumes the click-clacking of the typewriter. As the minutes pass, she loses track of time. Suddenly, she sucks in her breath and jumps. William's face appears before her in a break in the skyline of file folders along the edge of the desk.

"You didn't even hear me come in," he says. "I could be a mobster, coming to bump you off."

"Please, there are hardly any left, now that I'm on to them," she says with a wink.

William's grin calls forth a flutter in her belly. He hasn't looked this good since Riverbank. She knows it's because he finally took her suggestion and started meeting with Dr. Philip Graven, of the Washington, DC, Psychoanalytic Association. Dr. Graven has done extensive studies on everything from headaches to epilepsy and has emerged as a leader in the growing field of psychoanalysis. His work with veterans of the Great War has made him an expert in shell shock.

The men meet at Dr. Graven's office twice a week. While William is not specific about their conversations, he has indicated there's great deal of resurrecting the past, bringing memories to the forefront with the hopes of releasing them, in a sense, so they don't assert themselves at inopportune times.

"What's that look?" William asks.

"It's you. You look so good, Billy. So healthy and handsome."

"It's astonishing how having support frees one from burdens," says William. "A confidant. A confessor. Someone to help carry the load."

"I get your jab," she says, narrowing her eyes at him. "And I have help. Her name is Cassie. I have you to thank for her, as you well know."

Though she hates to admit it, Elizebeth doesn't know how she lived without Cassie. The incessant, unconscious breath-holding she was doing has disappeared. Barbara and Cassie adore each other. Elizebeth and Cassie adore each other. The women plan meals together, for which Cassie shops and prepares for Elizebeth to cook—her favorite way to unwind after a long day of staring at codes and ciphers. Cassie's deep, warm voice hums Baptist hymns all throughout the house, the music hypnotic, drowning out the jarring sounds of the city. Cassie has even moved in with them during the week, allowing for the occasional night out for Elizebeth and William, which they try to take advantage of, whenever possible, including earlier that week, when they went to see the film *The Black Pirate* at the Tivoli Theater.

In the film, Douglas Fairbanks was captivating as a man bent on avenging his father's death at the hands of pirates by posing as one himself to infiltrate from within. On the way home,

Elizebeth and William couldn't stop chatting about the story and the real lives of its actors.

"I read in the *Post*," Elizebeth said, "that in the last scene, Fairbanks's wife stood in for the actress playing the damsel in distress. Mary Pickford didn't want anyone else kissing her husband."

"Smart woman," said William. "She came by Fairbanks the bad way, didn't she? When he was married, and they went on the road with Charlie Chaplin, raising war bonds?"

"*Both* were married to other people when they had their affair."

"I don't understand how men and women think that's going to turn out. If one gets one's spouse via adultery, wouldn't the odds spell out a similar end in sight for that relationship?"

"Not everyone lets statistics rule as we do, darling."

"Then maybe they think their first marriages were mistakes, and now that they've found their true love, they're settled. But ladies, beware. '*Men were deceivers ever, One foot in sea, and one onshore, To one thing constant never.*'"

"Ah, the wisdom of Shakespeare," Elizebeth said. "But the Bard gives women too much credit. As if women aren't every inch the schemers, every inch the adulterers and pirates that men are. Never underestimate women, especially those with ambition."

Elizebeth returns her attention to her typewriter, while William continues to watch her.

"You could use more help," says William.

"What does that mean?" Elizebeth asks. "Should we hire a groundskeeper for our third-acre lot? A cook for our family of three?"

"Soon to be four. And I already did, with the groundskeeper."

"William."

"I've just gotten a raise. You know how busy I am, and with the baby coming soon, you will be, too. And I must have roses for you. Walls climbing with talisman roses. Oh, also, Tony, the security guard at my building, has an unmarried sister, Carlotta. Another out-of-work nanny. When the new baby comes, Carlotta can help with him or her."

"A nanny for each baby? William, you're mad."

When he flinches, Elizebeth regrets her words. He frets about his sanity often, and with good reason. She stands, heaving her considerable girth around the desk, and takes William's hands, kissing them.

"I'm the one who's mad," she says. "Tired. Uncomfortable. My brain is foggy. The backlog is so bad because I can barely concentrate. I'm sorry."

He nods and leads her to the worn leather couch by the window, helping her to sit with her back to him. He massages it, kneading away the pain and pressure. She sighs.

"It's all right," he says. "You don't have to apologize for speaking the truth. Dr. Graven has all but said I'm mad."

"What do you mean? I thought it was going well."

"He said I'm 'unsane.' Neither sane nor insane, but in a constant state of flux between the two."

"That describes almost everyone in the world. Especially war veterans. Especially those engaged in secret work."

"But not everyone in the world is plagued with nightmares, panic, and psychic giddiness. You, for instance, are involved in secret work without it wrecking you."

True, she thinks. *But it will not do to say so.*

"Billy," she says, "not only am I not a war veteran, but my secret work leads to catching criminals. Your secret work involves peering behind the curtain of the good and the bad alike, and that's a very special kind of burden. And that's only what I'm allowed to know."

"I so often feel like a character in a Poe story," he says. "Like I'm William Wilson. Like I have a double. Like there's two of me: one in the dark and one in the light. And I cannot reconcile them."

"You can," she says. "You are. Whatever you're doing with Dr. Graven, even if it's just having conversations, is working."

"Do you think?"

"I don't think, I know. Or do you not realize that it's been months since your last nighttime attack?"

She turns to face him and kisses him. Then she moves him around so his back is to her and massages his shoulders.

"If I'm short with you," she says, "I think what's also addling my brain is the upcoming Prohibition Agency Ball. I know it's silly, but I don't want to appear in public at such an advanced stage of pregnancy, drawing attention to my womanhood—my motherhood—in a sea of men and women, some of whom resent my success. You always look so good. I'll embarrass you in my circus tent of a dress."

"Nonsense," he says. "You're beautiful, always. Radiant and powerful. You'll outshine every woman there."

She knows he means this. It's one of the reasons she married him. William has always worshipped her.

"And you, every man," she says. "After all these years, you still give me butterflies in my stomach. More so, the older we get."

He turns to face her, cheeks flushed with love.

"Lizbeth, what did I do to deserve you? What would I do without you?"

"You'd hire a staff of ten. No, fifteen. A gardener for the front yard, in addition to the one in the back. A cleaner for the first floor. One for the second. One for the attic. An escort to the trolley. A food shopper. A breakfast cook. A lunch cook. A dinner cook. A midnight sandwich maker."

He tickles her, catching her laugh with his kiss.

FOURTEEN

MIAMI BEACH

Marie

In her kerchief and sunglasses, jewels flashing, riding in their new green Bentley, Marie feels like a film star. Charlie looks like one. Even Benny, in the suit Marie had custom tailored for him, has cleaned up well. Marie wants everyone in her entourage to look as good as she does. She thought the color of the car too garish, but she indulged Charlie. He behaves better when he gets what he wants.

Marie reaches over to the driver's seat and straightens the new gold tie peeking out of the copper-colored vest of Charlie's three-piece suit. Doing so, her knuckles graze the flask in his breast pocket. On impulse, she reaches in and throws it out onto the road behind them.

"What the hell?" Charlie says, swerving.

"I told you, only fools drink while they gamble," Marie says.

"When they gamble. When they work. When kids are around. When can I have fun?"

"When you learn to hold your liquor."

He scowls and throws the car into a higher gear, speeding toward the Fulford Raceway as if he's one of the men on its track. It's the grand opening, and everyone from the rummy crowd to the Fisher conglomerate, not to mention journalists, will be there. Marie will do her best to get herself and Charlie in front of the camera for some good press, but they have to make it there alive first.

"How about slowing down?" she says, white knuckles on the door handle. "Last I checked, you're not in the race."

"This time," he says. "But mark my words: I will race at Fulford. And I'll win. The boys told me there are beach races going in Daytona. The track runs from the road onto the beach itself and back, bootleggers beating everyone by a mile. The top speed there so far is one-hundred-eighty. I'm going to break it, and I've got my eye on a racer."

Marie is glad he can't see her roll her eyes beneath the sunglasses.

"We're getting that dance hall before we buy a race car," she says. "We need a legitimate business for when Prohibition is over."

"That'll never happen with the dries running this country."

"You're wrong about that."

Charlie glares at the traffic ahead. In this mood, he'll be sulky and unwilling to pose for newspaper pictures. Since she's deprived him of his liquor, Marie knows she had better placate him in some other way.

"But we'll have both race cars and dance halls in no time," she says. "With my plans."

He groans. "What now?"

"Cuba."

"What about it?"

"We're switching the majority of our routes from Nassau to Havana."

"Why? The pigeons don't know the way. And that town has criminals, plus corrupt government and Uncle Sam enforcers."

"The duty in the Bahamas is eating up our profits," she says. "Cuba charges a third of the cost. And I can put my brother there to broker."

"Angel?"

"No, Rogelio. He spends a lot of time in Havana."

"Rogelio? Ha! I'd trust Jimmy Alderman over him."

"You're one to talk. Not one of your lowlife siblings is worth a damn, except Benny," she says, throwing him a smile over her shoulder, which he returns. "Even your sisters. Do I have to remind you of the time I had to bail Bessie out of jail?"

"That was her husband's fault. He's the one who made her bring the hacksaw to the pen when she visited him."

"You didn't have anything to do with the escape plan? While you were in the cell next door for stealing tires?"

"What, are you a judge now? I got out. He got out. She's out. It all worked out."

Marie scoffs.

Traffic on the road increases, and by the time Fulford rises on the horizon, they're at a crawl.

"I knew we should have taken the shuttle bus from the Flamingo," says Marie.

"I want to be in charge of when I come and go. Not reliant upon some damned shuttle."

Parking and the ticket line take an hour, and they bicker the whole time. Charlie wants Marie in the three-dollar infield spots, to see the racers and pits up close, but she refuses.

"In these heels?" she asks. "Fuel fumes and dust on my face? You must be bats."

Marie is here to rub elbows with the best of Florida society, not with the grease monkeys in the pits.

"You know what? Good," says Charlie. "Buy as high up in the grandstand as possible. Anywhere I won't have to hear you yapping in my ear."

Marie purchases a ticket for the eight-dollar seats and leaves Charlie in her wake, grumbling.

Once there, her eagle eye tracks over the boxes until she finds her target: Carl Fisher. As Marie moves to her place in the grandstand, all heads turn to follow her. She swapped her kerchief for a cloche hat, but keeps her sunglasses on and walks with the kind of saunter she practiced in front of her life-sized gilded mirror. Her new heels are a pair of two-toned Alfred Cammeyers. They are the color of an ivory sailcloth on top and have a snakeskin print the aquamarine of Biscayne Bay on the bottom. She's never owned such an exquisite pair of shoes in her life and knows they'll be worth the blisters, worth every penny for what they add to her stature.

Her sleeveless dress is made of ivory lace, with a low aquamarine belt. Her lips have her usual Tangee rouge-turned-red, and for her eyes she found a perfect shade of ocean-colored shadow, the kind that makes her beryl eyes appear blue. She has also found a signature fragrance: Molinard's Habanita. It smells of honeyed tobacco and leather, with notes of jasmine and orange blossom. Like Marie herself, it's powerful and masculine up front, with a velvety smooth, feminine finish, and it costs a fortune.

Marie granted Charlie permission to bet ten thousand on the race, as long as he vowed to put it on the man she picked: an Italian named Peter DePaolo, whose Duesenberg 8 won at Indianapolis. Charlie wanted Harry Hartz and his flashy, new Miller race car—which had virtually no track record—and Charlie fought her tooth and nail, saying he didn't want to bet on "that wop DePaolo." Marie insisted. Her picks aren't arbitrary, the way Charlie likes to make them.

"I have a hunch!" he said.

Charlie finally relented. When it comes down to it, even though he won't admit it, Charlie knows his brains are no match for hers.

Marie pauses when she spots Cleo Lythgoe in the cheaper grandstand seats. Marie heard that Cleo had been bouncing between Florida hotels, sucking as much out of the scene here as she could before making her next move. When the women meet eyes, Cleo nods. Marie considers returning the greeting but decides not to acknowledge Cleo. Marie doesn't want any low associations, especially not today. Besides, Marie doesn't need Cleo anymore. Marie is closing in on half of what Cleo made in her whole career, and it's only been a fraction of the time. Cleo's eyes narrow, but the corner of her mouth lifts into a grin before she turns her back on Marie.

When Marie passes Fisher's box, she slows. From behind her sunglasses, she's able to see both Carl and his wife, Jane, look her over from top to bottom. Marie enjoys the way Jane leans forward to goggle at Marie's shoes. She takes her seat on the top row of the grandstand, directly across the walkway separating them, and is close enough to the Fishers' box to get snippets of conversation. Jane whispers about Marie's shoes to her lady friends. Carl brags about the track and the thirty-thousand-dollar purse.

"With these fifty-degree banked turns," Carl says, "drivers have to keep above one-hundred-ten miles per hour, or it's kaput."

There are whistles and headshakes, and ladies' voices saying how dangerous it is, wondering how the wives can stand to watch their men in such a perilous profession. Marie thinks maybe she will buy Charlie a car and let him kill himself on a racetrack so she won't have to get her hands dirty.

Engines roar, a gun blasts, and they're off. Twenty thousand people watch nineteen cars race two hundred forty laps. As the race goes on, cars that can't keep up speed slide and crash on the banked turns, puttering out of the way as the pack thins. Marie can scarcely believe it, but she's captivated by the race. The noise, the motion, the speed—there's a pageantry to it. Her mind drifts to her boat, thinking of the motors, of outrunning the coastguardsmen who are multiplying like mosquitoes. She's been listening at the Lucerne in Nassau and has heard about the men having Great War Liberty airplane engines outfitted on their vessels. The coasties don't stand a chance at catching them with that level of speed. If she adds those and radios to her boats, she'll be queen in no time.

The hours pass, the clouds providing a cover from the Florida sun. Marie buys a lemonade and a bag of popcorn. She listens to the people around her. She watches. She plans. When Jane Fisher steps away, Marie walks over to Carl at his box.

"Pardon the interruption," Marie says, allowing her voice to climb higher and come out breathless. "But I have to tell you, with this track, you've made the eighth wonder of the world."

Fisher beams.

Of course, he does, she thinks. *There's not a man alive who doesn't act like a puppy being petted when his ego's stroked.*

The men around him crowd closer, all eager to talk with a beautiful woman who's interested in cars. A newspaperman elbows forward and asks if he can snap a picture. Marie removes her sunglasses and flashes a smile, thrilled to be a part of the shot, giving the newspaperman her name, spelling it carefully, twice, so he gets it right.

Marie feels the glares of the women, of Jane's friends, women sweaty and wilting in the heat, women who wore sleeves, and dark colors, and heavy hats, northerners unaccustomed to the Florida sun. Marie takes her cue to depart, knowing she has spent enough time with Fisher to both leave him wanting and to recognize her when she next approaches him. She'll do so as soon as possible since his main supplier, Red Shannon, is now dead. When she excuses herself and saunters back to her spot, she feels Fisher's stare the whole way.

On the course, there are only six cars left, and DePaulo and Hartz lead the pack, neck and neck. Marie leans forward, searching for Charlie in the crowd. She spots big Benny first, towering over the men, and then—in the flash of sun on his Rolex—Charlie, jumping up and down next to him, yelling. Marie's lip curls in disgust to see his jacket soaked with sweat and smudged with grit.

In the final laps, the din increases. Hartz has a small lead. Marie clenches her fists, willing the man to blow a tire, lose his car on the bank, or drop an engine part like the dozens strewn like shrapnel over the course. She then turns her attention to DePaolo's car. She quietly encourages it, the way she does her sea vessels, seeking the spirit of the vehicle, urging it to find its full power. All at once, the Duesenberg remembers what it is. It leaps ahead, propelling with an incomprehensible speed toward the finish. The crowd has reached a level of mania that touches even Marie. Normally reserved, she finds herself clapping and cheering right along with them, feeling a burst of pleasure when DePaolo crosses the finish line.

Marie slips away, nodding at Fisher as she passes, and walks down to meet Charlie and Benny. She'll let Charlie buy a racer with their enormous winnings, and she looks forward to telling him so. In the crowd, however, it's impossible to see or find Charlie or Benny. She soon gives up and heads to their car.

As the time passes—one hour, then another—the crowds file past her. She grows hungrier, angrier, and more uncomfortable by the moment. The buses leave. The parking lot is nearly empty. She curses herself for losing track of Charlie. He could be robbed and beaten for all she knows.

Finally, with the sun setting, she sees the outline of Benny, pulling Charlie toward her. Charlie staggers and resists, until Benny finally has to grab his brother by the scruff of the neck and force him to the car. Marie shakes her head in disgust.

"How much did you blow?" she asks. "While I sat here, roasting, starving, for hours?"

Charlie's words are slurred, and he won't look her in the eye. Benny loads Charlie in the back seat, slams the door shut, and passes Marie the keys. Benny won't meet her eyes, either.

"With our win, I can't believe he didn't run up to meet me," she says.

Benny swallows and wipes the sweat from his brow with a handkerchief. Marie narrows her eyes at her brother-in-law.

"What happened?" she asks.

Benny looks down at his shoes, covered in dirt from the infield, and shakes his head.

"You didn't win," Benny says.

"What do you mean? We bet on DePaolo."

"Charlie changed it to Hartz. Last minute. Said he trusted his gut."

Marie feels her fury rise, uncontainable. She throws open the car door and heaves Charlie out with all her strength. Battering and beating him, she feels like a woman possessed. He doesn't fight back.

She kicks him over and over, until blood stains her new heels.

FIFTEEN

WASHINGTON, DC

Elizebeth

William escorts Elizebeth into the grand entrance of DC's exclusive Metropolitan Club. Men and women from the United States Coast Guard, the Bureau of Investigation, Customs, and all groups within the Treasury and Justice Departments engaged in the Rum War are joining forces for a night of fun and celebration.

"Goodness," says Elizebeth, noting the faces around her, "it's carte blanche for the smugglers tonight."

"Everyone needs a night off," says William, with a teasing twinkle in his eye.

As they were walking out the door, a courier delivered a locked bag to Elizebeth that she knew came from Leila. Elizebeth looked longingly over her shoulder at the documents that William had run up to secure in the library, and he knew as well as she that her mind would be half on them all evening.

As soon as their outer garments are hanging in the coat check, they pass through the elegant lobby—William redirecting Elizebeth from the magnetic pull of the library they pass—and through the arched doorway into the red ballroom. High ceilings, oak-paneled walls, red damask drapery, chandeliers, and ornate moldings create a luxurious atmosphere. The bar area—gleaming with bottles and crystal glasses—is inviting even without alcoholic drinks. In spite of feeling self-conscious about her condition, Elizebeth can't help but brighten. Such beauty and glamour would have been unimaginable in the plain, drab surroundings of her and William's childhoods. Now, they're a regular and welcome part of their lives.

Elizebeth catches sight of herself in a large mirror and stands a little straighter. The loose, drop-waist style helps camouflage her stomach, and under the dim chandeliers, the dress's midnight-blue satin shimmers like an inky sea in the moonlight. Her confidence wavers, however, when she spots the woman across the room. Wearing a slinky beaded number, bobbed blonde hair in perfect waves, is Leila Russell. She and a handsome singer from the orchestra chat while the musicians tune their instruments. When she sees Elizebeth, Leila excuses herself from the conversation, and makes the long walk across the empty dance floor, all eyes on her. William's nearly pop from his head. Elizebeth told William about Leila's beauty. Now he can see for himself. Before Leila reaches them, William looks at Elizebeth with wide eyes.

"I'll go get drinks," he says, kissing her cheek and heading to the bar.

As he exits, Leila arrives.

"I knew you'd be here," Leila says, air-kissing Elizebeth.

"That makes one of us," says Elizebeth. "What a surprise."

"I wouldn't miss it. We're all playing in the sandbox so nicely with each other now. That's worth celebrating."

"True," says Elizebeth. "I must thank you for your communication. It's been stellar. One of your bundles arrived as we were leaving, and my husband had to practically pry my fingers from the door to get me here."

"That took longer than I thought it would. I sent it nearly two weeks ago."

The music draws their attention. As indicated on the invitation, Paul Whiteman's Orchestra, with the Rhythm Boys, is playing symphonic jazz. Whiteman, the portly conductor, was a U.S. Navy bandleader during the Great War and now commands a large ensemble of fine-looking young men.

"That fellow you were talking to," says Elizebeth. "The singer. Is he your date?"

"No, and never will be."

"Why's that?"

"His name is Bing."

"Bing?" Elizebeth asks.

"Yes, Bing Crosby. I could never step out with a man called Bing."

The women laugh.

"Well, Leila, since there's not a man in this room who hasn't noticed you, you don't have to settle for any Bings."

"Please," says Leila. "When you walked in, everyone woman in this room groaned with envy."

"You must be joking. I'm the size of a zeppelin."

It's the first reference Elizebeth has made to her pregnancy outside of the house, and it feels strangely liberating.

"I didn't want to ask, but I'm happy for you," says Leila. "Your first?"

To avert answering, Elizebeth pretends to be distracted by Bing Crosby's voice.

After a few moments, Leila touches Elizebeth's arm.

"Aside from your beauty," Leila says, "you're absolutely glowing. You are successful, working at important things, and married to a devoted husband. Most of the women in this room are only here because they're 'wives of.' William is a 'husband of.'"

Elizebeth is surprised to feel tears spring to her eyes along with a bloom of gratitude. She thinks, *This pregnancy is doing a number on my emotions.*

"Thank you," she says. "I shouldn't have to be reminded of all I have to be thankful for, but I do. I appreciate your kind words."

"It's nothing."

A movement by the door and the appearance of another woman—Agnes Meyer Driscoll—causes an involuntary groan from Elizebeth that she regrets. She chastises herself inwardly. Women really should stick together, but this one is a thorn in the Friedmans' side. Before doing contract cryptanalysis with the coast guard, Elizebeth replaced Agnes at the navy, doing the same work. Agnes thought she'd go for the private sector, to make more money than she could in the government, but didn't have success. She enjoyed a lot of attention until Elizebeth and William came on the scene, and now Agnes feels overshadowed and left behind. Elizabeth would sympathize with Agnes if it weren't for the woman's malicious, gossiping tongue. She talks horribly about the Friedmans, especially William—for moving ahead of her with both the creation and breaking of cipher machines.

"I'm sorry. That was adolescent of me," says Elizabeth.

"Please, don't apologize," says Leila. "You must tell me all about her. I crave gossip like Charles Waite craves booze."

"Who?"

"Ah, that's right. You just got the bundle, so you haven't read my memo yet. We have our new King of the Rum Runners. The one who bought Red Shannon's *Goose* and renamed it *Josephine*. Charles Waite is his name. He and his no-good siblings have quite a record. Mostly small arrests and convictions for everything from drunk and disorderly conduct, to tire theft, to liquor distribution, but there's never enough to convict him or make him pay for long. And because the courts are so swamped, he's learned to play the game of pleading guilty, paying minimal fines, dodging jail time, and getting back to work."

Charles Waite, Elizabeth thinks, creating a new file in her mind. More than ever, she feels an urge to leave and get into that bundle.

When Agnes passes, she runs her eyes over Leila and Elizabeth from head to toe and tracks back to Elizabeth's stomach, taking no pains to hide her bulging stare. Agnes pauses as if she wants to say something, but must think better of it, because she continues to the opposite side of the room.

"Goodness," says Leila. "I see why you groaned."

Elizebeth nods and spots William, balancing three club sodas with lime, crossing the room to join them.

"Before my husband gets here," says Elizebeth, "A secret question. Commander Jack. Did my statement help him with the judge?"

"It did. Jack's out and back on the water."

Elizebeth exhales. "Thank heavens. I was worried that not appearing would lessen the force of my words and argument, but my doctor doesn't want me traveling until after the baby comes."

"It came through, perfectly. And we were able to find a witness to corroborate. A gondola driver. He had a perfect view of the whole exchange."

William reaches them and distributes the drinks.

"My husband, William Friedman," Elizebeth says. "This is Leila Russell, the assistant DA from Florida I've told you all about."

"Wonderful to meet you," says William.

"And you. You're both like royalty around here. The king and the queen."

"More like the queen and her jester," says William. "I hear you're a pilot."

The group chatters amiably, soon joined by Commander Root and a succession of others. J. Edgar Hoover arrives late, slinks in the shadows, and leaves early. Agnes avoids the Friedmans the entire night. Leila and Bing flirt between sets. When Bing starts to sing "Somewhere a Voice Is Calling," William and Elizebeth take to the dance floor. Under the soft glow of the chandeliers, in William's arms, Elizebeth feels as if time has slipped away and they are newlyweds, dancing one last time before William's deployment.

"Our war song," says William. "When we were apart. I could never bear such a separation again."

"Then there better be no more wars."

"We can dream."

"But we also know the magma is always boiling just below the surface."

"Indeed."

Once Elizebeth is thoroughly exhausted, they make their good-byes and take a taxi home. The house is quiet and dark, and they fall into each other in bed. As tired as she is, however, Elizebeth can't sleep. The pull of the bundle is too strong. She doesn't want to hear William's chastisement, so it's only once his breathing is deep and regular that she walks on bare feet to the library.

Once she's locked inside and the light clicks on, her eyes travel over the art and history books to the literature section. Elizebeth likes to do this, to find the quote—like a book's epigraph—to set her frame of mind before she works. Shakespeare is, of course, her go-to, but Poe calls tonight. In a few moments, she feels the draw from the first-edition, soft red leather volume that includes *The Purloined Letter*. She opens to the story and soon finds the words that will help her get into the mind of the pursued.

"'When I wish to find out how wise,'" she reads, "'or how stupid, or how good, or how wicked is any one, or what are his thoughts at the moment, I fashion the expression of my face, as accurately as possible, in accordance with the expression of his, and then wait to see what thoughts or sentiments arise in my mind or heart, as if to match or correspond with the expression.'"

Elizcbeth imagines Charles Waite—a petty criminal within a network of petty criminals—who suddenly becomes rich, and all the trouble that brings. Something feels off to Elizebeth, however. It's a nagging tingling, like electrical pulses, that tell her there's more to this. She tries to crawl in Charles's mind, but it's difficult without a picture. Once she sees what he looks like, she'll better understand. She'll be able to inhabit him, to tap into his very thoughts.

Elizebeth slides the Poe volume back on the shelf and approaches the desk. She unlocks the drawer and lifts Leila's bundle. Elizebeth skims Leila's memo on top—making a mental note that Al Capone's operations in Miami are growing, and the T-Men are on the hunt for an airplane pilot Capone has hired for smuggling—and then dives into the pile of newspaper clippings. She soon finds Charles Waite. His picture is with an article in the society pages of the *Miami News*. He's at a Mardi Gras party, at Carl Fisher's Flamingo Hotel, with a woman.

"Mr. and Mrs. Charles Waite," reads Elizebeth.

Even in black and white one can see how strikingly handsome Charles is. He has fair hair, a chiseled jaw, and cruel, pale eyes. The wife is also striking. She has dark hair, full, pouty lips, an arrogant tilt to her chin, and shrewd eyes. She looks like a portrait of nobility, like the haughty Catalina Micaela of Spain. Elizebeth returns her attention to Charles's face.

"So, Charles, you bought the *Goose*," she says. "Did you tip us off?"

Elizebeth takes a deep breath and closes her eyes, imagining crawling into the skin of Charles, trying to conceive the kind of man he is, the kind of plans he makes. Her thoughts return to the tip. The words.

Roja. Flamenco. Baile. Pescado.

Red. Flamingo. Dance. Fish.

Roja.

Spanish.

Elizebeth's eyes snap open and return to the newspaper, to the woman, to Mrs. Charles Waite.

Never underestimate women. Especially those with ambition.

"What's your name?" Elizebeth says.

She flips through the bundle, skimming newspapers, one after another, until she finds the wife in a photograph from the Fulford Raceway. She has the same dark hair, arrogant bearing, and shrewd eyes. Elizebeth reads as fast as she can.

Developer Carl Fisher, of Miami Beach, and businesswoman Marie Waite, of Miami, take in the sights of the inaugural Fisher Cup.

"Eureka," Elizebeth says.

Businesswoman Marie Waite.

"Got you."

SIXTEEN

MIAMI BEACH

Marie

Marie leads the children and their new nanny, Florence, to a set of reserved seats at the Roman Pools. Carl Fisher bought the large recreational complex and casino last year and updated the grounds to feature a windmill, which helps draw salt water in to feed the sparkling beachside pools. Fisher does not swim with the commoners, but he's known to have lunch often on the terrace with business associates or his wife, though today he's not with his wife, but another woman. The woman wears a white fox stole on her shoulders—*strange*, Marie thinks, *for the weather*—leans on his arm with familiarity, and even kisses him in broad daylight.

Shameless.

It's not the obvious fact of the affair that bothers Marie—she would take that woman's chair in a heartbeat—but the brazenness of it. At the moment, however, Marie isn't interested in an affair, but in a business arrangement.

"Will you swim with us?" asks Josephine.

Marie looks down at her heart-faced children, wearing little white robes over belted bathing suits, dark hair slicked back, large eyes gazing up with hope. The hope gives her heart a pang. The world is cruel and will likely break their hearts. She will do all she can to prevent it, but she's nothing if not a realist.

I can't coddle them.

"No," Marie says. "I have business to attend to, but Nanny Florence will swim with you."

Their shoulders fall. Florence is a plain girl, dry and colorless. Marie met Florence at Gesú Catholic Church, where she plays the organ and is a recent graduate of the school, where she was always on the honor roll. Florence is quiet, smart, and efficient, takes no nonsense from the children, and most important, will be absolutely no temptation for Charlie. Marie thinks the women who hire pretty, young nannies are fools.

"How about Uncle Benny?" asks Joey, looking over at the hulking form of the man in the shadows, the man never more than a shout away from his boss.

"No," says Marie. "Uncle Benny is working, too. However, if business goes well, one day we'll have our very own pool, where Mama and Uncle Benny will be able to swim with you at their leisure."

Marie can see they're still disappointed.

Life is nothing but a series of disappointments, Marie thinks. *But hopefully, not for much longer.*

"And Charlie will be able to swim with us then, too," says Josephine, eyes alternating with sparkles of challenge and shadows of suspicion. "Won't he? When he's all better?"

God, she's just like me.

"Yes, as soon as he's out of the hospital," Marie says.

Charlie has been at Allison Hospital for weeks, recovering from a bruised kidney, broken ribs, and a nasty concussion. Marie told the children Charlie was jumped at the racetrack, and it wasn't a lie.

As luxurious as a hotel, Allison Hospital was completed last year by its namesake, James Allison, and his dear friend and investor Carl Fisher. Rich men don't want sterile industrial buildings when they're sick. They want the things that Allison provides: Spanish architecture, three-hundred-sixty-degree water views, gentle wall colors, and world-class dining. Marie could have had Benny take Charlie to the clinic serving the poor, but she decided he'd been punished enough. Besides, they have a reputation to protect.

The nurses at the hospital have grown to love Marie, the "lovely, devoted wife who visits every day," especially because of the large donation Marie has just given them. Marie knows she must do good and do it visibly. It will lay a foundation for respectability when she no longer has to engage in illegal activity to support her family.

Josephine continues to stare at Marie for a long moment until a cheer from the crowd draws their attention. A man dives from the breathtakingly high ladder while barely making a splash. From the balcony, Fisher and his secretary clap.

I'm wasting time, thinks Marie.

She abandons her children and sets her course for Fisher,

Benny trailing. She takes the back stair and positions herself gracefully against the balustrade overlooking the ocean, in Fisher's line of sight. She has framed this scene in her mind. She knows what an elegant and striking picture she makes, the contrast of her black hair with her coral seaside dress, her sheer scarf blowing in the breeze, her turquoise high heels with pearly scalloped art deco edging. The endless blue sky and blue-green waves provide the perfect background to her stage. The wind coming off the Atlantic will send wafts of her perfume across Fisher's table.

Soon lunch is cleared and the mistress rises to take her inevitable trip to the ladies' room to primp, to keep her man on the hook. Marie glides along the walkway, looking down over the Roman Pools, pausing when she's near Fisher's table, pretending to be surprised to see him there. She's pleased at the bright spark of recognition in his eyes.

"Mr. Fisher," she says.

"Carl."

She nods. "Marie."

"I know," he says, leaning toward her, conspiring, eyes twinkling. "Spanish Marie."

Marie hopes her face doesn't convey her displeasure. She didn't expect a man like Fisher to engage in dockside gossip.

"The public," she says with feigned exasperation. "They love a tall tale."

His face falls into a pout. "I like the lore."

"Then for you, I'll answer to the name. For you, anything."

When Carl brings his sweating iced tea to his lips and grins around it at her, she feels a ripple of desire. His glasses make him look smart and refined, which, combined with his net worth, makes him very attractive.

"Since you brought up business," Marie says, "I hear you need a new supplier."

She knows this isn't true. Sensing the vacancy Red Shannon left, Jimmy Alderman slunk in before she could. Fisher's glance darts around, and he shakes his head.

"You have bad intelligence," he says, all flirtation gone.

"Not quite," she says, matching his serious tone. "I should have given this introduction: Because Jimmy Alderman cuts his liquor with water, and because he's dealing in human cargo, you should have nothing to do with him. Therefore, you need a new supplier. I can be that."

At the words *human cargo*, Fisher nearly spits out his drink. The mistress is on her way back.

"Have your men contact mine, at Theo's Lunch Counter, Miami," says Marie. "They'll give you my direct telephone line. *Hasta la próxima.*"

———

"'Pillars of the community,'" Marie reads aloud from the paper to Charlie, while Florence serves them breakfast. After more than a month, he's finally home from the hospital. "'Mr. and Mrs. Charles Waite's generous donation to Gesú Catholic Church has allowed for the addition of the new statue of Immaculate Mary,

Queen of Heaven, and funding for the missionaries serving persecuted Catholics in Mexico. ¡*Viva Cristo Rey!*'"

Back in Key West, when Raul Vasquez told Marie to tithe, she balked, but since she's started doing so, she feels better about herself and her income. Strangely, this is an expenditure of which Charlie approves. He thinks it's bringing them good luck, even if it is going to the Catholic Church. There's no luck about their success, only sound, smart business practices. It's certainly bringing them respectability. They are now regular features in the society pages, for one reason or another, including last week's coverage of the Easter egg hunt Marie coordinated for the parish children. She knows in September, there will be no trouble getting the kids enrolled at the school.

"Very nice," says Charlie.

At the hospital, as soon as Charlie regained consciousness, Marie explained the expense she'd taken on to keep him at such a fine facility, and how—from now on—she would be in charge of business operations. Marie remembers how pale Charlie got upon understanding how she'd claimed power, and how astonished he was, learning how successful she became in such a short time. It was much easier to work without him dragging them down.

He groveled.

"I deserved this," he said.

Marie was so stunned by his admission that she was speechless.

"I should have listened to you," he continued. "I know how smart you are. How you do research. It won't happen again. Never. I'll let you take the helm."

He reached for her hand and kissed it earnestly. It was such an unprecedented gesture of chivalric submission it softened her.

I must have knocked something straight in that brain of his, she thought.

Marie nodded at him, offering silent absolution. She didn't believe in her heart that such a thing would last forever, but she'd take it for the short term. Charlie was essential to her plans.

Now that Fisher and a growing network of his friends and associates are clients, the cash is pouring in, almost faster than she can keep up. Marie has been able to acquire enough boats to expand the fleet to vessels of varying sizes, including a seventy-five-footer named the *Cortés*, of which she's particularly proud. She's upgraded the smaller vessels with Liberty airplane motors for speed, and all are equipped with radios. She's hired a small navy of men for her armada and has gotten Benny and Theo an instructor to teach them to drive the boats.

Her brother Angel has opened a pirate radio station in Key West for her, and has picked up the trade quickly, learning from his friend—a Great War Signal Corps vet who abandoned his government job at the radio building of the Naval Air Station for private illegal industry, where the pay is much better. Her brother Rogelio has set up a cigar-shop storefront in Havana, and once Marie visits to get the lay of the land, their new channel between Cuba and Key West can open, and they can make a real profit.

The new Herschede Hall grandfather clock in the hallway chimes the eight o'clock hour. Its gorgeous brass face includes a moon dial and ship under sail. Marie feels the familiar tingle of excitement, anticipating tonight's huge run, followed by a rush of annoyance.

"Where's Benny?" she asks.

It's not like him to be late. If anything, he's usually early, hoping for a seat at the family breakfast table. Charlie shrugs.

Marie dismisses the children and Florence to finish getting ready for school. Once three sets of shoes are upstairs, and the water in the bathroom sink runs, Marie leans closer to Charlie.

"We're taking the *Cortés* and the *Josephine* to Cuba next week to meet up with Rogelio."

Marie sees the flash of anger on Charlie's face that he quickly stifles before he nods. Charlie has never been able to stand Rogelio, who's dazzlingly handsome, has the easy confidence of one who's instantly popular wherever he goes, and only speaks Spanish or French around Charlie, with the sole purpose of making Charlie feel talked about, which he is. She's both surprised and pleased to see Charlie learning to control his baser instincts. Maybe there's hope for him, after all.

"Will we keep using Peltz in the Bahamas or switch completely over?" Charlie asks, careful now to solicit her opinion before spewing his own.

"Variety keeps the feds guessing, and they're all over Peltz," she says, "Rogelio set up a cigar-shop front, with a big warehouse in the back, along the Prado in Havana. He's in with a wholesaler who can get us the booze, the false documents we need, and the officials who will turn a blind eye. Our vessels are also registered as commercial to carry the cigars, so if the coasties stop us, we'll have cargo that matches our papers and a legitimate tie to Cuba."

"Okay," Charlie says, nodding.

Marie feels a strange deflation that he isn't speaking with a confrontational edge, but rather asking and agreeing like a student. Charlie was more attractive to her when he was dangerous. He's become like a pet.

"So, tonight," she says, "it's hopefully our last run to the Bahamas for a while. Next week, we start Cuba."

"I can still go tonight, right?"

Marie has already decided she'll let Charlie take the helm again, to keep up the image of the king, while shielding herself. They'll show their competitors he's back on his throne. She's been seeding the rumor fields for weeks that they'll find the one who jumped Charlie and show no mercy. It has increased the paranoia level of the rummies substantially and put them all on guard. She enjoys the chaos she's created.

"Yes," she says. "You are the king, after all."

That brings the old sexy, devilish grin to his face.

"Peltz will have four hundred sacks for us," she says. "Which will put us firmly on the way to becoming millionaires."

Much faster than Cleo Lythgoe ever was, Marie thinks.

"Let's go over the plan again," she says.

"We'll run to the Bahamas and back," says Charlie, talking like a schoolboy reciting his lesson. "Then I'll drop you off to Benny at the Flamingo."

"Yes."

And that way, only you will get pulled in if the feds catch us.

"Then I'll tie up with the *Shadow K*," he says, "and unload to Fisher's men. When we finish, they'll radio the hotel manager in the tea garden, who'll give you the money."

"Then?"

"Then you and Benny will drive the truck along River Drive to the Twenty-Seventh Street Bridge, where I'll unload the rest to you two to take to Theo's place."

"And what are you to do with the boat if you get caught?"

Charlie swallows, unable to say the words. He thinks she's crazy for it. Maybe she is.

"Burn it," she says for him.

Legend says that, when threatened by marauders, Spanish explorer Cortés burned his own ships. Whether that's true or not, Marie would rather burn her *Cortés* as an offering to the sea than allow the enemy to take one plank of it. The coast guard knows the only hope they have of matching the speed of rumrunner vessels is to take them over. She won't allow it. One of Charlie's old army buddies got him a crate of hand bombs, little metallic pineapples that take five seconds to explode after the pins are pulled. That would be just enough time to detonate, jump overboard, and swim for dear life.

Brakes squeak outside the house.

"Finally," Marie says, standing and heading toward the front door.

The tide of relief is quickly replaced with fury at herself. Marie hadn't realized how dependent upon Benny's presence she's become. Independence is her goal, after all. When she opens the curtain and looks out the window, however, it's not Benny's truck, but a beat-up International. The men in it are wearing hats low over their faces and driving slowly, and she thinks she sees one taking pictures before they speed away. Heart pounding, Marie releases the curtain and recoils from the window. She couldn't get a good enough look at the men to decide if they were feds or smugglers.

Now you're being paranoid, she thinks.

Marie can't keep her mind from spinning. Her relationship with Fisher has gotten her in with Sheriff Bryan, whom she has on her payroll, and the feds don't usually bother with rummies unless they're part of the larger crime syndicates. That means it's likely a peer. Envious smugglers have confronted Benny at the racetracks over the past weeks. None of them are happy about Marie and Charlie's success. She'll have to beef up her security, and maybe even think about bringing Benny on to live with them.

As if conjured, Benny finally arrives, breathless and sweating, as a passenger in a truck that's not his. As he hurries up the front path, she throws open the door, her face aflame.

"Why are you late?"

"I'm sorry, Boss. It was my tires."

"What about them?" she asks.

"They were slashed. All four of 'em."

Marie's stomach roils. She's about to interrogate him further, but the children interrupt. They come pounding down the stairs, dressed for school, trailed by Florence. Joey runs to hug Benny, and the big man picks him up and kisses him on both cheeks.

"You be a good boy at school today, Joey," says Benny. "Listen to your teachers. Learn your letters and numbers, so you don't end up a big dummy like me."

"I promise," says Joey.

"You too, Josie," Benny says.

"I will, Uncle Benny."

Marie sees her daughter try to hide the doll in her cardigan. Marie holds out her hand and Josephine surrenders it, scampering outside as quickly as possible. Marie grabs Florence's arm as she passes.

"I've told you," Marie says. "Josephine is too old to take a doll with her outside of this house. Don't let it happen again."

"Yes, ma'am," says Florence.

"Bye, Florence," Benny says.

The nanny's cheeks turn crimson, and she ducks out. Marie shakes her head in disbelief, and once they're gone, she slaps the back of Benny's head to get his attention.

"Did you see anyone?" she asks. "Last night? This morning?"

"No," he says. "But the worst part was the truck was locked up in Theo's garage. They knew it was there, broke in, did the damage, and left, without anyone seeing a thing."

"What damage?" asks Charlie, joining them.

"Slashed tires," says Marie. "And a suspicious truck just drove by our house."

"Who do you think it is?" asks Charlie.

Benny and Marie answer at the same time.

"Alderman."

"Why is that here?" Marie asks, pointing at the pigeon cage in the bed of the truck.

"It's a Bahamas run," says Charlie.

"We have a radio now. Theo has a receiver. We don't need a bird."

"I'll keep my faith in pigeons, not machines," Charlie says, failing to confine his anger.

"Your faith should be in me. I'm the one who made this boat, this run, this supplier, and this buyer possible."

Seeing her anger, he swallows. He looks from her to the pigeon cage and back.

"I'll put it back," he says.

"It's too late. Let's go."

Once on the boat, the entire run, she tries to keep her eyes on the horizon to will calm into herself. The seas are turbulent, the clouds are low, and the bird won't stop cooing. It's driving her mad. She realizes, with some discomfort, that it feels like bad luck to have the squab onboard. She dismisses the thought, however, reminding herself that there's no such thing as luck, bad or good.

She slips her hand into her handbag and steals a nip from her flask so Charlie doesn't see. Her paranoia is at an all-time high, and she has to take the edge off to keep calm.

It takes them longer than she hoped to get to Nassau, longer than she anticipated to load four hundred sacks into the secret compartments, longer than she would have liked to haggle with Customs, more than she wanted to pay in duty. When they're finally ready to return, she sends out the first message to Theo, via radio, in Spanish. They agreed upon the word *siesta* to mark the time of them leaving, so he'll have a good idea of when they'll arrive. Once they get to Miami Beach and reach Fisher's boat, she'll send, *"Voy a pescar"*—*I am going fishing*—so Theo and Benny can get the onshore trucks ready.

As they pull out of Nassau harbor, Charlie releases the pigeon. It's all Marie can do not to draw her revolver and shoot it, as it flies off into the night.

The ride back is awful, with four-foot rollers, raging wind, and a clanging birdcage. When the rain starts pounding, she can take it no longer. She strides over to the empty cage and heaves it overboard.

Charlie shakes with fury, but he keeps his eyes forward and his mouth shut.

Even in a vessel this size, being so heavily weighted makes the boat ride slow and dangerously low to the water. She thinks of all the champagne, wine, whisky, rum, and gin they carry. If it weren't wrapped so tightly, she'd have broken into it by now. Her flask is almost empty. At least they shouldn't have to worry about the coasties for the last twelve miles. They don't patrol in these conditions.

At the time they should have reached Fisher's boat, the radio crackles. Marie hurries to pick it up.

"*¿Ya estás pescando?*"

"No. *Pronto.*"

Charlie looks at the radio with wide eyes, clearly impressed.

"Can your squabs do that?" she asks.

He keeps his mouth shut.

They don't have Miami Beach in their sights until two in the morning, and the weather has reached near-squall conditions. They go black—lights out on the boat—and Marie uses the dial to search for the Miami Beach pirate channel. She was able to buy the information, and a quick lesson in Morse code, for no small sum.

This is where it gets dangerous, she thinks.

The government men are constantly searching for these wildcat stations and transmissions. Some are in fixed locations; others are in the backs of vehicles, constantly moving. Because Miami Beach is smuggler-friendly, this station is fixed at the windmill at Fisher's Roman Pools and has excellent views. Every ten minutes, or if there's a change, the radioman she bribed will send the Morse code signal *XTAL*, for *Crystal*, meaning the coast is crystal clear. For a warning, he'll Morse *SKIDOO* for *Keep out*.

They must have just missed the last transmission because it's nine minutes until the next.

"*XTAL.*"

"Okay, go," she says.

With wide eyes, Charlie looks from her to the radio, then motors toward Government Cut and into the bay, where he drops Marie at the Flamingo Hotel pier. Before she goes, she points to the three hand bombs lined up in the opening under the steering column. He nods. Marie climbs onto the pier and sees Benny's reassuring shadow, his arm raised at the end in silent greeting.

Marie watches Charlie motor to the dark side of the *Shadow K* and then hurries in the rain to join Benny, who escorts her to the tea garden. They stand in the dark, under the awning, waiting. It's only been ten minutes, but it feels like years, and she's gotten a chill from her wet clothing. Just as she starts to wonder if something is wrong, the hotel door opens, and an arm passes out a fat pouch. She grabs it, unzips it, and counts the money inside, her heart racing as the tally grows.

We could stop now, she thinks. *We could buy a place in Key West and keep the house here. I could run dance schools, and Charlie could race cars. We'd be set.*

But they haven't done a single run from Cuba, and they'll really make big bucks from that.

Just a little longer, she thinks.

The storm is relentless. They run all the way to the truck, Benny opening Marie's door before getting in himself. Hair plastered to her face, clothing soaked, she curses and drinks what's left in her flask. Benny averts his eyes and puts the truck in gear, heading for River Drive, which runs along the waterway, where they can track Charlie's progress. When she sees the *Cortés* slip into the river, Marie exhales.

Riding parallel to the boat, windshield wipers scraping, they meet no road traffic. Hopefully, Charlie won't meet any on the water. They only have three and a half miles to go to reach the canal at Northwest Twenty-Seventh Street, where they'll unload, but every minute since Marie radioed Theo feels like an eternity. When Benny nearly hits a resting heron, it squawks and flies over the windshield, its feathers leaving a trail on the rain-soaked glass. Spooked, Marie tells Benny to go faster.

"You don't want to stay with Charlie?" asks Benny, nodding toward the *Cortés* as it snakes along the river.

The look she shoots Benny causes him to obey without a word.

As they pick up speed, Marie has a terrible premonition that something is wrong. While she has a fortune with her, she realizes, with horror, that Charlie has no will. They've been acquiring everything from their home, to lots, to boats at such a rate, many in his name only, that she can barely keep up. She resolves, at first light, she'll have Charlie make an appointment with their lawyer. Charlie won't like it, but she doesn't care. She's angry at herself for not thinking of this sooner.

When they cross the railroad tracks and arrive at the bridge, they park where they can see down the river. Charlie isn't yet in view. Heart pounding in time to the wipers, at first, Marie thinks she imagines the sounds of sirens. When Benny looks at her with wide eyes, however, she knows he's heard, too.

Benny puts the truck in gear and drives down the ramp— lights off—tucking the truck under the bridge. She crawls into the back seat and lifts the cushion, where she locks the money bag in a secret compartment, then returns to the front. In a few moments, along the river, she sees the running lights of the

Cortés, coming fast. Seconds later, she sees the flash of red on the light of the police boat closing in behind Charlie.

"What do we do?" asks Benny, panicked.

"Be ready to drive," she says.

"What about Charlie?"

"He'll have to figure that out."

Benny looks at Marie, his forehead wrinkled with concern. In spite of how poorly Charlie and his brothers treat Benny, he loves them. He has the loyalty of a dog. It won't do to have him worried. Scared people make stupid mistakes.

"Charlie will be fine," she says. "He'll blow up the boat, if necessary. We'll wait for him at Theo's."

Benny exhales. The relief doesn't last long.

They hear a gun blast. Shots fire back and forth between the *Cortés* and the police boat. Marie slips her revolver from her garter and Benny takes his from his breast pocket. The boats have stopped. They heave and groan in the wake from the chop and the storm.

"Did they kill him?" asks Benny, again in a panic.

Without a will, I hope not, Marie thinks.

When the police boat throws on a searchlight, Charlie's form can be clearly seen, hands in the air in surrender.

Marie thinks of the bombs.

How will Charlie deploy them if his hands are in the air?

Aside from the officer driving, there are three men in black trenches and hats on the police boat.

"Feds," she whispers.

Marie wonders if it was the radio signal, or if the feds have been tracking them.

Cleo and Raul might have been right about the dangers of getting more sophisticated, thinks Marie. She won't allow herself to acknowledge that maybe Charlie was, too.

No, she thinks. *We'll get out of this, and we'll have a fortune for it. A fortune that wouldn't have been possible without the new boats, the radios, and the connections.*

Suddenly, Benny's truck floods with light. A black car comes to a screech at Benny's door. Marie jumps out of her side, pointing her gun at the men—three more black-hatted, black-coated figures. Two men drag Benny from the car.

Time slows. She's at a crossroads. Does she lower or raise the stakes? The ball is in her court.

Fury rises in her. It feels uncontrollable, like a hurricane. Marie shoots the windshield of the car with lights pointed at them.

"Get off him," Marie yells.

"Drop your weapon!" orders a man, pointing his gun at her. "Now! Or you're dead."

Marie keeps her gun on him.

"Come closer, and you are dead," she says. "Who are you?"

"We are federal Prohibition officers, and you're under arrest."

Damn, she thinks.

"Prove it," she says.

A badge flashes in the light. The men holding Benny flash theirs.

Mierda.

Marie lowers her gun, facing the ground. Her heart feels as if it will pound out of her chest. The blood rushes through her body. It feels good, a high like nothing she's ever before experienced.

"You can't arrest me," she says. "I've done nothing wrong."

"You were waiting here to unload liquor from that boat."

"I was doing no such thing. I was trying to steal some time in the dark with my man."

Benny's eyes widen, nearly bulging from his head.

"You are a liar, Spanish Marie," the fed closest to her says. "And we're on to you."

"Search the car," she says. "You'll find nothing to incriminate me."

One of the feds does just that. She prays he doesn't tug at any of the seat cushions, but even if he does, it's not illegal to have a pouch of money. The man soon finishes and holds up his arms.

Shouting on the river draws their attention. Charlie has the *Cortés* underway, heading back the way he came, away from the bridge and the police boat, which has stalled. Ignoring the guns pointed at her, Marie walks toward the river's edge, the men in her wake. She stares through the dark at Charlie.

Do it, she wills.

They have enough money, and this boat might have a jinx, after all. Not that she believes in such things.

Seeing their men struggling on the water, the feds on land run toward their shot-up car. Marie thinks they'll try to track Charlie to a place they can intercept him. She can hear their curses as the glass on the seats from the shattered windshield cuts them.

Do it.

Before they put their car in gear, Marie sees Charlie run out of the steering house and launch into a graceful dive off the side. Horrified and thrilled, her eyes widen.

Five, four...

She raises her arms, as if conducting an orchestra about to reach its symphony's climax.

Three, two, one.

A spectacular blast lights up the night sky.

SEVENTEEN

WASHINGTON, DC

Elizebeth

E lizebeth can almost feel the heat of Leila's fury coming through the phone line.

"I can't believe what the Waites have gotten away with," Leila says. "Because of the weather, our men took too long to get to the *Cortés,* so she was likely able to get in a big drop on the coast before heading to the river. And because the boat they exploded was their own property, Charles can't be charged with destruction of it. Marie had nothing in her truck because Charles hadn't unloaded yet. If the feds had waited until the transaction was taking place, we could have hauled them all in. As it is, now only Charles is charged for the fees to tow what was left of the boat out to sea to sink. Shots fired can't be proven because he didn't hit anything, and no gun was on his person onshore. Marie claimed self-defense because she said she thought our men were robbers. They didn't flash their badges until after they accosted her and Charles's brother. We failed."

Elizebeth scans the papers on her desk, shaking her head in disbelief.

FEDERAL AGENTS IN GUN BATTLE.

WINDSHIELD SHATTERED.

MRS. WAITE IS THE BRAINS BEHIND THE OPERATION.

SHE'S NOT AFRAID TO SHOOT.

THEY CALL HER "SPANISH MARIE."

Elizebeth lifts the paper with the photograph, a lone woman, arms raised, silhouetted against a blazing conflagration. It's a film-worthy still. Elizebeth can't help but smile.

"We haven't failed, Leila. We've been outsmarted and we've lost a battle, but we won't lose the war."

"How can you be such an optimist?"

"I love a challenge," says Elizebeth. "Spanish Marie has thrown the gauntlet. She's set the table, knives out. We'll rise to meet her, and we'll triumph."

"What makes you say so?"

Elizebeth shuffles the papers until she finds more photographs of Marie. Marie at a church Easter Egg hunt. Marie at Pompano horse track. Marie at the Flamingo Hotel. Marie at the Olympia Movie Theatre. Marie at the Vizcaya mansion.

"Vanity," says Elizebeth. "Plain, simple vanity. Marie wants to be seen. She loves the theatrics. She can't keep herself away from the limelight."

"True."

"Trust Shakespeare," says Elizebeth. "*Richard the Second.* 'Light vanity, insatiate cormorant, Consuming means, soon preys upon itself.'"

======

As they walk toward the Treasury Building, William holds the umbrella over Elizebeth to protect her from the sideways rain and keeps his arm wrapped around her waist. At first, Elizebeth thinks the tightness she feels in her abdomen is from his embrace, but when he pulls away to shake out and close the umbrella, the squeezing remains.

It's just from the stairs, she thinks. It's a tall climb into her office.

"Morning, Captain," she says to the security guard stationed at the employees' entrance.

"Morning, Special Agent," he says, tipping his hat at her.

The Friedmans are overjoyed to be reunited in work. They've been asked to train T-Men in the high-frequency direction-finding equipment William helped design. Patrol boats and trucks are now equipped with portable electronics that will allow them to intercept the transmissions of the ever-growing population of radio-equipped rumrunners and their wildcat stations in real time, enhancing the moment-by-moment communication between the field and HQ.

As they proceed inside, Elizebeth stands straighter. She never gets over the feeling of pride when walking through these doors. After she gets a security check and passes the columns, her heels click over the parquet floors and up the curved marble staircase, the sound ascending the frescoed walls to the chandeliers high overhead. They soon reach the Cash Room, the large space that, since the days of Lincoln, has quite literally been where cash and coin from government vaults is handled. It's an open, two-story room with large windows and globed chandeliers, pilasters, gold-leaf plaster, and bronze railings lining a second-floor walkway. It's filled with suited men at tables, each with its own direction finder and manual. Up front are portable chalkboards—one for Elizebeth and one for William—and it's from here that America's First Cryptographic Couple reigns. Confidentiality paperwork is signed, introductions are made, and training begins.

Before Elizebeth starts her lesson, she scans the faces looking back at her, taking their temperatures. Some of the men have eager looks and pencils at the ready, but a good portion of them sit back with arms crossed, skeptical gazes leveled at her. Her obvious condition is not an asset for winning them over. Elizebeth knows she must start with her credentials or these men won't be able to get over the fact that she's a woman, and a very pregnant one at that.

"For the last decade," she says, "Mr. Friedman and I have been the foremost teachers of cryptanalysis in the world. It's a science we helped perfect and a term Mr. Friedman invented."

Though Elizebeth's stomach tightens, she doesn't allow herself to flinch.

"That's debatable," William says. "Special Agent Friedman and I share brain space. Who knows who said it first, but we all know the man gets the credit."

There's a low ripple of laughter. Elizebeth can see some of the cold ones thawing.

"In 1917," she continues, "the army sent eighty men to Riverbank, the think tank that employed us. We trained the first codebreakers of the United States military for the Great War, and now we'll train you to fight the Rum War."

She sees the slouchers sit up straight.

I've got them all now.

Ignoring the increasingly regular squeezing in her stomach, Elizebeth teaches the basics of solving coded and enciphered messages. As the morning progresses, William instructs the men about the new direction-finding technology. The students are both thrilled and unsettled, astonished by how much easier it will be for them, as hunters, to catch their prey. The mood is high for the T-Men, but Elizebeth knows William has spotted her discomfort. When they break for lunch and the men clear out, William touches Elizebeth's arm.

"Are you all right?" he asks.

"Fine," she says, hoping her grimace looks like a smile. "Just have to visit the restroom."

"You're not, uh...?" He looks down at her belly, the size of a large pumpkin.

"Surely not. It's too early. The baby's not due for another month, at least. I've been having Braxton-Hicks contractions. The doctor says that's more common, the more pregnancies one has."

"Then you should lie down. I'll take the rest of the afternoon. Grab a trolley home."

"And let you have all the fun? Absolutely not. Besides, Commander Root and I haven't had *the talk* yet, and he's supposed to meet us for lunch."

"The talk about what?" asks Root, striding in from the hallway.

Elizebeth sighs. Though her stomach makes her pregnancy obvious, men and women don't discuss such things in the workplace. This was not how she wanted to tell her boss she'd have to take off for two months.

"I'll let William fill you in," she says. "Be back in a jiffy."

Ignoring William's look of horror, Elizebeth walks out and crosses the hallway to the ladies' room, where Anna Wolf stands near the mirror, polishing her glasses. When she puts them on and sees Elizebeth, Anna brightens, but her smile evaporates when she sees Elizebeth's obvious discomfort. Elizebeth's next contraction is so intense, it forces her to lean against the stall door until it passes. Anna's cheeks turn red, as they always do when she looks at Elizebeth's belly.

"Are you," Anna says in a small, wavering voice, "all right?"

Elizebeth nods and closes herself into the stall, only just making the toilet when the gush comes.

Of all times, she thinks.

Thankful her waters didn't break when she was teaching a room full of men, but still mortified, Elizebeth takes a deep breath to steady herself.

"Miss Wolf," Elizebeth says, calmly as she's able. "Please get my husband in the Cash Room and tell him to procure a car. I have to get to the hospital immediately."

EIGHTEEN

CUBA

Marie

Marie wants to enjoy the trip to Cuba more.

She's at the helm of the *Kid Boots*, her sleek new boat, ironically named for a recent film about a gold-digging wife. A newspaperman got to the *Cortés* explosion in time to get a stage-worthy photo of Marie's silhouette before the conflagration that graced all the papers and took her to legendary status. The ink is still drying on the contract for the new building she's leased on the corner of West Flagler and Southwest Twenty-Third Avenue, less than a mile from home, for her new dance academy. And she made enough from the Fisher transaction to retire, not that she would think of it.

Marie can't fully enjoy the moment, however, because Benny isn't here.

She looks at the water next to her, where Benny should be captaining the *Josephine* to learn the route from Cuba and help transport the haul, but he didn't turn up in Key West, and no one has seen him. Not only does this anger Marie because—as much as she hates it—she's reliant on her bodyguard for security, but it also means they'll only make half of what they planned, and they'll have to disappoint one of her clients because of it. It will be a blow to her reputation.

Marie looks at Charlie, slumped in the passenger seat, with a hat covering his eyes and arms crossed over his chest, and feels her fury rise. She reaches out and punches his arm. He startles awake, dropping the hat, which blows out the door and into the water, disappearing fast behind them.

"Turn around!" he says.

"Not a chance."

"That's a genuine, handwoven Panama hat."

"I don't care what it is. We're not going back. Maybe you'd still have it if you weren't so hungover."

Charlie has made a return to bad behavior. Because his theatrics raised his "king" status, his ego is bloated. He kept the plastic crown Marie placed on his head the night of Red Shannon's death and sometimes wears it, looking more like a court jester than royalty. He's been at Nora's Cabaret, on the Miami River, every night, making a fool and a target of himself with his fancy watch and the money he throws around. Marie sticks to dances with the moneyed crowds, where Blue Steele and His Orchestra play, and everyone's favorite dance instructor, the handsome Professor Ted Hill, gives lessons in all the latest crazes. Charlie, on the other hand, can't keep away from the lowlifes. Now he's sulking because he doesn't want to add a Cuba run when they made so much off the Bahamas run. He forgets they've blown that route, quite literally.

Charlie pushes his sunglasses closer to his eyes and again crosses his arms over his chest.

"The last time you saw Benny was two nights ago at Pompano, right?" Marie asks.

"Yeah," says Charlie. "I told you that. He won a big pot and left around midnight."

"Was he drunk? Or were you too drunk to notice?"

"He was drunk," Charlie says, ignoring the second part of her question.

"Did anyone follow him?"

"I don't know. I drove separately and left before he did."

"How much did you lose, by the way?"

"Only a grand."

"Only a grand," she says. "A fine attitude."

"What's a grand when we have a fortune?"

"I'm not doing this so you can lose our money to that pack of thugs you insist on running with and shower the rest of it on those filthy whores at Nora's."

"*You're* not doing this?" Charlie says. "Who was the one who swan dived off an exploding boat?"

"I wrote the script for that whole run, and you know it," she says.

"Would you stop? My head is killing me."

"Your head? While you were off doing God knows what all day, Florence was sick, so I had to cart the children to the dance hall, where I was interviewing instructors and meeting with carpenters and electricians. Then I had to get an earful from my mother when I dropped off the kids about how we never see them. And Benny never made it to Key West, but he has to learn the Cuba route. And have you made that appointment yet to get the will completed?"

"You're pushing so hard for this will that it's making me think you want to off me. And will you settle down about Benny? If he didn't look like an ape, I'd think you were sweet on him."

"Ridiculous," she says with a scoff. "Don't you realize that without him, we'll only get half of what I promised from this run?"

"That's *if* we can rely on *your* brother as a supplier."

"You're one to talk. When your stupid brother didn't even show up."

As much as Marie gets a charge sparring with Charlie, Benny's absence casts a dark shadow. She senses something bad happened to him. If something bad happened to Benny, not only does it affect her operations, but it's meant to send a message to her. A thought about how devastated the kids would be if Uncle Benny is hurt moves through Marie's mind, deepening the shadows, but she doesn't have time to mull it because the mountains behind Havana Harbor appear on the horizon. Marie tries to relax, but she's too tense. When Charlie's not looking, she takes a long nip from the flask. She's been to Cuba once, on her honeymoon with her first husband, but certainly wasn't there with an eye on business. She hopes her brother Rogelio has laid a good foundation.

The closer they get to the island, the more the picture sharpens to reveal the rustling palms and the flaming red flowers of the flamboyant trees. Josephine, the little florist, would be in heaven. On their port side, they pass Morro Castle, rising from the rock, built to protect the island from pirates and invaders. The seas and air buzz from different kinds of invaders: wealthy American tourists. Bacardi has launched a full-scale advertising assault, luring those from the "Dry States of America" to the "Wet Paradise of Cuba." As they motor closer, they're dwarfed by cruise ships. Airplanes and seaplanes rise and descend like dragonflies. New hotels and clubs loom over the old city in a clash of ancient and modern, creating an electric kind of tension that's intoxicating in its own way.

At the Tallapiedra Wharf, seeing Rogelio talking to the harbormaster allows Marie to breathe easier. With Rogelio's slicked black hair, pronounced eyebrows, and pouty lips, he looks like he could be Rudolph Valentino's more handsome brother. He spots her and points at two vacant slips. While he walks toward them, movements smooth as a Florida panther, she pulls into a slip and directs Charlie to tie up the lines.

"Spanish Marie," says Rogelio, making an exaggerated bow.

"None other," she says.

Rogelio grins, white teeth flashing in the sun. He looks over her shoulder, out to the harbor.

"*¿El segundo barco?*" he asks.

She doesn't want to admit there's not a second boat because Benny was a no-show. It will reflect poorly on her.

"I decided to start small," Marie says, switching to Spanish. "In case you hadn't done your part."

"You doubted me?" Rogelio asks, pretending to be wounded.

"I doubt everyone. That's why I'm successful."

He grins.

"You've got the warehouse space to hold the extra liquor we can't take, right?" she asks.

"*Sí*," he says.

Rogelio holds out his hand to help Marie onto the dock, and when he sees Charlie, Rogelio's jaw tightens. The men nod at each other, unsmiling. Marie threads her arm through Rogelio's, and they start toward the taxi stand, Charlie in their wake, carrying their overnight bags and grumbling about the heat. Rogelio throws Charlie a look of irritation. He leans down, close to Marie.

"I don't trust him," Rogelio says.

"Neither do I," she says. "But he's easily manipulated. And he has his uses."

Rogelio meets her eyes, and the siblings exchange a long look, followed by a smile.

The music, the bustle, the color—all of it energizes Marie in a way she hasn't felt in a long time. There's such ebullience and vitality in the people around her. For a place with such a fraught history, there's a lot of joy and celebration, at least where she can observe. She knows she hasn't yet peeked into the shadows, but the facade is enchanting. She decides to forget about Benny and let herself get lost in enjoying the moment. Charlie, on the other hand, sweats profusely, his body emanating fumes of last night's alcohol.

"We better get Charlie fed," Marie says to Rogelio. "And watered."

"With the hair of the dog that bit you," Rogelio says in English to Charlie.

Charlie mumbles an unintelligible response.

"Sloppy Joe's," Rogelio says to the taximan.

Once Charlie loads the bags, they set off in bumper-to-bumper traffic—full of beeps, shouts, jerks, and near misses—toward the Malecón, the scenic esplanade along the seawall. While the taxi driver chatters away in Spanish, Marie hangs her head out the side, feeling the zephyr breeze run its fingers through her hair, while the sun kisses her skin. When a wave crashes against the seawall, soaking the well-dressed American tourists posing for a picture, Marie laughs. It's the first time she's laughed in ages. The cool, salty droplets reach her face, like a sprinkling of holy water. Charlie, green-skinned, looks at Marie as if she's crazy to be enjoying this.

After they pass the stone fortress, Castillo de la Real Fuerza, they head west, toward Old Havana. The taxi driver points out the bronze statue of the woman on the tower at the fortress.

"Isabel de Bobadilla, wife of de Soto. First female governor of Cuba."

Marie cranes her head to see the statue, liking the idea of a woman in charge.

"Was she a good ruler?" Marie asks.

"What is good? What is bad?" the driver says. "She was."

Marie ponders this as they continue to inch along, soon passing a Spanish baroque church, made of limestone.

"Catedral de San Cristobal, where Christopher Columbus's bones used to be."

"Where are they now?" she asks.

"Spain, some say."

A procession of women in white garments fills the streets ahead, forcing them to a stop. Elder women carry a statue of the Virgin Mary. Her ornate, jewel-laden cape is spread out like angel wings, and a large crown and halo of stars give her a royal appearance. In one hand Mary holds a cross, in the other, the infant Jesus. Her face is not like the gentle, passive, representations Marie is used to seeing in America. This Mary is stern, commanding, and a little frightening.

"Nuestra Señora de la Caridad, Patrona de Cuba."

"What?" asks Charlie, clearly frustrated by not being able to understand the language.

"Our Lady of Charity," says Marie. "Patroness of Cuba."

If only Marie had known about this likeness, she would have bought it for Gesú Church back home, instead of the Immaculate Mary, Queen of Heaven statue, which looks more maternal than regal.

Maybe I'll donate another one.

Marie meets the stare of one of the elder women—her look as stern and commanding as Mary's. Marie looks away and shifts in her seat.

As they snake through traffic, their driver explains that the side streets were designed tight to keep the narrow walkways in shade, and along the main avenues, the arcades and trees provide covering. Marie translates.

"Thank God," grumbles Charlie.

They arrive at a white three-story building, with iron balconies and a long line of tourists in the arched colonnade at its ground level, waiting to get into the famous Sloppy Joe's. While Charlie gets the bags, Rogelio tips the driver and walks past the line to the bouncer. Rogelio embraces the man, slips him a bill, and the bouncer lets the trio jump the line, though the look he gives Charlie tells Marie it's only because of Rogelio that Charlie's allowed inside.

"Behave," Marie tells Charlie.

Inside, the music of a three-piece band greets them. A few of the bartenders shout *Hola*s at Rogelio, and every woman he passes turns her head to watch him. He leads them along an endless mahogany bar to a table in the back where they can see the whole room. Once they're situated, he orders them three of Sloppy Joe's signature cocktails and three signature sandwiches.

Marie thinks, *It's a relief to go to a bar and not have to worry about it getting raided*. Clearly, rich Americans feel the same. They make up almost the entire crowd. The colors, the sounds of the mixing, the music, and the promise of cold drinks fill Marie with pleasure. She becomes transfixed by the closest bartender. He wears pants with suspenders and a white oxford shirt, with sleeves rolled up to reveal muscular forearms. When he catches her watching, he flashes his dimples.

The men, here, she thinks. *Guapo.*

Using a silver jigger, the bartender transfers one part pineapple juice, one part Martell's cognac, and one part port wine—topped off with grenadine and curaçao, dribbled over a muddler—into a tall glass. He finishes with a large scoop of chipped ice and pours it all in a shaker, its sound like maracas in time to the music. Once the drink is mixed, he strains the cocktails into the three champagne flutes. He places the drinks on a tray, along with a tiny cocktail souvenir book, and delivers them, giving Marie a wink. When Charlie sees, he jumps to his feet, nearly knocking the drinks over, but Rogelio shoots out his arm and pulls his brother-in-law back down in his seat. The bartender gives Charlie a murderous look and leaves them.

"I'll tell you once," says Rogelio. "None of that here. Or I'll leave you to the dogs. And some wouldn't think twice about killing you."

Charlie scowls. When Rogelio excuses himself to speak to the bartender, Charlie leans close to Marie.

"I knew this was a bad idea," he says.

Too furious to speak, Marie gives Charlie her most withering stare long enough that he looks away first. She takes a deep breath. She's not going to let him ruin her trip. The waiter soon arrives with three plates of *ropa viejas*, sandwiches spilling over with beef, simmered in tomato, onion, and peppers. Rogelio follows, and the three devour their food and drink. Once they get through lunch, Charlie is in a better frame of mind.

Marie treats, and once they've settled up, they start for the door. On the way out, Marie passes Joe Russell, from the Blind Pig in Key West. They see each other at the same time.

"Hey," Joe says. "What're you doing here?"

"I could ask you the same," she says.

"I came on the *Anita*. I saw an opportunity to try some of my own running."

"Then I'll remove you from my order this time," she says, relieved not to have to disappoint him, but aggravated that he's dipping a toe in her waters. "You know who to get in touch with when you realize rumrunning's not a sport for amateurs."

Marie leaves him shaking his head and follows her men back out into the sunshine. Rogelio starts to hail another taxi to take them to his place, but Charlie—hatless—seeing the traffic, shakes his head. Rogelio looks at the bags over Charlie's shoulders, shrugs, and leads them to the Prado, the tree-lined promenade through the heart of the city. There are few people walking in the midday heat, but Rogelio tells them, when the sun goes down, it comes alive.

They pass flower, souvenir, and cigar stands. Marie enjoys the attention she gets in her red polka-dot sleeveless dress, and Charlie is too busy wiping sweat and swatting bugs to notice or care. She enjoys watching him struggle. Mingled in the alcohol fumes oozing from his pores, Marie detects a definite female scent. Once she figures out who it belongs to, she'll decide her course of action. She won't think about that now, however. She has an empire to grow.

Rogelio's place is in a small but charming building on the Bahía de la Habana. He opens the wooden door to his apartment: a two-bedroom, with soaring ceilings, ornately tiled floors, and walls painted in bright teal and coral, with arched windows leading to a balcony looking out at the water. Entranced, Marie walks to the balcony and inhales the salty air.

"This is heaven," she says.

Charlie's look is incredulous.

"You like it?" asks Rogelio. "There's a place on the third floor—a three-bedroom—that's for lease. That one has its own bathroom, instead of having to go down the hall. If you're going to make this a regular stop, I recommend it."

"Yes, we wouldn't want to interrupt any of your trysts, staying with you," says Marie. "I saw the looks you got from the dames at the bar."

Rogelio raises his arms as if to say, *What can I do?*

Marie looks back out at the bay and has a sudden image of herself and the children setting up camp here, buying a large house in the hills overlooking the bay. The house could have a garden teeming with flowers for Josephine and a swimming pool for Joey. It could be an escape. Maybe she'd even invite her parents to show them what she's made of herself. She notes, with curious detachment, that again, Charlie is not in her dream, and wonders if that's a premonition or a hope.

She hears Charlie inside, retching.

It's both, she thinks.

NINETEEN

WASHINGTON, DC

Elizebeth

It was an easier labor than Elizebeth's first—which had put her in a brace, her back never quite the same since. However, because John Ramsay was early, he had to stay in the hospital. It nearly broke his parents' hearts to leave him, but they knew John was in good hands. Barbara, however, didn't hide her pleasure that the baby wasn't home. She was terribly disappointed not to have a sister.

"Where's Dorfy?" she asks, when Elizebeth is discharged.

"We don't have a Dorothy," Elizebeth says. "We have a John."

"I want a Dorfy."

"How about a cat?" William asks.

Barbara is happy to have a cat, a little black one they name Pinkle Purr, after the A. A. Milne poem. The cat is endlessly patient with being loved to death by Barbara, and their daughter continues to thrive. Crypto loves the gardener, who takes him to his country house some days for long runs, and the dog and the roses thrive. William, still seeing Dr. Graven, thrives. John, though small, makes steady progress, which can be characterized as a kind of thriving. Elizebeth doesn't feel as if she thrives, but she's certainly productive. Not having an infant home yet at night means Elizebeth sleeps, for now. When she's not at the hospital during visiting hours, she continues with her work. She can't stop. She realizes she's become obsessed with Marie Waite.

Elizebeth doesn't know if it's because her adversary has had such an enormous increase in success in such a short time, or because she's a woman, or because she's a glamorous woman, or because she's a mother, but Elizebeth can't get Marie out of her mind. Elizebeth has a growing file on Marie—including an incomplete but evolving family tree and client tree, and a supply route map—complete with newspaper clippings and scores of photographs. Whether Marie is at a race, a dance, or a charity drive at the church, her striking, proud face is always on Elizebeth's mind. She knows it's silly, but it feels as if the woman is taunting Elizebeth, daring her to catch her. It's only a matter of time, and Elizebeth hopes she can somehow be there to see the woman in the flesh, to understand what could make a wife and mother, with a mind like this, engage in so dangerous and unlawful a profession.

Marie would make an excellent double agent.

Elizebeth now sits across from her boss at his desk at HQ, while they await a delivery. The coast guard has spent months developing a new code they consider unbreakable, and Elizebeth will spend her last day before Baby John comes home and leave starts trying to crack it.

"Since you've come onboard with us," says Commander Root, "liquor traffic from Vancouver to the West Coast to the Florida region has been reduced by fifty percent. Specifically, from fourteen million gallons of liquor a year to five million gallons."

Elizebeth beams with pleasure.

"So, that's why hooch has gone from thirty-five to one-hundred-twenty-five dollars a case," she says. "Goodness, I'm glad I don't drink."

Root cracks a rare smile.

"I can't say the same for Miamians," she says, pulling a new stack of newspapers from her satchel and spreading them across Root's desk.

Leila's most recent bundle has quite the intelligence. Through her law network, Leila found out Charles made a will for the ever-expanding list of boats and property the Waites have acquired, including a new building close to their home. The latest newspapers have photographs of Charles, Marie, and dance instructor Ted Hill announcing the upcoming grand opening of Marie's Miami Academy of Dancing.

"Is she starting a business to launder money?" asks Root. "Or does she want to get out of rumrunning?"

"Leila and I think it's both," says Elizebeth. "And this might have something to do with it. Look at these headlines. Charles's brother. Quite jarring."

BENNY WAITE, BOOTLEG WAR'S LATEST VICTIM.

BODY FOUND WEIGHTED DOWN WITH A RAILROAD
JACK IN THE MIAMI RIVER.

"And here's an ad," says Elizebeth. "Taken out by Charles, offering a thousand-dollar reward for information on the killers. The T-Men say there's little doubt it's Alderman. He resents the Waites' success, poaching his accounts, so he made an example of Benny. Of course, it can't be proven. Alderman's too slippery. The water leaves no prints or tracks."

"We'll get him one way or another," says Root. "The faster you get back, that is. When does the baby come home?"

"Tomorrow."

Root scowls, but quickly rearranges his face.

Elizebeth thinks Root should have masked his reaction and is glad for the quick correction. She feels torn enough as it is and doesn't need pressure from her boss to make it worse. He's lucky to have her at all.

"I'm glad the baby's thriving, of course," says Root, reading Elizebeth's displeasure. "But I hadn't realized we'd lose you so soon. When will you be back?"

"I've decided on a month. Once I fold John into the household routines."

"You have a nanny, yes?" he asks.

"Yes, and Cassie is a living angel. She can't wait to have two precious little ones to look after."

Knowing how Root depends upon Elizebeth and will do anything she asks to make her domestic life easier, she's comfortable with what she's about to propose.

All the hours Elizebeth takes typing transcriptions of the codes she breaks for Root are not only a waste of her time, but something anyone can do. Codebreaking is not. If she had a secretary to handle the typing and moving of correspondence between her home and HQ, Elizebeth would have more time for codebreaking. William was thrilled over the idea, especially because Elizebeth came up with it, instead of him. He's delighted that she's finally becoming an advocate for herself.

"When I do return, I have a request," she says.

"Yes?" asks Root.

"Miss Wolf is an excellent secretary," says Elizebeth.

She notes, with irritation, it takes Root a moment to recall who Miss Wolf is.

"Ah, yes," he says, the light going on. "With the glasses."

"Yes. If Miss Wolf is amenable, and we can get approval, I'd like her to be transferred to me. To be a courier between my home and HQ and to be my typist. She already has security clearance, and I think she would enjoy being my right-hand woman. I see an ambition in her that could use nurturing."

After a moment's consideration, a light goes on in Root's eyes.

"And if you had her for secretarial tasks," he says, "it would free you up for more codebreaking."

Making your life easier, Elizebeth thinks.

"Exactly," she says.

"Which means we'd intercept more criminals," he says.

"And the powers that be will give us even more money in the budget."

Elizebeth feels no guilt about feeding what is self-serving in Root.

"For more boats," he says. "We only have two hundred vessels to patrol five thousand miles of shoreline. We'll need more men. Maybe seaplane patrols."

"Raises for staff," she says.

At the word *staff*, a new idea is born in her mind. She has a vision. Her library and her desk expand to become a room full of books and desks, women and men, pencils scratching away, in a think tank like Riverbank. Instead of a domineering, hedonistic narcissist like George Fabyan at the helm, however, she sees...

They're interrupted by a knock at the door of Root's office, and an officer salutes and strides in with a briefcase. He gives Root a key, places the case on the table at the back of the room, and quickly exits.

Elizebeth moves to the seat at the table. She takes out two soft leaded pencils, a stack of graph paper, and a stopwatch from her bag. Once settled, she looks at Root expectantly.

Root unlocks the briefcase and removes the codebook, placing it in front of her.

"Five men," he says. "One hundred hours. Unbreakable code. Good luck."

Elizebeth thanks him, picks up a pencil, and hits the button on the stopwatch. She hears Root snort with derision before heading back to his desk. She can read his thoughts, knows he doesn't think she can crack this before she goes on leave, or maybe ever.

Elizebeth opens the first page and scans, taking in the letters and numbers, starting her frequency table. She imagines the men who made this. Men with sharp focus. Smart men. Military men.

Elizebeth's hands move furiously. Her eyes dart up and down, left and right. The room around her falls away. The pages turn. The eraser shrinks. She takes the second pencil. The soft lead making marks, neat columns, bringing glimmers of clarity, deciphering. She feels a tinge of pain in her lower back but doesn't move her hand from the pages to massage it. She's close. Getting closer every minute. Every second.

Suddenly a light. A flash of clarity. Heat on her skin. An avalanche of symbols of letters. Letters arranged in ways that make sense. Readable words.

Five men. One hundred hours. Unbreakable code.

Exhaling, she slams down her pencil and hits the button on the stopwatch. Root looks up at her from his paperwork, bemused.

"Nine minutes," she says.

TWENTY

MIAMI

Marie

Suicide. The police tried to say Benny committed suicide. That he somehow tied a one-hundred-pound railway jack to his own legs and threw himself off a bridge into the Miami River. His body was found by two children. It had been in the water for an untold number of days.

On Benny's grave in Woodlawn Park Cemetery, Josephine lays a beautiful bouquet—palm leaves framing orange lilies and birds of paradise—made from the garden Benny planted with her. Marie's family sobs, openly. She's surprised to feel her own tears. She can't remember the last time she cried. She hates weakness and vulnerability. Numbness is easier. She could not have anticipated the heaviness of grief in her heart at losing her right-hand man. Benny was like a loyal dog, purehearted and devoted. He was, perhaps, the only man to ever adore and even love her perfectly, without any motive or lechery.

I will avenge you, Benny, she thinks.

Marie's bitterness is enormous because this should be a time of celebration. It's the grand opening of her dance academy.

She's been working day and night to turn the building into a palace with gleaming dance floors, a large bandstand, floor-to-ceiling mirrors, crystal chandeliers, enormous fans, and perfect acoustics. Though Charlie has sulked through every hour of the process—he reminds her daily that he still doesn't have his race car—he's agreed to form a corporation with Marie and the best instructor in Miami, Professor Ted Hill, a former vaudevillian, who toured with dance companies all over Europe. Marie secured Blue Steele and His Orchestra, and she and Ted have been practicing the opening dance with the musicians for weeks. She has invited the best in society, has hired and trained the most attractive staff to check coats and hats, and serve drinks and hors d'oeuvres. She's invited the newspapers and has created a signature virgin cocktail, the Spanish Marie, which is a virgin red sangria with apples.

In spite of the cocktail's nod to Marie's alter ego, everything the public sees at the dance academy will be aboveboard. Only Marie and Charlie know about the undercurrent that will wash other money clean, and that will only be until the academy flourishes, which Marie has no doubt will be very soon. Sign-ups for lessons in ballroom, tango, popular crazes, and children's ballet and tap are nearly filled for the fall season. Once the pupils begin next week and start paying, the academy will be in the black.

Marie stands behind Charlie at the gilded mirror in their bedroom, while wind assaults the house. She has tucked their wedding photo in the corner of the mirror to try to conjure happier times. It's not working.

At Marie's eye level, the knife scar on the back of Charlie's neck, from his first wife, invites contemplation. Its latitude lies below the clean line of his blond hair and above the crisp white of his starched collar. It was the price he paid to have Marie. He used to say it was worth it. As much as Marie has always hated Charlie's first wife, now that Marie knows Charlie as well as she does, she's surprised to feel a flicker of kinship with his ex.

Marie smooths Charlie's collar and turns him around to face her, straightening his bow tie and looking up into his white-blue eyes. Since Benny was murdered, what was left of the light in Charlie's eyes has gone out. She misses the gaze that was once infused with desire for her. Contrary to what she predicted, the more money they make, the less he looks at her. His stare drifts, haphazard and reckless, like currents on the Straits of Florida, and often toward younger, pretty things, other things, always the next thing. Marie has done her best to detach herself from Charlie. She tells herself he is only there to be useful to her, and once he's not, he's gone.

"Do you want your crown?" Marie jokes, nodding toward the plastic accessory.

Before Charlie can answer, the shutters bang, the wind howls. If Benny were alive, she would send him to check the marinas to secure their boats from the coming storm, but he isn't and there's no time. Tonight is for dancing.

Though it fills her with dread, Marie invited her parents to the grand opening of her dance academy. She wants her mother, especially, to see what Marie has made of herself. Since the event must be dry, Marie and Charlie have each consumed a large amount of alcohol at home, Marie no longer hiding it. She makes sure to stop just short of drunk, at a place where she can play the part without getting sloppy. She'll leave her flask at home so she won't be tempted to indulge at the event. Charlie is incapable of such self-discipline.

He walks into the closet to put on his sleek black tuxedo jacket. She still gets a thrill every time she looks at him. If they have nothing else, they have lust. Still, she's annoyed at how her costumes have been relegated to boxes on the floor. His appetite for new clothing rivals hers, and he's encroaching on her territory. They nearly came to blows over the *Hamlet* skull. She insisted he keep it on the center shelf—the first thing one sees walking in the closet.

"It's repulsive," he said. "A graven image."

"You pull out religion at strange times," she said.

"I could say the same for you. I don't need constant reminding of your bizarre Catholic rituals and idols."

"It's not a ritual or an idol. It's a reminder. *Memento mori.* Remember your death."

"Why should I do that?"

"So you'll live better. So you don't end up in hell."

"What, you don't think you'll be right there with me?"

He let the matter drop, and now the skull watches.

Over his watch, Charlie fastens the new golden beryl cuff links Marie gave to him as a gift. She thought he would enjoy the reminder of her eyes, but he scarcely masked his irritation.

Fair, she thought. *He read the message that I'm always watching.*

When he exits, Marie walks into the closet, and lets her robe fall to the floor so she wears only a brassiere, panties, and gartered stockings. She looks over her shoulder, beckoning, but his back is to her. There was a time when he couldn't take his eyes off her. She scowls and pulls on her new flapper dress—art deco gold with glittering accents—and slides her new buttery-soft gloves up her arms. She steps into her golden, T-strapped Latin high heels, slips a tiara into her hair, and walks out to the mirror, awaiting Charlie's praise. Over her shoulder, she can see him look from her tiara, to her dress, to her shoes, which he stares at long enough for Marie to know he's thinking of the day at Fulford Raceway when she attacked him. After a long moment, he slips his flask into his jacket and starts out of the room.

"Hurry up," he says over his shoulder. "We're gonna be late."

———

The building is like a star fallen to earth, a glowing spectacle of monied electricity. Moving spotlights, beaded dresses, cigarette tips, camera flashes, chandeliers upon chandeliers, from the ceiling to the endless wall-mirrored reflections. The large fans are no match for the cross breezes of what will no doubt be an epic storm coming in from the open windows running along two sides of the dance floor, charging the air. Though the event is dry, it doesn't appear to be. The music, the crowd, and the energy are intoxicating.

I did this, Marie thinks. *My vision morphed from vapors to reality.*

My dreams projected out like a film on screen, taking on flesh, bone, and beads.

Marie feels emotional, and even sad at the thought of leaving rumrunning. Her focus, however, has shifted to her reputation as a businesswoman and a leader in the community. Living a double life cannot go on forever, especially not while she's trying to get her kids in the right schools and activities. Benny's death has shown their lives are all in danger, and Marie can't have that with little ones dependent upon her.

A movement near the bandstand distracts her. Marie has forbidden Charlie from inviting any rummies, so he has found a flock of admiring flappers. They are the daughters of society women, girls like Marie used to be—fresh, flirty, and ready for fun. These tarts, however, have money, and with it, the kind of careless confidence that Marie despises, the kind that fuels the fires of her envy and adds names and faces to the lists of those who have crossed her.

Marie tears her attention away from Charlie and back to her creation.

I did this without Charlie, she thinks. *Hell, in spite of him. And his usefulness is waning.*

Marie stiffens when she sees her parents arrive. Her father wears a suit from the last decade that probably smells of mothballs, and her mother wears a dour burgundy frock—more fitting for a funeral than a dance—and her graying blonde hair in a bun. Looking out from behind glasses that magnify her reach, the woman's lightning gaze takes in the entire room, targeting

Charlie before landing on Marie. Her mother appraises her from head to toe, her disdainful look mirroring Marie's for the hens, just moments ago. Marie feels a flash of hatred for her mother, for Charlie, and herself.

Why did I invite her? Marie thinks. *I must be a fool to think anything would ever impress her.*

If there's anything Marie is good at, however, it's acting. She narrows her eyes, finds her haughtiest expression, and walks across the room to greet her parents. Her father brightens to see her, but her mother's scowl deepens.

"I'm so glad you could make it," says Marie.

"You should have called this off, with the storm coming," says her mother.

"A storm wouldn't dare interfere with my grand opening."

Her mother mutters something in Dutch. A distant rumble of thunder, however, transforms the woman's scowl to a smug smile. Marie hopes the flame she feels in her skin hasn't turned her as red on the outside as she feels on the inside. She's desperate for a drink. As if on cue, a server arrives, encouraging each of them to take a "Spanish Marie." She and her father take their drinks, but her mother wrinkles her nose.

"It's virgin sangria," says Marie.

Her mother doesn't respond.

The blackness inside Marie threatens to pull her under. If Benny were here, he would rescue her. He would see her distress and find a way to intercept. Luckily, she's able to catch Ted's eye. He clinks his champagne flute and takes the microphone.

"Welcome, one and all," Ted says in his smooth baritone.

Her stomach flutters. With his black hair and blue eyes, Ted's a dish, and it will be good to be seen with him. Charlie doesn't know it, but Marie and Ted are kicking off the opening with the first dance. She hopes it fires a jealous rage in Charlie's belly.

"Now that everyone has their 'Spanish Marie'—our signature *virgin* cocktail for the night..." He draws out the word *virgin* long enough to send a ripple of laughter through the crowd. "We can raise a glass to the drink honoring the woman, Marie Waite, whose drive, creativity, and vision have started what will surely become an institution in this great city."

Marie burns with pleasure. She looks at her mother and sees a shadow cross the woman's face. In the shadow, it dawns on Marie that it's her mother's jealousy that makes her behavior so ugly. The woman is bitter about a life where she must not have fulfilled her own dreams, whatever those were, and she resents her daughter's success. It briefly occurs to Marie that she has never asked her mother what she wanted to make of her life, but her mother's scowl removes all sympathy.

To hell with her.

Marie looks around to see if Charlie sees her success, but he's leaning over his favorite blonde, the shameless tart who's a daughter of one of Carl Fisher's rich friends. The girl wears a dove-gray dress with feathers, like a damned carrier pigeon.

Marie tears her eyes away, taking in the women, most of whom don't conceal their envy. The men don't conceal their lust. They only want her because they want something of hers. Marie realizes she wanted independence, and she has it. That's all she's got. Total aloneness. Without Benny, she doesn't have a friend in the world.

It takes a monumental effort of will for Marie to tap into the fire in her belly, but she manages. She places her empty flute on a server's tray. The chandeliers are dimmed, and the crowd recedes to the edges of the dance floor. Marie imagines the curtain opening on a stage while she slips into the skin of another. Marie and Ted walk toward each other. In the walk, she's able to abandon reality and move to the space outside of time, where it's just her and Ted and the music.

In the hush, the rumbles of thunder get closer. The wind gusts get stronger. Marie inhales a great breath of the charged air. Ted passes her a white lace fan, and she flares it.

They picked a blend of *son cubano* and *danzón*, music and dance originating in Cuba from Spanish and African roots. Guitars, clave, bongos, and maracas provide the smooth, sultry soundtrack to accompany the flirtatious dance. It starts with a slow promenade facing out, but quickly draws the dancers together. Though arms are held high, hips and legs are entwined, rhythmically undulating to the music. Ted draws Marie closer with each pass.

After the first verse, the instructors promenade in a circle around Marie and Ted, then fall into their own dances, all in time with one another. Marie is at once lost in the performance and aware of how they captivate the onlookers. There's a hush, a communal harmony, heavy breathing of many in time to the same heartbeat. For the last verse, the crowd is invited in, and it's then that Marie fully allows herself to watch the others. She can read the thrill on the guests' faces. She can almost hear the bell of the cash register, see piles of money—money that is clean and legal and will not only continue to fund her empire, but also make her truly respectable.

Charlie dances with the tart in feathers. He doesn't venture a glance at Marie. Was he even jealous? Marie maneuvers Ted closer to Charlie. Once she's closed in, she makes an abrupt change, pushing the girl away and gripping Charlie as if her hands are claws. She feels his resistance, but she doesn't let him go. She stares into his ice-blue eyes and tells him with her thoughts that he has crossed her, and he will pay. The longer the music goes on, the more infuriated she becomes. He doesn't submit. He is restored to his old dominant, forceful self, and he wants the upper hand. She won't allow it.

At the song's end Charlie wrenches himself from her grip and turns his back on her. A man appears before Marie, asking her for the next dance. Then another man and another dance, and another. A line of men and of women who want lessons trail her and Ted. They look greedily at the instructors. The storm rises outside, lightning flashes. Her parents leave without saying goodbye. Thunder booms louder, closer. Rains starts, pelting sideways, pouring in the open windows on her new wooden floors. The crowd thins. The guests who remain are drunk.

Where did the alcohol come from?

It disturbs Marie that she didn't know about the booze. She thought everything at the dance hall was under her control.

Charlie is drunk. He disappears.

She feels reckless, dangerous. She seeks out Ted to use for revenge, but he's in a corner, necking with a rich girl. This isn't what Marie envisioned. Nor is the party ending early, which happens precisely at ten thirty. Lightning strikes close by, resulting in a blast, followed by the ballroom going dark.

TWENTY-ONE

WASHINGTON, DC

Elizebeth

T his isn't going how I planned, thinks Elizebeth.

Baby John is so mercurial that his fits and fussing are a constant distraction and make Elizebeth worry there's a greater problem. Barbara is so easygoing. Elizebeth can't figure out how two such different children came from her and William. She's finally forced to acknowledge how a second nanny would help and hires Carlotta, the woman William suggested. Even with Carlotta, however, Elizebeth is having trouble concentrating. She tries to return to writing her children's alphabet book but feels like a dog perpetually circling, unable to lie down. She can't get her mind to calm and to focus. After a month and a day passes, Root calls.

"When will you return?" he asks. "The volume of intercepts is profound."

"It's difficult to know," she says. "The baby hasn't settled in as easily as I thought he would. There are too many distractions."

Root calls after a month and a half. "You could come into the office to work."

"I'll think about it."

She doesn't want this. Not yet, anyway. That much she knows.

Root calls at two months, then two and a half. "I have an office with a window for you. A big cherry desk."

The idea intrigues Elizebeth, and William fully supports it, but she feels too guilty to fully consider it.

Why do I feel so drawn to work when I have two children? she thinks. *Why are other women content to stay home and keep house? Is there something wrong with me?*

William tries to assuage her guilt, to assure her that she has a calling and a very special and unique skill set. The world needs her. But returning to the work somehow doesn't feel right, either. Between overnight feedings and her mind spinning, she loses sleep. Now William is the one comforting her, and she hates it.

Her sister Edna's words haunt her.

No one can have it all, without suffering in some way.

Maybe Edna is right.

Months after John's birth, Elizebeth is at her desk in the library, staring at the next blank page in her alphabet book—the *P*—and nothing fitting comes to mind. If she doesn't have the mental faculties to focus on completing a book for children, there's no way she'll be able to return to codebreaking, here or in the office. She turns to her baby record book. There are pages and pages for Barbara, and barely any for John. What would she write? He doesn't eat or sleep well. He works himself up so angrily, his face turns beet red. He vomits up half of every feeding. He only has eyes for William. She pushes the baby book aside, and staring at her is Marie Waite. It's an ad in the *Miami News*, offering discounts on dancing lessons at her academy in a building spared from the hurricane. Marie's ad has a stink of desperation to it. It gives Elizebeth a strange pang of regret for the woman who might have been trying to move into legitimate business and away from rumrunning, before a hurricane sidelined her.

In Leila's last few newspaper bundles, the vast destruction of Miami from the storm that arrived at two in the morning, September 18, 1926, is laid out before Elizebeth. The 128-mile-per-hour winds and a devastating surge left two feet of sand on Collins Avenue, over twenty-five thousand Miamians homeless, a thousand hospitalized, and over one hundred dead. The glass dome from Carl Fisher's Flamingo Hotel was shattered, his Roman Pools were filled with sand, and his Fulford Raceway was reduced to a pile of splinters.

Leila says Fisher and other investors have been working hard in their own desperate ads to emphasize Florida is hurt but not dead, but the writing is on the wall. Florida weather is too temperamental to draw investors. A second, smaller hurricane in October was the nail in the tourist season's coffin, and now Miami business owners are scrambling.

There's a soft knock at the library door.

"There's someone here to see you," says Cassie. "From HQ."

"I'm not expecting anyone," says Elizebeth. "Please take a message and send him away."

"Pardon, but your visitor is a she," says Cassie. "An anxious-looking young woman, with glasses and a suitcase."

Elizebeth looks over her shoulder at the closed door. Realization dawning, she feels a knot of tension release, followed by wave of gratitude for Root, followed by a pang of anger at herself for assuming it was a man. If she can't rid her mind of that stereotype, how can she expect others to do so?

Elizebeth stands and hurries to open the door, her smile mirroring Cassie's.

"Please, send Miss Wolf upstairs."

———

Not only did Root reallocate Anna Wolf as a secretary for Elizebeth, to work with Elizebeth from home, but he got Elizebeth a salary of twenty-four hundred dollars a year. Both came with the stipulation that Elizebeth would no longer work on short-term contracts, but as a full-time special agent of the Treasury Department, within the coast guard's Communications Section. She agreed, and immediately felt her mind clear.

Mornings, while Cassie and Carlotta prepare the children for the day, Elizebeth cooks a big breakfast for all of them— including William and Anna—where they sit down together in the dining room at seven thirty sharp. In a short time, and once Baby John is big enough, even he falls in line with the routine, eating cereal and banging his high chair with spoons, delighting in Crypto vacuuming crumbs from under his seat. Cassie and Carlotta are as good as members of the family, and Anna, though still shy, contributes to the conversation more and more. Every day before William leaves for work, he kisses Elizebeth and the children goodbye, telling John how lucky they are to have so many wonderful, brilliant women in their lives. Then Elizebeth kisses the children and she and Anna head up to the library to get to work.

Elizebeth is astonished at their progress. Anna's fingers fly over the typewriter as fast as Elizebeth can decode, and Anna provides a welcome sounding board for Elizebeth. It's a relief of enormous proportions to have someone with whom she can discuss the work, which is not only stimulating, but often amusing. Deciphered and decoded messages reveal important routes, contacts, and landing points in the smuggling trade, but also funny personal messages. Elizebeth and Anna share many laughs over everything from requests for size sixteen boots and extralarge underwear, to an announcement from a shore station to a rumrunner about his wife birthing twins, with the swift reply that the rumrunner has no wife. Their favorite so far is the call from ship to shore for a new glass eye, the old one having popped out somewhere in the Atlantic, off the coast of Savannah.

"Good heavens," says Elizebeth. "We really are dealing with pirates."

And pirates they are. Jimmy Alderman, now known as the Gulf Stream Pirate, is getting more brazen with his poaching of others' cargo and has started runs to and from Cuba. With Alderman still considered the prime suspect in the murder of Benny Waite, Elizebeth often thinks that he could be the avenue for nabbing Marie and Charles Waite, either for use as double agents, or because of their likely desire for revenge. If only

Elizebeth could get down to Marie's world, and even observe Marie and some of the others, Elizebeth could learn so much more about the woman of her fascination. She floats the idea to William, in the context of a family trip to the beaches there, and his enthusiasm overtakes hers. They both think, maybe they'll go in the new year, in the spring, when John is a little older and the weather is better for travel, and Edna could even join them to help with the children.

The new year arrives, and with 1927, an increase in radio traffic.

Elizebeth and Anna sit side by side, Elizebeth working her frequency tables, and Anna typing away, her fingers like a pianist's on the keys. Elizebeth looks up and sighs, taking in the scene. The window across the library frames Pinkle Purr, watching a gentle snow. They are surrounded by books. On the desk, a blue-and-white Chinese porcelain pot of green tea—sent from the U.S. Coast Guard Pacific Office of Operations—rests next to matching cups on their coasters. The aroma of chili simmering downstairs and Cassie's humming reach them. With Anna's support, the women have solved the backlog of several months for both coasts and are caught up to real time. Elizebeth is again sleeping, again content. She asked for help, and she has it. She has a healthy, happy family. William has graduated from his sessions with Dr. Graven and remains steady and well.

What did I do to deserve this? she wonders.

She doesn't know, but she's grateful.

Still, though, her mind is untamable, forever ping-ponging between the work and her family. The tethers never go away, her reactions to those around her almost barometric. Can a woman ever turn off the noise, the incessant mental traffic? Can anyone? That is a question to which Elizebeth thinks she might never find the answer.

She returns her attention to two piles of intercepts, from what appear to be different criminals. When her mind is exhausted from one, she pivots to the next, tacking to and fro, as if on a sailboat. She's close to solving each—one to do with the corrupt Sheriff Bryan in Miami, the other from a batch involving a new Key West pirate radio station communicating with a fleet of rumrunning boats of unknown captainage that has made several crossings from Cuba to various points along the Florida coast. Elizebeth knows one key word will crack the whole thing, but it's still out of her grasp.

According to Jack, in the rummy's fleet, there is one pilot boat outfitted with guns, and four smaller boats—which likely keep the contraband—that scatter when trouble arises. Last week, there was an exchange of gunfire between the pilot boat and the coasties, while the other boats escaped. Once gone, the pilot boat flew off into the horizon, easily outrunning the coasties. Between the speed of the pilot boat, the rough seas, and what looked like a tarp hanging over the side, blocking the name, Jack's crew wasn't able to get a good visual on any men or boat details. This is clearly not the work of an amateur.

"Anna," says Elizebeth, "I want you to clear your mind. I'm working a transposition cipher, and I can't figure out the key word that will unlock it."

This is what Elizebeth and William used to do at Riverbank, when one would get stuck. Often, the freedom of the other mind lends a clarity to the mind in the weeds. While William is a technical and statistical genius, Elizebeth's intuition borders on the mystical. She thinks it's because she's a woman, and maybe Anna, also being a woman, can help find the missing puzzle piece.

Anna stops typing, takes a deep breath, and closes her eyes.

"After I give you a series of nouns that represent various players, boat names, et cetera, I want you to say the first word that pops into your mind. Don't overthink it, just go with your intuition," Elizebeth says.

"All right," says Anna.

Elizebeth looks at Anna, eyes closed, face eagerly poised to help her boss. The young woman is a treasure and is finding her wings. Elizebeth wonders if Anna would like to be trained in codebreaking someday. Elizebeth has started dreaming about her own unit within the coast guard, an intelligence unit that she could oversee. She would love if it were staffed with a balance of men and women, creating a perfectly oiled and complementary machine.

"Here are the words," says Elizebeth. "*Angel. Malecón. Isabel. Charity. Danzón.*"

"*Danzón*," repeats Anna, in a whisper, the word clearly triggering a thought. "*Havana.*"

Anna opens her eyes.

Of course, it has to do with Havana, Cuba, but no one would pick such an obvious key word.

"Anything else?" asks Elizebeth. "Maybe a little more complicated or less evident?"

Anna's cheeks color, and Elizebeth feels a stab of guilt for dismissing Anna's idea.

"I'm sorry," says Elizebeth. "I'll start with Havana."

Anna nods and returns her attention to typing.

Elizebeth starts to scribble, and within seconds the lights go on in the strand. Not only do the messages reveal themselves, but they are clearly related to another pile of intercepts she hadn't connected. Her hand scribbles like lighting now, and she has the rush, the feeling of unlocking, the thrill of the successful hunt, especially when the scribbles unfolding before her, the connections between papers, the boat names, and the maps open up a lead Elizebeth has not anticipated. The words can all be traced back to the Key West pirate station regularly sending and receiving messages from the woman of Elizebeth's fixation. The woman who invades her waking thoughts and sleeping dreams.

Elizebeth sits back and laughs. Anna looks up, a question in her eyes.

"I really do owe you an apology," says Elizebeth. "With your intuition, you just helped me crack open a whole new operation by my favorite adversary."

Anna beams and glances over the desktop until she finds the picture never far from staring out from under the mess. She reaches for the paper and holds it up.

"Spanish Marie?" Anna asks.

"*Sí*," says Elizebeth.

TWENTY-TWO

KEY WEST

Marie

S till crushed with grief and fury from Benny's death, after the Miami hurricane, Marie and Charlie decided to head to Key West. After the storm, Charlie suffered fresh heartbreak when he discovered his pigeons had died, the doors to the shed having blown open. Marie could barely hold back her delight when Charlie found the squabs in wet piles of feathers, with broken necks. He hadn't come out and blamed Marie, but she knew he thought if they had ever built the dovecote, the birds would have been saved. This hasn't helped the rising tension between them.

Though their home and the dance hall suffered only minor damage, the roads were impassable for weeks, and the city was shut down. They piled the children, Florence, and their new staff into the *Josephine* and the *Kid Boots*—also untouched by the storm—and set their course for Key West, where they rented a bungalow near Angel's home, where he operates the pirate radio station. It was only after they signed the rental papers that Marie realized Hal and Eva Bennet lived next door, and the woman is always peering out her window at Marie's comings and goings. Eva also won't let her girls play with Josephine and Joey—a sin for which Marie will never forgive the woman, especially because Marie thinks Josephine and the older Bennet girl, Mariella, are kindred spirts. At least Raul Vasquez—who has retired from rumrunning—and his family live nearby, and they are happy to allow the kids to play.

While Charlie visits with his mother, Marie buys Raul's boat and renames it the *Malecón*. Marie approaches Hal Bennet to buy the *ForEva*, but he won't sell it. He's using it as a fishing boat and hopes to have a charter business someday. She asks Joe Russell for the *Anita*. He won't sell, having been bit by the rumrunning bug, but he refers her to another speakeasy owner, one who wants out of the trade, which results in Marie's next boat, the *Isabel*, named for de Bobadilla, the first female governor of Cuba. Marie has the new boats repainted and outfitted with Liberty motors and radios and commissions retractable tarps to be made to cover the names, in case of engagement with the coasties, and all before Charlie even realizes what's happened. When he returns from a week, allegedly staying with his mother, Marie tells him what she's done.

"Are you trying to sink us?" he asks.

"Quite the opposite," she says. "With my new plans, and the number of players getting out of rumrunning, we'll corner the market."

"Haven't you heard about the mobsters coming in to fill the void? The guys at the track said Al Capone is around Miami more and more, and has even hired a pilot to smuggle booze and who knows what else in from the Bahamas. He's using airplanes, for God's sake."

Though Marie finds it jarring that Charlie has intel she didn't, she's impressed, but she won't show it.

"Of course, I heard," she says, her mind racing to catch up. "But airplanes are unique, so that puts a target on them. Not only that, guys like Capone have a lot of work to do, building their networks. We're established and connected, and our possessions were mostly spared in the hurricane. It feels like a kind of blessing."

"I thought you said you made your own luck."

"I have the brains to find opportunities when they arise. This is a golden opportunity."

A month after the hurricane, they were shocked to hear about another, less destructive hurricane in Miami, but devastating to Cuba. It took weeks for Rogelio to radio Angel with an update. In Havana, throughout the entire city, not a palm was left intact. A tidal wave crossed the Malecón, flooding the Old Town and washing out the aqueduct, leaving no water or electricity. Forty boats in the harbor were sunk and over forty people in Havana alone were killed. Hundreds more were killed on the rest of the island and in Bermuda, where the October storm finalized its deadly path.

Luckily, Rogelio had enough warning and caution to board up the cigar shop and his apartment building, so both sustained minimal damages. Because it was inland, their wholesaler's warehouse fared well. Much to Charlie's chagrin, Marie asked Rogelio to keep his eyes open for seamen who wanted to sell their boats. Even those with damage could be considered.

"How many boats are you going to buy?" asks Charlie.

"Enough to enact my plan."

"What's this plan?"

"The less you know, the better. Just do what I tell you."

Marie's answer infuriated Charlie, but he didn't raise much protest. Over the winter months in Key West and into the new year, Marie has been giving Charlie a long leash. Charlie is clearly messing around with other women. In such a small town, it's impossible for him to hide it. Drink makes him careless, so he takes minimal pains to hide the lipstick stains and wash the perfume out of his clothes before Florence gets to the laundry. Marie tallies up his indiscretions on a scorecard. He will pay dearly at the right moment, but that time has not yet come. She needs him at the helm of one of the boats in the fleet.

They have only made two trips from Cuba, but the runs have already taken them to new heights of wealth. They soon rent an even larger house—a private compound, just outside of Key West—and put the boats at the marina on Stock Island, which is as close to Cuba and as far from the coast guard base as they can get. Marie hires a private tutor to oversee the children's schooling. Marie also hires a cook, a maid, and Theo as her new bodyguard. He's always in her sights, even now at mass, where he stands in the shadows of the choir loft, at St. Mary, Star of the Sea. Though he doesn't have the size or dogged loyalty of Benny,

Theo used to be a boxer and is always looking for a fight. Also, he'll do anything for money, and Marie pays him well.

At church, Marie sits with the children and Florence in a pew with a view of the grotto. After a hurricane in 1919, one of the nuns at the school commissioned it and raised funds to have the grotto—containing a statue of Our Lady of Lourdes and the child who saw the vision, Saint Bernadette—built. There hasn't been a direct hit on the island since. Marie thinks she will have a grotto built in Miami if they ever fully move back to the city. They've made a few return visits, but with the failing dance academy, and the city still struggling to come back to life after the hurricane, it depresses Marie too much to remain for any length of time. Not only that, but the feds enacted a massive raid and arrested Sheriff Bryan and all six of his deputies for conspiring with smugglers, so Marie's Miami shield is gone.

Her new longing is to settle in Cuba, but Havana is also struggling under the weight of rebuilding. Because of the storm, however, she was able to buy a house in Cuba cheaply, in the sleepy fishing village of Cojimar, just outside of Havana. The house is situated on an overlook, with views all the way to the sea. It has four bedrooms and a gurgling fountain in an enclosed courtyard, with space for a pool. She's having Rogelio oversee the pool construction, renovations, and landscaping. She's having every room painted a different jewel tone, and every floor replaced with glittering mosaics, and all of it is dirt cheap since the hurricane has scared away other investors. Her favorite part: Charlie doesn't know a thing about it and, hopefully, never will.

Charlie never came home last night. When he does this, he says he stays at his mother's, which is a lie. Keeping her fury at bay is getting increasingly difficult, but Marie manages. She's a performer, after all, and knows how to use everything for her roles.

At church, Marie plays the role of the elegant mother, a model of decorum and piety for her beautiful family. Without Charlie, however, she can't fully inhabit the role. Raul and his wife smile when they see Marie and join her pew, but Marie sees how Raul notices Charlie's absence and gives her a look of pity. The feeling of humiliation is quickly replaced with rage. She clenches her fists. As if sensing the heat, Josephine watches her mother's skin turn red, from her chest to her face. When Joey gets restless and fidgets, it's Josephine who shoots out her arm and hushes him.

Marie's gaze finds the warm smile of Raul's beautiful wife. It's excruciating for Marie to have to answer it. The woman has it all. A loving husband with a business now operating aboveboard, adorable children, the love of the community, and a calm and placid nature. Marie and Raul's wife organized a charity drive to help the victims of the Cuba hurricane, kicking off the drive with their own large donations, and the *Key West Citizen* took their picture. Marie has added it to her growing press collection, but even press coverage no longer gives Marie the thrill it once did, especially when she has to share the spotlight with another woman.

Marie has a sudden desire to find Cleo Lythgoe, to commiserate with someone more like her in temperament. Marie wants to return to simpler days, to a husband who was interested in her, to having a friend in Benny. That time is gone, however. All she has is her empire and the future. Seeing the vacant place where Charlie should be, she fully allows what he does to her to settle in her brain, to acknowledge the weeds and thorns it has wrapped around her heart and lungs, coiling up and down her spine, invading her thoughts, choking her womanhood, leaving it cold, dry, and empty.

The irony is not lost on Marie that today is the Feast of St. Joseph—a feast celebrating a good husband and father. In the priest's homily, he praises men who use St. Joseph as a model of manhood. The priest suggests that St. Joseph might not have been the old man so often depicted in art but could have been a young man. It would have been difficult for an old man to protect Mary and Jesus on a long journey and to be a guard for his family. What is clear is that Joseph was loyal, disciplined, faithful, and true.

Marie's father comes to mind. All she can see when she looks at him are slumped shoulders, exhaustion, and no fight left in him against Marie's mother. A whine from Joey gets her attention.

"Hungry," he says.

Of course, he is. A typical male, ruled by his senses.

Josephine hisses a warning at him. He scowls at her, but he quiets.

Marie looks from her children to the empty space at her side, where Charlie should be. She feels a rush of heat and anger. There is nothing loyal, disciplined, faithful, or true about him, and she allows herself to admit there never will be.

The incense lifts her mind from her body, but instead of elevating her thoughts heavenward, they leave her body and fly out over the water to her fleet. To the routes. To Cuba and the Bahamas. To a run, a final run—the last twelve miles for the man who has held her back and betrayed her more than could ever be forgivable. To a plan to enact justice on him, cutting him off like the railroad tie he has become, dragging her under, drowning her.

It's time to finish Charlie, once and for all.

TWENTY-THREE

KEY WEST

Elizebeth

E lizebeth can't believe they're all here in Key West, seated around a table at the Victoria Restaurant. Their bones are thawed from winter. Their noses are pink from the sun. Their hair glistens with highlights and is coarse from the salt water. Their glasses are full of citrus juices. Now that Baby John is nine months old, Elizebeth is delighted to be able to again fit into her linen pants and sleeveless shirt, and—captivated by the somewhat revealing outfit—William can barely keep his hands off her. Edna joined them and is having the time of her life. She has rarely left Indiana and has certainly never traveled to a place like Florida, which has opened her eyes to a new world.

"You've made a grave mistake taking me along with you," says Edna. "Because if you ever try to go to Florida without me, I'll be raving mad with jealousy. I can't believe you're getting paid for this."

"I know," says Elizebeth. "Hard to call this work, isn't it?"

"You deserve it," says William. "I don't know anyone who works as hard as you do. I would hire you for my team, if I could, but then we wouldn't get trips to sunny places, and we certainly couldn't take the family. The kinds of places we'd go... Never mind."

Elizebeth smiles.

"It's so unfair," says Edna. "You get to work from home. You have a staff. Then you get to go to places like this and meet exciting people. All this, along with a handsome, doting husband who supports anything you do. It's a good thing you're my sister, or I might hate you."

Edna follows her impassioned speech with a fake laugh that doesn't touch her eyes.

Maybe it was a mistake bringing Edna, thinks Elizebeth.

Years ago, when Edna first met William on a visit to Elizebeth at Riverbank, Edna was so taken with William she wrote letters to him that fell only just short of pitching herself as the better sister. They've all joked about it over the years, but it has always left a bad taste in Elizebeth's mouth.

Elizebeth is saved a response by the arrival of Commander Jack with his visibly pregnant wife and their toddler. On Jack's recent visit to HQ for a conference, it was Root who exposed Elizebeth as a wife and mother, and Jack was delighted to hear it. Forced to let down her guard, it was a bit of a relief to not have to hide such things from her coworker in the field. Seeing the families together around the table brings Elizebeth a joy she couldn't have anticipated. Baby John is taken by Jack's towheaded toddler, seated next to him, and when Barbara learns the girl's name is Dorothy, Barbara makes everyone laugh by calling "Dorfy" her "sisser."

"I'm afraid she's never gotten over having a brother instead of a sister," says Elizebeth.

"Dorothy also wants a sister," says Edie, Jack's wife. "I hope she'll be happy either way."

"Just get her a cat, if it doesn't turn out," says William. "Pinkle Purr has more than made up for Barbara's disappointment with Baby John."

They laugh, and once all orders are in, they fall into easy chatter. Tucked away in the corner of the restaurant, the music of the Cuban trio is far enough away to be able to talk over, yet close enough to provide lovely background music. Because of the extended families there, Elizebeth and Jack can't speak about the rumrunners or the pirate radio station they're allowing to keep broadcasting so they can gather more intelligence, or the fact that William and Elizebeth have been commissioned to write the first official codebook of the coast guard, together, but there's enough about the beautiful island, and Jack's family recommendations, so the conversation never lags. Elizebeth amuses the group describing Jack's anxiety during her first trip on a coast guard patrol, and Jack makes them all laugh when he tells them about finding Elizebeth slipping out of a speakeasy the last time she was in Key West.

"I'm shocked," says William. "Every time I even hint at a little Manischewitz for Passover, I get shot down. And sacramental wine is perfectly legal. Just ask the Catholics."

"It was purely for research," she says with a wink.

The adults laugh. Baby John, however, is starting to squirm in his high chair.

Edna rises to lift him, but Elizebeth places a hand on her sister's arm.

"I'll walk him around," Elizebeth says.

Edna appreciates being able to stay at the table, and Elizebeth could use a stretch, her back giving her fits if she sits too long. She lifts John out of the high chair and bounces him over to the musicians.

Three men play a lively Cuban song, and John loves being danced by Elizebeth. As she points out the maracas to John, other children join them, watching the musicians. With her dark eyes and plaited dark hair, the little girl nearest Elizebeth, bossing her younger brother, is a beauty. The way she mothers the whining boy reveals she's old beyond her years. With her wise eyes, she looks somehow familiar. The girl keeps looking from the boy to a table over her shoulder by the door, and Elizebeth follows the girl's alert stare to a couple arguing.

Must couples always argue here? Elizebeth thinks, recalling her last visit to the restaurant.

The shadows block their faces, as does the body of the waiter who appears unsure about whether to leave. When the man pushes back his chair so it falls over and storms out of the restaurant, the waiter also scurries away. It's then that Elizebeth gets a good look at the woman, and when Elizebeth does, she nearly drops Baby John.

Elizebeth knows that gorgeous face almost as well as her own.

The shrewd eyes catch her staring. Elizebeth feels her heart racing and she cannot look away. All she's able to do is turn John so he can't be seen by the woman.

How can I return to the table without her seeing our families? Elizebeth thinks. *She won't know me, but she might know Jack. It was foolish for us to meet in public for dinner like this, putting our families in danger.*

The girl saves Elizebeth by distracting her mother and breaking the connection. The children return to the table as their mother throws down a wad of cash. Though not a bite was eaten, she grabs the boy's arm and drags him toward the door. The woman casts one more look over her shoulder at Elizebeth before storming out of the restaurant.

Once Elizebeth is sure the woman is gone, she hurries back to the table and places John in his high chair. She sits heavily on her seat and tries to tune in to the laughter and conversation, but she can't free her mind from the woman. Elizebeth longs to follow her, to speak with her, to tell her there's a better way, but that's impossible. William's hand on Elizebeth's arm breaks her spell.

"Are you all right?" he asks. "You look as if you've seen a ghost."

"I have," she says.

At this, she turns to Jack and gives him a long look, telling him in her mind who she's seen. He tries to read her thoughts, but he cannot parcel them out. He's not connected to her the way that William is. He can't hear that Elizebeth has come face-to-face with her adversary, her obsession, in the flesh.

Marie Waite.

TWENTY-FOUR

KEY WEST

Marie

At the Victoria Restaurant, glaring at her drunk husband, Marie thinks back to several nights ago, when Raul and his family invited Marie and hers to dinner. Charlie said he was going fishing with friends but promised he'd be back in time and said he would meet Marie and the kids at Raul's house. She should go on ahead of him.

Six o'clock came and went. Six thirty did, too. At seven, Marie insisted they eat without Charlie.

Throughout the excruciating evening, Marie had to endure the poorly masked pity from the perfect couple, the perfect family, in the perfect home. She had to watch a man insist on washing dishes while the wives had a drink, and the children play with the perfect dog in a perfect garden, where the white-eyed stare of the statue of Our Lady of Charity, surrounded in roses, pierced Marie's heart so it ached. The bile in Marie's belly was so nauseating she could barely swallow. She had to choke down her dinner, her drinks, her vitriol, her very self. It felt as if she were drowning in an angry sea, while others tried to throw her lifelines to boats on which she didn't want to climb aboard. She would have to gasp and claw and crawl, but she would make it back on her own boat, on her own terms.

When the sun had set, and Marie could take it no more, she made her excuses. As she was leaving, Raul followed her through the thick waxy canopy of foliage, placing his hand on her back to stop her. His kind, fatherly look repelled Marie. It was all she could do not to turn and run.

"The business becomes a cancer," he said. "You've done very well. Too well. And now the corruption has set in. I felt it, too. In my soul. It began to erode my family. Please, get out, now. You are so young. Every day of your life you have the chance to start again, until it's too late."

Marie looked into Raul's eyes and saw that he was earnest. She could see his heart and his faith and his belief that people could change. Marie did not believe people could change, and she refused to suffer because of Charlie any longer. She didn't agree that the business was the cancer. Charlie was the cancer.

"Thank you," she said, meaning it.

Thank you for caring. Thank you for selling me your boat and your corner of the market. Thank you for showing me what a real man—a good man—is like. Thank you for the clarity.

From that moment on, Marie actively started planning her coup. She would overthrow the king. She would extract the cancer. She would start immediately.

Now, at the Victoria Restaurant, Charlie has to use the restroom as soon as they arrive.

"Order for me," he slurs, just as her eyes alight upon the special.

"Happy to," she says.

Marie orders, and when he returns, he's somehow drunker and barely able to keep his eyes open. The older couple at the table nearest them keeps shooting dark glances at Charlie, and Marie becomes concerned they'll tell the manager about him. Joey doesn't notice, consumed only with whining about how hungry he is, but Josephine's eyes, astute as ever, track between Charlie and Marie. Increasingly, Josephine takes cues from her mother's behavior. The girl has recently been fighting less and aligning more with Marie. Josephine didn't even try to ask about bringing the doll to the restaurant. Marie finds Josephine's scrutiny both endearing and unsettling.

Joey's increasing fussing leads Josephine to take him to watch the musicians. Once they're gone, Marie digs her nails into Charlie's knee.

"Ow," he says.

"You're a disgrace," she says through gritted teeth.

"Say grace?" he says, confused.

"Sure. Grace. You need it."

"Pray for me. You're the one who goes to church."

I don't think mass counts if I'm fantasizing about killing you, she thinks.

Charlie looks over his shoulder at the musicians and utters a curse, dragging his hands up to cover his ears.

"I thought we were in Key West," he slurs. "Sounds like we're in damned Cuba. Godforsaken place."

"That godforsaken place has made us a million dollars."

"And nearly got me killed. Those damned Cuban bartenders, looking for a fight. Your damned brother and his shady connections. The damned coast guard shooting at me. I'm not going back."

"Really?" she says. "And just what do you think you'll do? Retire? Keep house while I work? Fish all day long? You certainly smell like it now."

He scoffs.

"I'm going back to the Bahamas run," he says. "No more Cuba for me."

This is easier than I thought it would be, she thinks. *So easy it's almost boring.*

"That route is blown," she says.

"It's had time to cool down. A few Miami racetrack guys told me business is picking up again. They want us to supply now that Alderman's doing more Cuba routes."

"I thought you said Miami was Capone's territory now. Do you want to ruffle his feathers? And have you forgotten that Sheriff Bryan and his men have been arrested? The new guy, Sheriff Lehman, is not going to look the other way."

"Everyone has a price. And Capone doesn't care about us small-timers."

She bristles at the description. Millionaires are not small-timers. She is not a small-timer.

"Your radiomen will warn you," he continues, "if the coasties or the feds are patrolling. You can send me some kind of signal."

"It's too risky."

"If you're afraid, you stick to Cuba. I'll do the Bahamas. We'll see who makes more."

"Are you trying to compete with me?"

"Oh, I wouldn't dare compete with the notorious Spanish Marie," he says, taking a mocking bow. She yanks him back down into his seat. The old couple gives them another nasty look. From across the room, Josephine stares at Charlie. Marie can see how mortified her daughter is. It fills her with fresh hatred for Charlie.

"Shut up," she hisses. "You're making a spectacle. You'll never be respectable."

He snorts and takes a long drink of water, his watch flashing in the candlelight. The watch is a constant torment to her. Every time she sees how he splurged on himself on their first big run, and how he has never bought her a single piece of jewelry, it reminds her what a stupid, selfish animal he is. He parades the watch in front of her face as often as possible. It's a constant reminder that Charlie, and how he wants others to perceive him, will always be his first priority. She never will be.

The waiter arrives with their entrées. Marie braces herself, an electric thrill, underlaid with terror, coursing through her veins. The waiter removes the covers, the steam dissipating to reveal the squabs.

"Grilled pigeon de la Mancha," the waiter says with flourish.

Charlie recoils, cursing, knocking over his chair.

"You bitch," he says, before stumbling out of the restaurant.

The waiter scurries off, and in his wake, Marie feels someone watching her. There's a woman holding a baby, standing next to Josephine and Joey near the musicians. When Marie locks eyes with the woman, she looks as if she's seen a ghost.

Why is she staring at me like that? thinks Marie.

It's more than a look that a passerby would give, even at one whose husband has just stormed off. The woman knows Marie. Her first thought is wondering if the woman is dallying with Charlie, but that's not right. This woman looks sharp, wise, and elegant. She's above Charlie. Maybe she recognizes Marie from the newspapers, but why would she go white when they made eye contact? There's something else.

Marie's thinking is cut off by the return of the children. They've broken her concentration, forcing her to be first to look away. Marie feels as if she's somehow lost the upper hand and, along with it, her appetite. She feels like a caged animal.

Disgusted, Marie throws a wad of bills on the table and drags the children from the restaurant, casting one last glance over her shoulder at the woman, impressing her face upon her memory before leaving.

TWENTY-FIVE

WASHINGTON, DC

Elizebeth

At HQ, the twenty-one-year-old radioman, Hyman Hurwitz, interrupts Elizebeth's incessant nail chewing to pass her his pack of cigarettes.

"You could use a drink," says Hyman. "But since that's frowned upon, have a smoke."

"I haven't smoked in ages," she says.

"No time like now to start again, Boss," he says, flashing his dimple.

Goodness, she thinks. *He looks like a young William.*

Elizebeth takes the cigarette and leans down for the radioman to light it. She inhales and holds it for a few moments. On the exhale, it feels as if she's slipping into a warm bath.

"See, Boss?" he says. "Better."

"Boss," she says. "You keep calling me that. You know very well who your boss is."

"Yes, but one day I think it'll be you. Everyone knows, the minute you want to come to work in the office, you'll have a whole unit under your direction."

Elizebeth feels a warm burst of pleasure. She has allowed herself to imagine this, to fantasize about being the first woman in history to head a cryptanalysis team. She has told William, Anna, and Root about her dream of leading such a group, once the children are school age. Prohibition likely has a shelf life, but the smuggling of narcotics and human beings is just getting started.

"If you're lucky," Elizebeth says with a grin. "Let's see how you do with communications while we catch a pirate."

She enjoys seeing the color on Hyman's cheeks, but quickly feels a warning flag rise, like a mariner's gale pennant. The young man's admiration has sent an electric jolt through her, giving her new insight into the dangers of power.

She takes a step back, putting a more formal distance between her and Hyman, but when Root and a few other men arrive, the entire team crowds around the radio telephone. They've all come into the office in the wee hours of the morning to listen to the coast guard take down Charles Waite.

Seeing Marie in Key West, and tipping all the dominoes of intelligence in motion, has allowed Elizebeth to open up the Waites' impressive operation. Within days of the meeting, Elizebeth was able to find and decipher the intercepts that allowed her to map out the entire organization, and what an organization it is. Marie's brother Angel operates the Key West pirate radio station and employs a man to create the ciphers, translating them into Spanish and transmitting everything to Marie, who captains the pilot boat when they do the Cuba runs. Her other brother, Rogelio, works with a wholesaler, operating just outside of Havana. Charles's family are also employed driving boats and acting as bodyguards. The Waites have been operating out of Key West since the hurricane, but recent intercepts show a surprising run: a return to the old Bahamas-Miami route.

By all indications, and confirming Elizebeth's instincts, intelligence has revealed that Marie is the brains of the operation. This trip is a strange risk. With larger mob syndicates infesting Miami and the new sheriff, Manuel Lehman, firmly on the side of the law, Elizebeth can't understand why Marie would allow this. She has to be up to something. Elizebeth has cautioned Commander Jack, reiterating that Marie is armed and extremely dangerous, and this could be a trap.

Seeing Marie in person has only stoked the fires of Elizebeth's obsession, and she looks forward to the day when she can meet her adversary again, in court. Elizebeth has no doubt she will catch her mouse and enjoys the thought of the triumph of seeing realization dawn on Marie's face that it wasn't a man at HQ who took her down, but another woman.

Elizebeth can't help but laugh to herself.

"What?" asks Root.

"She's short. And I think her eyes are brown, not blue. And she has two young children."

"Who?"

"Spanish Marie."

"The one whom the rumors report is six feet tall?" he asks. "With a Mexican father and a Swedish mother?"

"Yes, and a sapphire glare that will send you straight to hell, if her revolver doesn't first."

The men laugh. Elizebeth joins them, delighting in the irony, the legend, the vanity. Marie is the one who wanted radio communication to make her operation larger and more sophisticated. Marie craved the coverage. By all intelligence accounts, Charles wanted to keep it smaller. Because of the growth, they've come on Elizebeth's radar, which means it's all but inevitable they will be caught. They should have stuck with carrier pigeons.

A crackling sound draws them all closer.

"Patrol," says Hyman. "What's your position?"

"Twenty-five point five degrees north," comes the coastie's voice. "By eighty point two degrees west, Biscayne Bay. Tucked in between two beautiful Tetas."

Snickers come through the radio telephone.

When discovered in the 1700s, the two mounds on the small island in Biscayne Bay reminded the Spanish explorer of breasts, thus, the names "Paps" or "Las Tetas," the Tits. While the men around Elizebeth attempt to stifle laughs, two red circles color Hyman's cheeks. He looks at her, mortified.

"Should I tell him a lady is in our presence?" he asks.

"Please," she says. "I spend my days reading the intercepts of criminals. It takes a lot more than that to offend me."

He nods and turns back to the radio.

"Do you have a visual yet?" he asks.

"Negative. Night glasses fixed on the horizon. Picket boat ready to make the chase."

Root crosses the room to mark the war map while Elizebeth breathes a sigh of relief. Commander Jack told her he'd stay on his seventy-five-foot patrol boat and dispatch Harvey "Two-Gun" and two others on a thirty-six-foot picket boat to intercept Waite. They'll require a smaller, more maneuverable craft, in case Charles takes to the shallower creeks and mangroves. Elizebeth is glad Jack will be safe.

She closes her eyes. She imagines being onboard the patrol boat, the rollers lifting and dropping the vessel, the salty air in her face, a waxing gibbous moon lighting the night. She imagines looking for the horizon's first rim of light in the east, where Charles Waite should soon appear. She feels a pang of anxiety, wondering if he'll show. She knows no matter how many times she proves herself to the men around her, most are still surprised when she's right. Many still have doubts that a woman is truly responsible for so much of their success.

Elizebeth has no doubts about herself. She knows her work is impeccable, and Charles should soon be appearing, Miami bound with four hundred sacks of liquor. If the King of the Rumrunners doesn't arrive, it's because he was swamped by a wave, or killed in a Nassau bar fight, or thrown overboard by another rummy who wants the crown. Still, if he doesn't show, it will make Elizebeth look bad, so she'll hold her breath until he does.

A vivid vision of the night she saw the Waites in Key West comes to mind. Marie's obvious hatred for her drunk husband pulsed from the woman like a bomb blast, its heat reaching all the way to Elizebeth, all the way to Marie's daughter. Those small keen eyes were so like her mother's. Seeing all. Judging all. Weighing and calculating all. Intelligent eyes. The brains behind the operation.

"We have a visual," comes the voice.

Elizebeth takes the last drag of her cigarette and stubs it out. It takes all of her willpower not to ask for another.

"Is it him?" asks Hyman.

"Affirmative."

An idea suddenly bursts in Elizebeth's mind, and she widens her eyes.

My goodness, she thinks. *This is a setup. But not of the coasties. Marie has set up her husband.*

TWENTY-SIX

MIAMI

Marie

Alone in her truck, Marie watches.

From her vantage at Black Point, she can see over the waters of Biscayne Bay to the horizon, where Charlie should soon arrive on the *Josephine*. Now that they lack the alliance of local law enforcement, they have a new warehouse, tucked within the secluded bug- and gator-infested mangroves of south Miami, and it's here that Charlie thinks he's going to unload his haul. Marie knows he'll never even make land.

She chose the boat bearing her daughter's name as the sacrificial lamb for two reasons. First, as much as Marie hates to admit it, she thinks Red Shannon's blood might, in fact, have cursed the vessel. In spite of their success, the darkness has grown since they acquired it, so it's time to let it go. Second, in a strange burst of maternal protection, she no longer wants her daughter's name touching anything associated with the trade.

In Key West, Marie has begun to see her daughter with new eyes. The child is the spitting image of Marie and is almost exactly like her in demeanor, save one thing. Josephine has a capacity for love, affection, lightness, and even joy. Marie has started to wonder if she might have been the same kind of child before the poverty ground down her father and the bitterness poisoned her mother. Marie can't remember, but somehow senses that protecting Josephine, and also Joey, might allow her children to grow up to be happier people. Maternal feelings have been largely foreign to Marie up to this point. She doesn't know why the feelings have grown in her, and she's pleased to know she isn't entirely dead inside, that there isn't something horrifically wrong with her. With it, however, comes a foreign sensation, and one she does not enjoy.

Fear.

In the past, Marie would have pushed away any hint of these emotions, particularly the ones that made her feel weak. Maybe it's because of Raul's words, or the echo of Cleo's, or maybe Marie is getting older and more mature, but she allows herself to inspect the good and the bad emotions. She picks them up like sea glass on a beach, turning over each piece, observing their shapes, forms, and colors, and placing them in a treasure box, instead of tossing them back in the sea.

The radio crackles.

"Skidoo."

Keep out.

Her heartbeat quickens.

The coast is not clear. Warning. Turn back.

Marie lifts the night glasses to her eyes and scans, and in seconds she sees the coasties. In the shadows of Las Tetas, there are two looming forms, like a mother tiger shark and her pup. Marie's lip curls in hatred at the sight of them, but tonight, they are strange allies.

The enemy of my enemy is my friend.

My enemy is my husband.

Marie moves her watch to the horizon, and her heartbeat further quickens when she spots the *Josephine*. Though her running lights are dark, the moon illuminates her form. She rides low and slow, laden with four hundred sacks that will soon be an offering to the ocean. Marie feels a tug in her heart for the vessel. The *Josephine* has been lucrative, if nothing else, and marked the beginning of Marie's ascendancy. She also feels a wave of nausea at the loss of the cargo, but it must be done.

Marie reflects that she feels no tug or sickness at the loss of the man at the helm.

"Skidoo."

Marie has one last chance to signal Charlie and call the whole thing off. Since he has refused to learn to use the radio, they agreed she would flash her headlights three times, at intervals of ten seconds, if there was danger.

Marie tries to kindle some kind of emotion toward the man she married. She thinks back to the early days, and the way Charlie held her in his arms when they danced, and gazed upon her with want, and played with her, and made her laugh, and made her body sing. Marie now realizes, however, his hold was a possessive grip—a claiming of territory that wasn't his—and there was never love, only lust.

Marie thinks back to the night of Charlie's stabbing. Over his shoulder, Marie can still see the wild-eyed, drunken, jilted wife lunging toward them in bed. Marie will never forget the squelching sound of the knife going into Charlie's neck, and the terrifying chorus of the women's screams. She can see the blood all over the sheets she used to cover herself, while Charlie staggered, naked, to standing and punched his wife, knocking her to the floor. He held a gun to her head while Marie called the police.

Marie now feels a kinship with the woman. Even though Marie's ex-husband betrayed her, too, she thinks with unease of Joe's hurt, the disappointment of her parents, the hyena pack of Charlie's friends at their wedding, and how he got so drunk he couldn't consummate the marriage until the following day. She thinks of the times Charlie has knocked her around, his filthy language, the fights, and the squandering of money.

How could I allow such a man in my home with my children? How could I have hated myself so much?

"Never again," she says.

There is no love left for Charlie. Like war, when blood is spilled, there can be no reconciliation, only more violence, and violence is how this will end. At least it won't be directly by her hand. She somehow knows that's the only hope she has to escape a blood curse.

Before Charlie left for the Bahamas yesterday, she told him to leave his Rolex Oyster watch at home.

"That thing will be the death of you," she said. "Either by

getting you jumped at Nassau, or by its reflection making a target of you for the coasties."

"You think I'm the only rich man in Nassau? That I can't defend myself? And I'm running in the dark. There's nothing for it to reflect."

"Have you forgotten the moon?"

He narrowed his eyes.

"Do you want to pawn it or something?" he asked.

Yes, she thought.

"I'm just looking out for you," she said quietly.

Marie put false love in her voice and softened her features to speak her lines. It made him pause. He kissed her goodbye, longer than he had lately, but he didn't take off the watch.

While she continues to watch the *Josephine* move closer, she's surprised by a thought.

Leave rumrunning.

It doesn't seem like the thought comes from within her, but from outside of her.

Maybe she could sell her extra boats and the lots she and Charlie have acquired. The watch will be a loss, but she could sell every other piece of jewelry and the house. She could tithe from the proceeds and put a statue of Nuestra Señora de la Caridad on the grounds of Gesú Catholic Church. She could buy a smaller place in Miami, near the dance academy that she might try to resurrect, but will keep the house in Cuba as an escape. Maybe Marie could teach dance at a Cuban hotel. Maybe she could start a flower shop in Havana, supplied by her own garden, where

Josephine could work. The girl has real talent for floral design, the kind that can't be taught. She has an eye for color, form, and meaning that comes from *su alma vieja*, her old soul, as a Cuban florist's mother observed, on their last trip.

No matter what Marie chooses, imagining a future without Charlie feels like a blank slate full of fresh, colorful possibility. It looks like a round, juicy, ripe fruit waiting for her to reach out and pluck it.

"Skidoo. Do you copy?"

Marie takes a long draw from her flask, wiping away the whisky that slides down her chin with the back of her arm. She pulls a knife from her garter, feels behind the radio that Benny installed, and cuts the wires.

TWENTY-SEVEN

WASHINGTON, DC

Elizebeth

Now that Elizebeth is certain Marie has hand-fed Charles to them, Elizebeth feels deflated. She hasn't outwitted her adversary; they're working together. Elizebeth thinks about telling her hunch to the men in the room but censors herself. It wouldn't change anything. She can't prove it, and they still have to take down Charles. Telling these men would only detract from what looks like her accomplishment. Still, it feels unsavory keeping a secret, but Elizebeth is used to keeping unsavory secrets.

What's one more?

The more Elizebeth engages in top-secret work, the better she becomes at storing intelligence in places away from her family and public life. She finds no difficulty in sliding information into endless file cabinets in her mind, away from her heart and even her morals. Her practicality suppresses any scruples that might arise over her interior second self. She's convinced that her work and her skill set are needed and special, so this must be done. It's interesting to Elizebeth that, as time goes on, while she gets better at the duality, William gets worse at separating his selves. Or maybe, he's privy to much darker intelligence than she is. Maybe if she worked in the "Black Chamber" she would feel as unbalanced as he does. He has alluded to as much.

"Waite just rounded into Biscayne Bay," says the coastie. "Headed south."

Root moves the flag on the map.

"Passing us now," says the coastie. "He hasn't seen us."

They wait, tense. Hyman holds up the pack of cigarettes to Elizebeth. She takes and lights another. After a long drag, she exhales into the smoky air of the radio room, adding to the fog. It takes her anxiety and even paranoia down a notch. Though she knows it's not possible, Elizebeth has the strangest feeling that Marie is watching. The woman's presence is so large it feels as if it casts a shadow.

"Now!" says the coastie.

They hear warning shots.

"Waite threw his engines into high gear," says the coastie. "He's not going down without a fight."

As they listen to the drama unfold, not for the first time, Elizebeth thinks what a great book, film, or radio program the Rum War would make. Based on the enthusiasm with which the radioman reports, he would agree. High-stakes adventure on the high seas, vivid settings, colorful characters, women on either side of the law. Maybe she'll write it one day. That way, she can control the narrative.

According to the coastie, Waite is throwing sacks overboard, while trying to navigate his vessel. With every ham that hits the water, the boat becomes lighter and faster. Like Red Shannon, Waite has incredible control over his vessel, and is able to maneuver the boat between ships at anchor much better than the coast guard helmsman. The patrol boat joins pursuit as long as possible, but the closer Waite gets to the mangroves, the more the large vessel has to fall back. Once the patrol boat loses sight, Harvey "Two-Gun" on the picket boat takes over. His radioman gives short dispatches that don't have nearly the color of the patroller's broadcast.

"Headed toward Black Caesar's Creek," he says.

After a few seconds, shots are fired, but the man doesn't say by whom. Then the radio goes silent.

Hyman groans. Root adjusts the map. Elizebeth smokes. The other men pace. Nearly thirty agonizing minutes pass before the line again crackles to life.

"Picket, you okay?" asks Hyman.

"All three CGs okay. Waite fired first."

"Waite's condition?"

"Harvey shot him. Easy target, with that flashy watch he was wearing."

Elizebeth and Root look at each other, silently communicating. There will be a trial, and somehow, the coast guard never comes out looking good to the public, especially when the one they call "Two-Gun" fired the shots.

"Is Waite dead?" asks Hyman.

"We don't know."

"Why not?"

"Waite went overboard. Never resurfaced."

TWENTY-EIGHT

MIAMI

Marie

Long after the picket boat had left Black Caesar's Creek, Marie and Theo searched for Charlie's body. She told Theo someone cut the wires in her truck so she couldn't give the warning signal. He paused only a moment before resuming the search. They found nothing but birds, wretched birds, noisy birds. Startled, a gull fluttered in Marie's face, drawing forth a scream from her. She found a feather on her truck seat and one in her hair. If she were superstitious, she'd think Charlie was haunting her.

That night, Marie returned to the marina where the coasties had towed the *Josephine*, and she set the boat on fire. The feds may have gotten the liquor Charlie had not been able to heave overboard, but she would never let them commandeer her boat.

Theo's despair over losing another brother was enormous. Marie's despair over not seeing Charlie's dead body was equally so. Both hate the coast guard—Theo, because they killed his brother, Marie, because they did so without leaving proof.

Without a body, no legal evidence of Charlie's death is possible, which means Marie can get nothing from the will.

Now, a week later, Marie's bitterness has made her even angrier than when Charlie was alive. She remains chained to him. He's still deadweight, tied to her legs, dragging her under. She didn't think it was possible to hate Charlie any more than she had. She was wrong.

The phone rings off the hook. The newspapers want a statement. Raul wants to offer his condolences. Charlie's mother wants to know if they've found a body. Her parents want her to bring the children to stay with them. Rogelio wants to know when she's doing another run. Angel wants to know when to transmit. Eventually Theo and the rest want to know, too. Her whole empire is waiting on her to make a move, but she feels paralyzed.

Josephine continues to watch Marie's every move. The child's demeanor has relaxed since Charlie's disappearance. Even Joey is more placid without the incessant, electric tension Charlie's presence caused. At least there's that.

The nightmares, however, are awful, and relentless, and always the same.

It's the night after Charlie was shot. Marie crawls into bed but can't sleep. A storm grows outside, raging. In a flash of lightning, she sees Charlie in the bedroom doorway. There's a bloody bullet hole in his forehead, his eyes are eaten out by fish, his blue skin is slimy with seaweed, and ocean water drips on the floor. A soaked carrier pigeon sits on his shoulder. It takes flight and aims for

Marie's eyes, attacking her. She screams over and over and is only awakened when Josephine shakes her.

"Mama, are you okay?"

No, Marie thinks. *And I might never be again.*

Floods of condolence cards, flowers, and food flow in. Josephine takes the helm. She arranges and rearranges the flowers and moves them all around the house. She heats the food for them. Joey eats until his cheeks are round and pink. He doesn't whine anymore.

A package arrives with a letter inside, on stationery from the Hotel Tuller, in Detroit.

"A timepiece for the queen, so she's mindful of when it's time to leave the ball."

Marie opens the box and draws in her breath. It's a slender gold-plated Bulova wristwatch, with golden beryl stones inlaid around its rectangular face. She winds it and puts it on.

"If you're ever in town, I have a guest room for you in my suite. My sincerest condolences. Cleo."

Is it time to get out? Marie wonders. *Maybe.*

She goes to confession. She drives all the way to Fort Lauderdale, where the priest won't know her voice. She tells him everything. For the first time in ages, she cries real tears. He asks if she would consider turning herself in to the police. She tells him her children would then lose both parents. The priest sighs, long and heavy.

"You are truly sorry?" he asks.

For a brief, shining, holy moment, Marie convinces herself

she is. She thinks she could have reached out to the coast guard or the feds to turn Charlie in, instead of setting him up to be killed. She knows part of this regret is because there's a lingering thought that Charlie might not be dead. It was dark. The coast guard could have missed. He's an excellent swimmer. Maybe he's biding his time, waiting to murder her.

"I am," she says. "It was wrong to go about it that way. There were other ways—legal, moral, and upright—that wouldn't have involved bloodshed."

"Then you are absolved," he says. "But for your penance, you must get out of the business forever. Never look back. Do everything in your power to make a good and holy life for your family."

"I will."

"For your penance, you must also have a mass said for your husband's soul. If you do not do either of these things, you are not absolved."

"I will do them," she says.

Marie has the mass said immediately, but—after two phone calls—the second part of her promise feels impossible for her to fulfill. The first call is from dance instructor Ted Hill.

"I'm out, doll," he says.

"What do you mean?" she asks.

"I've tried. We can't get anyone in the academy. We're not making numbers. My instructors are bored and leaving. I'm bored. I can't waste my talent any longer. It's over."

Marie is glad Florence has the children out for a picnic at

the beach because the storm of curses Marie unleashes result in Ted's hanging up on her. When she tries to call back, no one answers. She can imagine the phone at the academy ringing, screaming, echoing off the polished floors, floors with barely any scuff marks. Chest heaving, Marie bangs the earpiece down over and over, until the fingers on her right hand bleed. The phone rings again.

"How dare you hang up on me," she says.

"Mrs. Waite, this is your lawyer."

She groans and apologizes.

"Were you able to get the coastguardsmen's statements?" she asks.

If the coastguardsmen will say they witnessed Charlie die, that will be proof enough in court for her to get the estate. The coasties were put on leave for internal investigation, however, and have not been accessible.

"Not yet, and I have bad news," he says.

What more can possibly be wrong?

"Recent calls have revealed that your husband's debts have considerably dwindled the estate."

Marie feels her blood go cold. The fire of her rage turns to ice, freezing her body from head to toe.

"By how much?" she asks.

"It would appear Mr. Waite amassed a great deal of gambling debt. In addition, he made copious loans to his, uh, associates. And he had considerable bills from area hotels, jewelers, clothiers, et cetera, that have to be settled."

The thugs. The women. They've taken more from her than she ever could have imagined.

"How much?" she asks, clenching her jaw.

"There's less than a hundred grand."

Marie exhales, her skin color returning to normal.

"Less than a hundred grand, off a million, isn't as bad as I thought," she says.

The line is quiet for a moment, followed by the awkward clearing of his throat.

"No, ma'am," he says. "There's less than a hundred grand left in the estate."

Marie hangs up and looks from the closet, where Charlie's clothing has overtaken hers, to the skull, to the plastic crown on Charlie's nightstand. She thinks of all the times Charlie wore the crown, and how stupid he looked. She thinks about how the papers liked to call him the King of the Rumrunners when he was nothing more than her fool.

After a long moment, she pulls the revolver from her garter. She points it at the wedding picture tucked in the floor-to-ceiling mirror. She shoots Charlie's face, shattering it.

TWENTY-NINE

MIAMI

Elizebeth

With Leila piloting the seaplane, the drops through air pockets, the roaring and rushing, Elizebeth feels as close to religion as she ever has. She both fears for her life and is in awe of God's creation.

From four hundred feet up, Elizebeth takes in Florida's Atlantic coast. Her eyes follow the meandering rivers that feed the ocean with their lifeblood, stirring up the salt, sand, and water in dramatic and colorful eddies. As they pass over Miami Beach, Leila tips the wings and her voice comes over the headpiece. She points out everything from Fisher's Flamingo Hotel, to the windmill at the Roman Pools, to Las Tetas, and finally Black Caesar's Creek, where all that's likely left of Charles Waite are bones, picked clean.

"Have you heard of the legend of Black Caesar?" Leila asks.

"No," Elizebeth says.

"Supposedly, he was six and a half feet tall and of royal African descent. Highly intelligent and handsome. He escaped slavery and went on to become one of the most successful and notorious pirates on the East Coast. They say he buried treasure on the strip of land just south of Las Tetas, on Elliott Key, and haunts the islands."

"What happened to him?"

"After he fell in with Blackbeard, some say he got nabbed in Virginia and hanged. Others, that he escaped and lived a long, wealthy life."

Elizebeth's mind turns back to Charles Waite.

Did he escape? It's possible.

As Elizebeth predicted, Marie used Charles as a scapegoat, pinning everything shady and underhanded on her missing husband, pretending she knew nothing of his rumrunning. Charles was finally declared dead, months later, by statement of the coastguardsmen in pursuit. They said after Charles fired many times upon them, nearly striking Harvey, he administered a shot that went right through Charles's forehead and sent him backward overboard. Though a body was never found, Harvey said there's no chance Waite could have survived the injury. Because no one contested that Harvey fired in self-defense, the coasties were cleared and are back at the helm.

Marie was finally able to collect on Charles's will, but because of gambling debts and other bad investments, the papers reported, only one hundred grand was left out of what was once a million-dollar fortune. Elizebeth has crawled into the thoughts of the mastermind and felt the rage that must remain in Marie. Elizebeth knows Marie will not retire, going quietly into the night. She's biding her time but will be back in blazing form. When that happens, Elizebeth vows to catch Marie once and for all.

The flight is every bit as thrilling as Elizebeth could have imagined. When they come to a splash landing in the water, she hates for it to be over. Leila promises they'll do it again. She says she'll fly the whole Friedman family to Key West. Elizebeth is giddy at the thought.

Once grounded, Leila drives them to Fort Lauderdale. Elizebeth has been working with Base Six for a week, training coastguardsmen in codebreaking for real-time intercepts. This afternoon, she has been given special permission to ride along with CG-249 on patrol and can't wait to hit the open water.

"From a train, to a plane, to a boat," she says. "I can't believe I get paid for this."

"You deserve it," says Leila. "You're special. And your fearlessness will inspire other women."

"I can't claim fearlessness," says Elizebeth. "But I do have enough curiosity to overcome it."

Leila leaves Elizebeth with kisses on both cheeks and speeds away in her red roadster, her kerchief blowing in the wind.

Shortly afterward, Commander Jack comes out to greet Elizebeth, along with his crew, and they head to CG-249. As they motor offshore, Elizebeth is grateful for the breeze. She feels as if she's inside an oven.

"Should be quiet today," says Jack. "No rummy in his right mind would be out in broad daylight in these temps."

"I can think of at least three who would."

"Don't remind me. You know how anxious it makes me to have you onboard."

"Goodness, Jack, when are you going to see me as one of the boys?"

"Never, I'm afraid," he says. "Especially now that I know your husband and children."

Elizebeth sighs and heads to the pilothouse to listen to the radio. In spite of Jack's prediction that nothing will happen, her nerve endings have been tingling since they set out. She hopes they'll hear Marie on the airwaves. An hour passes, however, and there's only silence.

Her hackles rising, Elizebeth steps outside the pilothouse and stares at the horizon, wiggling in the heat. The water is flat, strange, and silver, moved only by things unseen, the glaring sun making liquid mercury of it. She feels something coming and it doesn't feel good.

A disturbance in the water calls her attention and makes her heart race. Sprays of white announce a vessel. Jack lifts his glasses to his eyes.

"Can you see the vessel ID?" she asks.

"Not yet," he says.

"Coming in from the Bahamas at that speed, it might be a rummy."

"Unlikely, this time of day."

Elizebeth puts her hand to her forehead to shield the sun but can only make out the growing sprays of white foam coming closer, indicating the boat's high speed.

"Okay, I see," says Jack. "Vessel labeled V-15997."

"I'll check the books," says a boatswain.

A spark ignites in Elizebeth's mind.

While the coastie heads for the pilothouse, Elizebeth allows the numbers to move swiftly through the hallways and files in her mind until she finds what she's looking for. When she does, she sucks in her breath.

"Alderman," she says.

Eyes wide with horror, Jack shoots a glance at her, just as the boatswain runs out.

"Alderman," he says.

Jack swallows, the sudden flush of red on his face betraying his fear.

"Special Agent Friedman," he says, as calmly as possible. "Get in the pilothouse and stay there until I allow you out, do you understand?"

Elizebeth knows enough about Jimmy Alderman to obey without argument. Once inside, she tells the radioman, who patches through to Base Six to alert them.

"Alderman in our sights," he says. "Heading toward Miami from the east, the Bahamas, roughly three miles offshore."

The message is received, and Elizebeth positions herself near a small rectangular window at eye level that gives her a good view of the action while keeping her concealed. The vessel kicks into gear, moving fast toward Alderman. In a short time, they're near enough to see there are two figures onboard. The coasties fire two warning shots, and Elizebeth is surprised to see Alderman slow to bobbing. She guesses he saw the size of the vessel and assumed he couldn't outrun it. She can't imagine however that the Gulf Stream Pirate will go quietly, so she feels no relief.

Soon they are close enough for Elizebeth to see Jimmy Alderman's green eyes staring, soulless and flat, from his weathered face. His gaze flicks down to his helm and back up. Her stomach roils.

What is he looking at? she thinks.

The coasties have weapons pointed at Alderman and his mate and order them to put up their hands. After a stutter of motion from Alderman, the rummies obey, and Jack orders two of his crew to board the vessel. Elizebeth can't believe she's within yards of a man who throws human beings overboard to be eaten by sharks. She can feel his dark energy, even from here. She longs to run out and tell Jack to be especially careful, but that's impossible.

After they tie the boats together and make a quick search, the coasties aboard report over a hundred hams. They lead Alderman and his mate at gunpoint to the coast guard vessel, and then to the engine room to be detained. Once they disappear inside the door, Jack makes eye contact with Elizebeth, giving her a quick nod of reassurance before ordering two other coasties to make an official count of the contraband and thoroughly search Alderman's vessel.

Elizebeth's nerves remain on high alert. This is all proceeding too smoothly for what she knows about Alderman's past run-ins. As the coastguardsmen load the liquor onto *CG-249*, the tension and the heat become unbearable. When they're about halfway through, Elizebeth hears a shout, followed by a shot.

Alderman and his man come flying out of the engine room, guns pointed.

Elizebeth feels as if she'll be sick.

The coastguardsmen on deck put up their hands, as do Jack and his mate on Alderman's vessel. She can see the sweat on Jack's underarms, feel his fear for her. The distraction of her presence is not good for him. He must forget her and think only of how to reclaim control of this situation.

The radioman taps a Morse distress signal. Elizebeth feels as if she's suffocating.

Alderman orders the coasties to start reloading the liquor onto his vessel, and Jack tells his men to obey. She has never seen the crew move so fast in her life. Once the work is done, Alderman orders all coasties to his vessel. They have no choice, but to obey, the radioman hissing at Elizebeth to stay hidden while he exits the pilothouse.

Her hands shaking, she crouches under a counter, pulling a large satchel to cover her. She can barely hear the voices over the sound of her own labored breathing. She can smell her sweat-soaked clothes. She thinks about how shattered William and the children will be if she doesn't make it home. Guilt overwhelms her.

Why did I put myself in this position?

"Cut the gas lines and set the boat on fire," says Alderman. "Show the coasties what happens when they mess with the Gulf Stream Pirate."

For the second time that day, Elizebeth finds religion. She prays to God like never before.

In moments, she hears shouts and scuffles, followed by shots. There are awful wails and more shots. An eternity passes before the radioman comes to find her. She stands, shaking with relief that it's him and not a criminal, and tries to leave the pilothouse. He puts up his hands, stopping her.

"No, Special Agent," he says. "You must remain inside. You're safe and we have control of the situation, but don't leave."

Elizebeth starts to argue until something out the window catches her eye. Alderman and his mate are handcuffed and bleeding, wincing from wounds. In addition, the coasties carry two of their own, covered in blood, bringing them back onboard the patrol boat. The first man, Elizebeth recognizes as one of the crew who led Alderman to the engine room. He's shot, but still conscious at the moment. The other's big chest is covered in blood, and his eyes are closed. Elizebeth feels her own heart lurch when she sees who it is. She cannot stifle her cry.

Commander Jack.

THIRTY

CUBA

Marie

Marie stands at the interior doorway of the canary-yellow kitchen, the smell of fresh paint in the air. Her gaze follows the floor tiles—geometric floral mandalas in white, teal, and grapefruit red—to a set of arched double doors that open to a pool and garden, with a view all the way to the sea, to Santa Maria del Mar. Filmy white curtains move lazily in the breeze, nudging the American newspapers spread across the breakfast table to life, the headlines singing like a Shakespearean chorus.

ALDERMAN ARRESTED.

GULF STREAM PIRATE IN THE BRIG.

COASTGUARDSMEN DEAD IN A RUMMY SHOOT-OUT.

Marie looks at the picture of the murdered coastguardsmen and recognizes one as the big teddy bear. She reads the story.

Commander Jack Wilson was a husband, a father of two, and another casualty of the Rum War, just like Charlie. She feels nothing but relief. All these men can go to hell as far as she's concerned. Justice has taken care of her enemies, making her the queen.

After dousing the fires of her rage, Marie realized all signs pointed to the fact that she should continue rumrunning. She knows this cancels her absolution from the church, but since she was remarried without an annulment of her first marriage, she didn't have it to begin with. She will try to do business with as little violence as possible, and for as short a time as possible. She can work on reconciliation once she retires.

In the meantime, Marie has systematically scrubbed Charlie from her life. She sold the garish green Bentley he loved and fired Theo and anyone Charlie had brought on. From now on, she'll work only with her family and her recruits. She sold every piece of clothing in Charlie's wardrobe, every shoe, every tie, every hat and accessory, down to the golden beryl cuff links, and reclaimed the Miami house closet. With her fleet of five vessels, she'll continue running between Cuba and various points along the Florida coast. She'll man the *Isabel* as a decoy, pulling the coast guard away on chases they cannot win, away from the other four boats that will carry liquor. Her men have orders to scuttle the smaller boats if they're apprehended. The amount she makes even landing one or two of the boats in the fleet will more than pay for losing the others. She thinks she should invest in a new code system, but her contact charges a fortune, so that will have to wait.

Marie inhales the rich Cuban coffee in her mug and walks outside to survey her property. Under Rogelio's supervision, Joey swims laps in the pool—an oasis of sapphire-blue water surrounded in terra-cotta tile. Joey swims hard, with all his little might. Rogelio looks at her and smiles. She nods back. Rogelio has taken the boy under his wing, and Joey thrives. Rogelio is strong and stern but loving. He gazes with obvious affection at Joey and is patient with the boy, and Joey has responded by whining less, needing less coddling, and growing more sure of himself. Hopefully, a good male influence in Joey's life will undo what Charlie did.

An influence like St. Joseph, Marie thinks.

When Marie was a young bride and her first husband, Joe, insisted upon naming both children after himself, she first was charmed, then aggravated. Now, she loves that both of her children are named for St. Joseph: a strong, hardworking protector. If she ever lets herself fall in love again, she will look for this in a man.

Josephine also continues to bloom. Marie bought Josephine a book—*Flowers, Shown to the Children*—an illustrated floral guide the girl reads constantly, making little notes in the margins. Unlike with the doll, when Josephine asks to bring the book places with her, Marie allows it. It gives Marie a pang of guilt to know she must undo what she has done with the girl, but Marie is trying every day. She often has to remind herself that she is not and will not become her embittered mother, and Josephine is not Marie, so that relationship need not repeat itself.

Josephine's long dark hair spills around her shoulders, over her white nightdress. She walks barefoot through the grass, snipping blooms for today's bouquet. She feels the weight of Marie's stare and turns to look at her mother, her face brightening like the sun. Marie feels a burst of pleasure. It's still a surprise when good emotions come, showing her that she's not entirely made of ice and stone.

"Which flowers today, princess?" Marie asks.

"White ginger and plantain lilies for the Feast of the Assumption," says Josephine.

A shadow flickers over Marie's thoughts as a cloud covers the sun. She wouldn't have planned the run tonight if she had remembered it was a Marian feast, but it's too late to call it off.

———

In spite of her ominous feeling, Marie pushes on. The *Isabel* cuts through the black water, using only the moon to light its way. Marie knows the Straits of Florida like the back of her hand, as do the men trailing in her fleet, so she tells herself that all will proceed smoothly.

It's roughly ninety nautical miles from Cuba to the Florida Keys. Her fleet's cargo is legal for seventy-eight of those miles. She knows the regular routes the coasties take on their patrols, has impeccable counterfeit paperwork, and is certain no one in Key West will apprehend them. It's only those last twelve miles in so-called American waters that present a risk, but her boat engines can cover that sea in half the time a coast guard vessel can. What are the odds that they'll intercept any of them in so great a space in the dark? She has herself so convinced all will be well that it isn't until she sees the spotlight of the picket boat illuminating her like a stage lamp that she realizes what's happening.

"Ahoy, *Isabel*," comes a voice over megaphone. "Fancy meeting you here, Spanish Marie."

Marie curses. She knows she has no contraband onboard, but she still doesn't like getting snagged. She goes to radio, gives the scatter signal to her fleet, and drops her engines to idling. The patrol boat approaches portside. She scans the faces of her enemies, fixing her stare on the one with the big lips—Harvey "Two-Gun"—who killed Charlie.

"Funny time to take a pleasure cruise," Harvey says. "Alone. Middle of the night. No running lights. It's almost like you're doing something illegal, but that can't be. You swore in court that your late husband was the criminal in the family."

"I do my best thinking on the water in the moonlight. Can't a lady enjoy a night ride without getting hassled?"

Marie sees the young coastie nearest her sigh, enamored. She flutters her eyelashes at him.

"I don't see a lady anywhere," says Harvey.

Marie returns her stare to Harvey and narrows her eyes.

"You're quite puffed up," she says. "Is it because your boss is dead, leaving a vacancy for you to fill? Did you orchestrate that so you could be king? Nah, you're just a puppet."

And I pulled your strings, she thinks.

Even in the dark she can see, Harvey goes pale.

"Search her," he says.

His crew jolts to action, tying lines, jumping aboard, their boots stomping all over her shining decks, scuffing them. They throw open doors, hatches, cabinets, lockers, and find nothing because there is nothing. They shout about a locked floor. She pretends to search for the key, taking as long as possible to give her fleet time to land the liquor.

"I thought I had it," she says, voice high and confused. "No, it's not here, hmmm."

Harvey looks as if he is going to shoot her.

"Ah," she says. "Here it is."

Marie reaches in her brassiere and pulls out the key, passing it to the coastie who has a crush on her. He gives it to another, who unlocks the floor, shines down his flashlight, and groans.

"It's only cigars," the coastie says.

"I have the papers for those," she says, passing them to lover boy. "And my clearance papers. My vessel manifest. It's all here. You're wasting my time and yours."

As she produces each paper, Harvey grows redder. Finally, with nothing unlawful to cite her for besides failing to have her running lights illuminated, the men climb back aboard their vessel.

"Just think," she says. "While you were messing around with a *lady*, you might have missed dozens of hard smugglers. Uncle Sam won't like that."

"We know you're up to something," says Harvey.

"Do you? Well, you'd better tell your man at HQ he'll have to do better than this if he wants to trap the queen."

Harvey gives Marie a strange look that doesn't escape her notice, but she can't fully read it. She can't stop herself from taunting him, though. She'll take this as far as she can, as long as she can, to make sure her fleet lands, and this night is a success.

"Especially," she says, "because very often, very quickly, the board changes, and you all play right into my traps. So, gracias, Boy Scouts. You've been so helpful to *Spanish Marie* in so many ways. Keep up the good work."

Harvey reaches for his gun. Lover boy pulls Harvey's arm and tells him to go. Marie keeps her eyes and her grin on Harvey the whole time the coasties untie the boats. They ride her trail all the way to sunrise, all the way to Key West. At the marina, she sees her fleet has landed, unloaded, and bobs happily, emptily, lightly in the morning sun. A wave of fresh joy washes over her. When she hops off the *Isabel*, Marie winks at the coasties, salutes, and walks away.

THIRTY-ONE

WASHINGTON, DC

Elizebeth

Elizebeth feels as if she's unraveling, as if her whole world is coming apart, one thread at a time.

Losing Jack was a turning point. Codebreaking no longer feels like a game. It's personal. If Elizebeth had already worked too much, Jack's murder pushed her over the edge. She can't stop. She tells herself, *Just one more telegram, one more code*. If she stops, men will die. If she had worked harder and longer, maybe she would have known Alderman was coming and prevented the death of Jack. She knows she's wearing out Anna, her nannies, William, and herself, but she can't stop.

Her employer feels the same about her importance.

Elizebeth is called to the West Coast on a grueling train trip across the country to read thousands of intercepts in advance of opium-smuggling court cases. She feels guilty enough leaving her family so quickly after returning from Florida a shell of her former self and is further pained to learn, by telegram, the children have whooping cough. William assures her, they have good care, and her returning will do nothing, but it still keeps her up at night. Not only that, but with Elizebeth's blessing, William has allowed the gardener to take Crypto full-time. The Airedale is too confined in a city house. Crypto has been with them since Barbara was a baby, and in spite of frequent visits, Barbara is saddened, so this feels like a failure of another kind. When Elizebeth returns home, the children are on the mend, but William is again plagued with night terrors and anxiety. He returns to Dr. Graven's care and is diagnosed with manic-depressive disorder. As much as Elizebeth tries to convince herself the trip didn't contribute to William's psychotic relapse, her heart doesn't believe it. If she'd been home from both trips, maybe he'd be better.

As the months pass, Elizebeth feels a coldness come over her, freezing her except for a pilot light keeping her anger at rumrunners constantly simmering, making her more determined than ever to capture Marie Waite.

Alderman was likely doing the Bahamas run again because Marie has taken over the Cuba route, so—as far as Elizebeth is concerned—Marie shares blame for Jack's death. One of their undercover Prohibition agents in Havana, Mary O'Kane—a sharp, fearless Venezuelan woman married to an American businessman—has befriended Marie's wholesaler and sent a detailed report of Marie's empire. From coast to coast, Marie is not only smuggling, but destroying everything from her peers' assets, to their reputations with customers, to their actual boats. Marie and her henchmen also might be behind a rise in sabotage of coast guard vessels. From small mechanical issues of cut gas lines and ignition wires, to manipulated starter buttons causing explosions, Marie is clearly determined to push the envelope. In the name of intelligence gathering, they've allowed Marie and her radio station to operate for too long. It's time to clamp down and catch her. Because of a sharp decrease in intercepts to do with Marie's old code and an increase in another, Elizebeth suspects Marie has a new system, one that Elizebeth has not yet broken. It's driving her mad.

Elizebeth lights a cigarette and passes one to Anna. With smoky air, files strewn everywhere, piles of newspapers, and a large map on an easel showing Florida, the Bahamas, and Cuba and pinned with vessels, pirate radio stations, and warehouses, the library looks like a war room.

"The disorder in this library is killing me," Elizebeth says, rubbing her eyes. "Marie Waite is trying to kill me."

"Us," says Anna, giving Elizebeth a grin. "She's trying to kill us."

Elizebeth returns the smile. She can't believe the young woman wearing red lipstick and sharing a cigarette with Elizebeth is the same mousy girl she poached from HQ. In addition to her increased confidence, Anna has become an excellent partner and is even starting to pick up codebreaking. There isn't much spare time for teaching, but Elizebeth narrates whenever possible, and the girl is catching on at a promising rate.

Since starting with the coast guard, Elizebeth has solved twelve thousand coded messages and has cracked over thirty distinct systems of ever-increasing complexity. Anna transcribes and binds Elizebeth's top-secret work into one-inch volumes for filing at the coast guard, and there are already fifteen of them on the shelf. From coast to coast, Elizebeth has trained dozens in cryptanalysis, and she and William have completed the first official codebook of the coast guard. The work is marvelous and stimulating, but it doesn't take a genius to understand she cannot do it all alone. Elizebeth must have a staff of codebreakers and secretaries, and it should be sooner rather than later. As soon as she cracks Marie's code and they bring her down, Elizebeth will write an official memo laying out her plan for a future intelligence unit.

"I'm stuck," Elizebeth says. "Let's have William pick up crab cakes for us, and then we'll jump back in after dinner."

Anna looks down at the desk.

"I'm sorry," she stammers. "Tonight, I can't."

"No apologies. I'm sorry I presumed. What, do you have a handsome date?"

The girl's face turns red, and Elizebeth coughs on her cigarette smoke. She was joking. She had no idea Anna was dating, but it makes sense, now that Elizebeth thinks about it. This metamorphosis of confidence couldn't only be because of the work.

"I do," Anna says, failing to suppress a smile. "A lieutenant commander from HQ. The one I exchange your decodes with each week for new intercepts. It's our fifth date."

"This sounds serious," says Elizebeth. "How wonderful!"

"It is. He is. I'm sorry to leave you. But he bought us tickets for a film at the National Theater. Otherwise, I'd call him to reschedule."

"No, no. There's no reason for you to work late. What film is it?"

"Cecil B. DeMille's *King of Kings*."

Elizebeth sighs. She can't remember the last time she and William went to the theater or had any kind of date. They've both been working like mad. He's been so fragile lately. She knows she's been distant. Whatever resources she has in her, she gives to the children, but that's not the order of priority in which she should be doling out her attention. She resolves they will go on a date as soon as possible. Elizebeth can't allow her marriage and family to suffer for her work. She will draw boundaries for herself and keep them. She'll learn to tell Root no. These are her New Year's resolutions.

Right after her January trip to Florida for Alderman's trial, that is.

James Horace Alderman is being charged with two counts of murder in the first degree on the high seas, and if convicted, according to U.S. Criminal Code, Section 275, he "shall suffer death." Leila has called Elizebeth as a witness for the prosecution, and Anna has been working around the clock to help assemble and clear all documents associated with Alderman's long and evil legacy. Elizebeth has also written and submitted a formal statement detailing what she saw and heard on the water that day.

Elizebeth has never felt so conflicted about appearing at a trial. This case has been in the papers nationwide, and the stakes are high. Elizebeth doesn't know how she feels about capital punishment, but that's not for her to legislate. She must report the facts and let the law do the rest. Her biggest concern, if she's truthful with herself, is that this trial will put the spotlight on her like never before. It feels as if she's blowing her cover.

"Thank you, Anna," Elizebeth says. "You've reminded me that life is not work. And the world will keep spinning whether or not I'm at my desk."

Anna smiles and stubs out her cigarette. She checks the wall clock.

"We still have seventeen minutes until I have to leave. Let's see what we can accomplish."

THIRTY-TWO

MIAMI

Marie

The courtroom for Jimmy Alderman's murder trial is so packed it's easy for Marie—wearing a black kerchief and sunglasses, a modest gray coat, and low, sensible black heels—to blend in, becoming one of the nameless spectators in the crowd. The room is like a twisted kind of wedding—guests divided by association and a general air of expectation. For all Jimmy's thuggery, he has quite a cheering section, revealing just how many clients he had. For future business purposes, Marie makes a note of the faces she recognizes and takes mental pictures for further investigation of the ones she doesn't. Based on the overflowing seats on the prosecution's side, however, it's obvious Alderman has more enemies than friends.

Marie is absorbed by the theatrics, imagining how she would play it, and is fascinated by the actors.

All the world's a stage, she thinks.

On the defense's side, one soulless man represents another. Alderman, a man who has likely never before put on a suit, wears an ill-fitting dove-gray number that showcases his sunburnt face.

The lawyer likely wanted a light color to make Alderman look innocent, but with the contrast of his red face with the light fabric, it's impossible not think of him pirating on the high seas.

Alderman's defense is his nonsensical assertion that he fired in self-defense, without knowing he was shooting at coastguards-men. Marie can't believe Judge Henry D. Clayton would allow such a bold-faced lie, especially with the large picture of *CG-249* blown up so everyone can see how clearly it is a coast guard vessel. It's almost as if the judge is too exhausted to poke the bruise. Marie is sure he is. Liquor cases have flooded the courts so thoroughly that judges can hardly keep up. Not to mention, the man looks hungover. Everyone knows the judge likes to spend his weekends drinking in Havana. She's seen it with her own eyes.

On the side of the prosecution, the pitiful mother of one of the dead and the plump wife of Commander Jack Wilson are in attendance. The attorney was smart to invite them. Mrs. Wilson's wide, perpetually leaking eyes and innocent face will move the jury. Alderman's wife and children are not in attendance, which Marie thinks might be a miss for the defense. Although, if Alderman's wife feels about her husband the way Marie felt about Charlie at the end, it's probably better to keep the wife away, to hide her relief and even glee at the thought of her husband's incarceration and possible execution.

The woman of Marie's fixation, however, is the assistant DA, Leila Russell. If she weren't on the wrong side of the law, Marie would spend more time admiring a dame working so deftly in a man's world. Leila is sharp and aggressive while managing to remain charming. Her height and beauty are assets, as is the direct way she speaks. She knows how to use cadence and pause in her oratories to keep the jury leaning forward in their chairs. Marie has no doubt Leila has spent time on the stage.

Leila is visibly agitated today, however. Her final witness— the celebrated codebreaker from HQ, who was apparently riding along on the coast guard vessel that murderous day—is late. Marie is dying to finally see the man who has caused her so much trouble and relief. They've been working together, after all, and she likes to know her coworkers, especially when they're also her mortal enemies. His train from Washington, DC, has apparently experienced multiple delays because of icy tracks up north and is hours overdue. He should be in quite an agitated state when he arrives, which will not serve the prosecution well.

Not wanting to hold up anyone any longer, Judge Clayton cracks his gavel, adjourning for the day. Marie groans with frustration, and the people stand, all of them disappointed by the unwanted intermission. Suddenly, the back doors burst open, and a guard escorts someone to the front of the court. Marie is too short to see what's going on, but when she hears the judge's gavel and call to reconvene, she knows the prosecution's witness has arrived.

Marie's heart races with anticipation. As audience members take their seats, Marie leans forward and removes her sunglasses, staring at the front of the room. She experiences a moment of confusion watching the diminutive woman in pearls, her chestnut hair in a tidy bun, wearing an elegant navy-blue wool dress take a seat. The woman's cheeks are flushed becomingly, and though shadows below her eyes betray her fatigue, the twinkle in them, her posture, and the catlike grin she gives Leila Russell show she's in good form.

I know her, Marie thinks. *How?*

"Please, state your name and position for the court," says Russell.

"Special Agent Elizebeth Smith Friedman. Cryptanalyst, United States Coast Guard Intelligence Department."

With every word the woman utters in her deep, commanding voice, Marie feels her temperature rise.

The crowd bursts into chatter so loud the judge has to bang his gavel to call order. The deepening of the Cheshire cat grin on Friedman's face reveals she's enjoying the controversy.

As Leila Russell questions her star witness about Alderman's notorious history and the proof of that history through cryptanalysis, a word Friedman has to define for the audience, Marie's mind races. She thinks back to the strange look Harvey "Two-Gun" gave her when she said, "your *man* at HQ." She thinks of Cleo Lythgoe's warning about the "new man in the government" who knew where rummies were before they got there. Marie thinks of Peltz's operations being pushed farther out. Red Shannon's death. Charlie's death. The codebreaker's extreme attention to detail. Intuition. The quick response to tips. The ability to keep fifty balls juggling at once, managing the routes of just as many smugglers. Each notch of realization cools Marie's skin, and by the time Elizebeth Friedman gives her version of events on the day Alderman shot the coastie, Marie has to stifle a laugh.

"Of course, the codebreaker is a woman," Marie says.

Eyes turn toward her. She must have spoken aloud without realizing. The courtroom is so quiet, her voice must have traveled.

Elizebeth's eyes find Marie's. As soon as their gazes lock, Marie's skin again heats. It doesn't escape her notice that Elizebeth's face also turns red, before all the color drains out of the woman.

Instantly, Marie remembers exactly where she saw Elizebeth. It was in Key West at the Victoria Restaurant. This time, however, it's Elizebeth who looks away first.

THIRTY-THREE

MIAMI

Elizebeth

In all Elizebeth's anxiety about the trial, she never anticipated the nightmarish scenario that would actually play out.

It was bad enough to be away from the family again and still unable to break Marie's new code, even with all the weather delays on the interminable train ride. To be late for court, and then, once there, being plunged from dizzying heights of confidence and self-satisfaction to deep grief and guilt—warranted or not—recounting the terrible story of Jack's death while his sweet widow watched, not to mention the mother of the other young coastguardsman who ended up dying. Being a witness at this trial has been excruciating, and it's made exponentially worse by seeing—and being seen—by her archenemy.

When Elizebeth notes Marie's recognition, Elizebeth goes hot, then cold. She feels naked and exposed. She loses her place in the narrative. She falters, stammers, and has to look away. It's as if she's lost all her power. Leila rescues her.

"You were saying," Leila says. "Jack ordered you to the pilothouse so you'd be safe."

"Yes," says Elizebeth, mention of Jack setting her back on course. "His bravery was profound. He knew the kind of man they were dealing with. But it happened so fast. No one realized Alderman had grabbed his gun."

Elizebeth thinks with nausea about the glance Alderman made down at his helm, the stutter of motion. She should have realized what he was doing. She should have warned Jack and his men. She takes a deep breath and trains her gaze on Alderman. Seeing the blank expression in his soulless eyes allows her to again find the steel for her spine.

"Alderman waited until the liquor was unloaded before his cowardly ambush," she says.

"Objection," says his attorney. "He fired in self-defense."

"Sustained. Continue."

"If Alderman had cooperated," says Elizebeth, "he probably could have gotten away with a simple fine. But his murderous instinct has ruined two families' lives, three if you count his. Though—after what I've seen with human smugglers—I can't imagine having a man like that in a household is good for women and children."

"Objection," says his attorney, standing.

"Sustained."

"Thank you, Your Honor," says the defense attorney. "I want to make a motion to strike everything this witness has said. Her commentary is disputed and unwanted. Cryptanalysis sounds like voodoo. Why should we trust what her so-called decoding has turned up? None of it should be admissible."

"Objection," says Leila. "He's only insinuating magic because he doesn't believe a woman could be so intelligent. Just because one doesn't understand the science does not mean it should be thrown out. Do you understand the intricacies of aerodynamics? I don't, but I know how to fly a plane."

"'If this is magic,'" says Elizebeth, "'let it be an art, lawful as eating.' Shakespeare."

The courtroom again comes to life, stimulated and intrigued by not only a female cryptanalyst and a female lawyer, but also a female pilot.

And a female rummy, thinks Elizebeth.

Her gaze searches for Marie's. Elizebeth is both alarmed and relieved to see her adversary has disappeared. It helps Elizebeth concentrate on the rest of her testimony and on the closing arguments, but when they adjourn for the day so the jury can deliberate, she can't curb her paranoia. She feels like she sees Marie watching her from every corner, even from the restaurant where she and Leila dine. They eat quickly and Leila drives Elizebeth back to the law office, locking the door behind them.

Elizebeth lights two cigarettes and passes one to Leila. The women stand at opposite corners of a large picture window, looking down over Miami. Neither removes her coat. The daytime temperature only reached sixty-three degrees and the newspaper said the nighttime low would be in the thirties, with wind gusts up to forty miles an hour. Looking down from Leila's third-floor office over Miami, sirens flash in every direction. Elizebeth knows Al Capone has officially moved to town and is looking for a permanent residence on Little Palm Island. This, in spite of the fact that lawmen and politicians are doing everything they can to keep him out. Everything about this trip and this place feels wrong.

"Did I make a wrong turn and end up in Chicago?" asks Elizebeth.

"Feels like it, some days. Especially with this miserable weather. I haven't been able to fly in weeks, and I'm itching to take to the air."

"Speaking of, did you ever find out the fate of the pilot the coasties shot over the Atlantic, the man flying for Capone?"

In a previous bundle from Leila, there was a Base Six coast guard report about a plane believed to be owned by Capone getting shot at after takeoff in Miami, after a suspected liquor delivery. It dipped toward the coast guard patrol boat as if to attack, but after shots were fired, the pilot allegedly flinched. The plane then banked, lifted, and flew east.

Leila laughs and takes a long drag.

"The man? How about the boy?" she says.

"The boy?"

"Robert Hanley. Seventeen years old. Student at St. Patrick's High School during the week, smuggling pilot for one of the most notorious gangsters in the world on the weekends."

"A Catholic school student," says Elizebeth. "Do you think he went to confession for it?"

"If not, his soul still has time. Since the bullet only hit his leg, he's expected to make a full recovery. Hanley says he won't press charges against the coasties. It was a *misunderstanding*. He says he wasn't attacking the patrol vessel, only playing with it. And he continued on, flying the plane to the Bahamas empty of liquor, so there's nothing to charge him with. He's become quite the local celebrity, and surely the most popular boy in school."

Elizebeth shakes her head.

"It's starting to feel like pandemonium, isn't it?" asks Leila. "The public cheers them on. Even children are getting involved. That's what scares me. In a biblical sense, that is."

"What do you mean?"

"In the Bible, when a civilization goes so off the rails the children in it have no hope of being brought up with decency, God takes his vengeance. God's vengeance is His justice."

"I wasn't really religious until the day Jack got shot," says Elizebeth. "And I haven't been since. But this does all feel apocalyptic."

The women stub out their cigarettes, pull the curtains, and turn on the lights. They sit at Leila's table and go over trial notes.

"The defense was foolish to put that red-faced pirate on the stand," says Elizebeth.

"Alderman insisted."

"He surely signed his death warrant. The man couldn't conjure up a shred of emotion."

"I don't imagine the jury will need much time."

"No," says Elizebeth.

Silence falls heavily. Elizebeth mulls the fact that a man will likely be sentenced to death tomorrow. While Alderman engaged in evil practices, he's still a man with a family. If sentenced, he will the first rumrunner in history executed for killing government officials.

"Do you want to talk about today?" Leila asks, not looking up from her papers. "When you were on the stand. What happened?"

"Marie Waite was there."

Leila looks up at Elizebeth. "What?"

"Yes. Wearing a kerchief. Bland clothes. Just a shadow, a mere slip of a woman. But it was her. We made eye contact."

"And you're only just telling me this?" asks Leila.

"I've had a lot to process today. I feel like I'm in a fog."

"I'm so disappointed I didn't get to see her, in the flesh."

"You sound like you're as obsessed as I am."

"Are you obsessed, too? I would think all rummies are the same to you."

"Don't be silly. Brilliant women are always intriguing, especially those who inhabit men's worlds."

"I could drink to that," Leila says, with a wink. "But we better wait for repeal. Too risky."

Elizebeth smiles and stifles a yawn.

"Poor thing," says Leila. "I should have driven you straight to your hotel."

"This was a good detour," Elizebeth says. "It gives me a chance to ask if you have any contacts among the T-Men in Miami."

"I do."

"Good. I think I'll require one tomorrow, and for the rest of my trip."

"I'll get you in touch right now," Leila says, walking to the phone. "What, do you want to tip him off about Marie?"

"Yes. And if possible, I'd like them to dig, ask around about Marie's family. Anything you can tell me about her parents, her siblings, her background. Even if it looks inconsequential, it could be key to breaking her new code. But, in truth, it's more about me."

Leila looks at Elizebeth with a question in her eyes.

"Now that she's seen me," says Elizebeth, "I want a bodyguard."

THIRTY-FOUR

MIAMI

Marie

Marie stands at the door of her closet, surveying the space with pleasure. Since selling everything of Charlie's, in addition to having ample space for her clothing and accessories, she has room again to hang all the costumes she's collected over the years. On the highest shelves, she has set her old Shakespeare scripts and playbills, facing out. Marie's eyes land on the skull, which keeps its place of honor. Her mind goes to the words she heard the codebreaker speaking as Marie slipped out of the courtroom. The woman quoted Shakespeare, *A Winter's Tale*.

If this is magic, let it be an art, lawful as eating.

The codebreaker knows her Shakespeare. She likes drama. Theater. This, Marie will give her.

With her archenemy in attendance at Alderman's trial, Marie knows she can't go back to court without a disguise.

Last night, Marie mulled hiring someone to bump off the codebreaker, but quickly dismissed the idea. Marie is enjoying the game of cat and mouse and wants to be triumphant because of her wits, not her fists.

Marie turns her attention back to the costumes. If only Benny were still alive. She could trust him to go to the trial for her and report back immediately. She considered sending Florence, but since the deaths of both Waite brothers and since Marie no longer attends mass—only sends the children—Florence looks at Marie with the side-eye.

Marie has taken pains to keep her dark business dealings secret, but the nanny is suspicious, especially since Marie recently sold the dance academy—a fact that made her sick, imagining her mother's triumphant sneer—but the cash keeps flowing in. Florence also scowled when Marie had a real estate agent out to the Miami house to prepare it for listing. Marie can't wait to be rid of this place. It's haunted by Charlie. Marie feels like he watches her from every corner, and the nightmares continue. Once she sells the house, her plan is to rent small places here and in Key West and to spend most of her time at her Cuba estate, where she'll eventually retire. Florence can decide for herself if she wants to continue in Marie's employ. One thing is sure, Marie will not take the girl's judgment much longer. Marie owes her nothing. Everyone is replaceable.

The house is blissfully quiet because Florence left to take the kids to "school" at their tutor's home and to run errands that will keep her busy for the day. Marie moves into the closet, touching the fabrics, the sequins, and the fringe, until she spots the burgundy velour. The dress was one she hated wearing at the time, when she played Thaisa in Shakespeare's *Pericles, Prince of Tyre*. The costumer had gone with what a young, sexy Marie found frumpy, overly modest, and boring. Today, it will be perfect for both the unseasonal cold and Marie's desire to disappear in the crowd. She finds the wig that also went with the costume—equally modest, boring, golden blonde—and adds a pair of fake spectacles to complete the look.

Marie has only the mirror in her bathroom now, the other having been shattered, so she can't get the full picture. When she walks in to appraise her disguise, she shudders. It could be her mother looking back at her. With no time left to change, Marie puts on her dullest, lowest heels and drives her truck to court.

—————

Marie should have taken the bus.

Parking is a nightmare, and by the time she finds a space, she has to run. On the way, she stirs up a flock of pigeons, bringing on a breath-stealing panic. Hurrying, she joins the crush of the crowd outside court. Once she gets past the press and squeezes inside, it's standing room only. The only good news is that she really is anonymous. There's no way she'll be recognized.

Elizabeth Friedman sits in the first row, her arm wrapped around Mrs. Jack Wilson, the codebreaker whispering reassurances to the widow. The intimacy of the women fascinates Marie. She has never had a good female friend, or any kind of real friend, for that matter. Her mother so soured Marie on women, so made her on guard against other females, Marie never considered how a sisterhood might have made her life different. Would women make better business partners? Should Marie hire women for her business instead of men? Women have always been competition for her, but she'll reexamine this jewel and all its facets another time.

The jury and Alderman soon arrive, the whispers growing. Alderman wears the same ill-fitting suit, but his skin has gone paler. Marie wonders if the lawyer powdered him to take the edge off the sunburn. His family is still not in attendance. He still wears a blank expression. His lawyer should have coached him on acting contrite, but it's too late for that now. The jurors also wear blank expressions. Did they find him guilty of murder in the first degree? How could there be any other outcome?

The crowd is so unruly Judge Clayton has to bang his gavel almost immediately.

"This is not a circus, and if the peanut gallery doesn't behave, I'll send every one of you out."

The room quiets until all that can be heard are the whispers of the palm trees outside in the cold January gusts. Marie closes her eyes and yearns for Cuba. For her home there. For the foliage and the color. When she opens them, she looks back at Elizebeth Friedman. The woman steals glances over her shoulder.

She's trying to find me, thinks Marie. *Never.*

Marie is all her children have. She will never let this puppet of Uncle Sam take their mother away from them.

Marie's hatred of the codebreaker rises. The woman is tucked safely in her government office, far away from danger, meddling in affairs that are none of her business. Much of her success is because of Marie's help. The woman will never be able to break Marie's new code, but if by some miracle Friedman does, Marie will be untouchable, drinking sangria at Santa Maria del Mar, while sitting on a fortune.

"Has the jury reached a verdict?" asks Judge Clayton.

"We have."

The bailiff takes the envelope to the judge. He opens it and reads, the lines in his forehead deepening, the darkness in his eyes growing. He nods, puts the paper to the side, and takes a deep breath.

"James Horace Alderman, rise," says Judge Clayton.

Alderman stands. Only the sweat soaking through to his jacket betrays his unease. His face remains blank.

Rumrunning makes poker players of us, Marie thinks.

And kills something in the soul.

That thought didn't come from her, but to her.

"You have had a fair trial, and a jury of your peers has made a ruling. James Horace Alderman, of two counts of murder on the high seas, you have been found…"

Judge Clayton pauses. The crowd leans forward. No one breathes. The waiting makes Marie feels as if she'll explode. She thinks that for a judge who just reprimanded the crowd for being a peanut gallery, he sure knows how to increase the tension and deliver a line.

"Guilty."

The crowd explodes. The judge again bangs the gavel. Alderman remains expressionless.

"As a punishment, you will be hanged by the neck until you are dead."

At this, the crowd sobers, the gravity of the trial descending upon them. Only the soft crying of Commander Wilson's widow can be heard. The codebreaker pulls the woman tighter in to her side.

Marie tries to imagine how she would react if she were Alderman. She thinks of her life, of her children. She resolves even more deeply that she will never let the feds do this to her. She will beat Elizebeth Friedman and all of them at this game.

She looks at her watch, the one that Cleo sent her.

Time to go.

Marie snakes through the crowd and, once outside, takes a big breath. She walks swiftly to her truck, careful to avoid birds, and drives home as quickly as possible.

THIRTY-FIVE

WASHINGTON, DC

Elizebeth

The train ride back to her family allows Elizebeth to reflect, to eat, and to sleep. She doesn't work a single code.

When she steps down on the platform and sees William and the children, she rushes to meet them. William places John on the ground next to Barbara and swoops Elizebeth into an embrace. In spite of being in public, they kiss long and passionately. William pulls back and takes Elizebeth's face in his hands.

"I saw the newspapers," he says. "Are you all right?"

Elizebeth nods.

"Are you?" she asks. "Did you sleep while I was gone?"

"Like a baby," he says. "Dr. G gave me some meditations to try. They're working."

Elizebeth gives him another kiss.

"Mama!" says Barbara. "Daddy helped me write you a code!"

The four-and-half-year-old passes a paper with large scrawled letters facing this way and that into Elizebeth's hands.

I	Y	O	A
L	E	U	M
O	V	M	A

Elizebeth draws in her breath.

"Your first rail fence cipher!" she says. "Barbara, I'm so proud of you!"

"It says, 'I love you, Mama,'" says Barbara, pointing at the paper with her pudgy fingers.

Elizebeth and William laugh, and Elizebeth crouches down to give Barbara a hug and kiss.

"And I love you," says Elizebeth. "You're so grown up!"

"And Cassie, Carlotta, and I taught John to do Ring around the Rosy!" says Barbara.

"You did?" says Elizebeth. "Mr. Impossible? I won't believe it until I see it."

Elizebeth picks up John and tries to kiss his cheek, but he scowls and squirms out of her arms. Then he runs away, yelling, "Twains!"

William chases after John, followed by Barbara, and when he catches the boy, he picks him up and tickles him. The three of them laugh, while William kisses John's plump cheek. John doesn't pull away from his father.

Elizebeth's heart feels a pang of jealousy, followed by a burst of love at seeing her happy family. It's both freeing and agonizing not to be needed.

That is the nature of motherhood, she thinks.

———————

Marie is also a mother, thinks Elizebeth.

Alderman, a father. Peltz.

What is the legacy they'll leave? Will the children follow their parents' lawbreaking lead or head in the opposite direction? Will they grow up resenting the feds for their interference, or does it bring them relief?

Elizebeth's mind spins for days. She's grateful for the weekend, the time to reengage with her family, and it's mostly satisfying. William and Barbara are their usual delightful selves. John Ramsay boomerangs from tantrums to bear hugs. As calm as Elizebeth and William are, and also Barbara, John's mercurial temperament continues to perplex and frustrate Elizebeth. By Monday, she's thrilled to have Cassie and Carlotta back. She's relieved to climb the stairs with Anna to the library.

The restored order steadies Elizebeth. Her organized files. Her pencils and erasers. Her tidy stack of graph paper. The water pitcher and glasses. Everything is in its place. She takes a deep breath, pulls the chain on the lamp, and she and Anna take their seats, sharpening pencils and laying out papers like synchronized swimmers.

After the women catch up on the trial, they attack Marie's

new code with renewed intensity. As days become weeks, however, Elizebeth's frustration grows. Jack's death and Marie's recognition have increased the stakes, and this has made the work harder. Elizebeth finds it more difficult to be separate and impartial. Her mind is shackled. She works other intercepts for breaks, but Marie looms always, haunting, taunting.

In late February, two phone calls change everything. The first is from Root.

"Our woman in Cuba says Marie spends a lot of time there," says Root, "and might even have a house."

"As in a permanent residence."

"Not yet confirmed but suspected. And she's connected with a local florist. She's supplying flowers, of all things."

"Interesting," says Elizebeth.

She feels a flash of hope for Marie. Maybe after seeing Alderman's trial and sentence to death, Marie realized she's all her children have, and she'd better get out of the rum business and into the flower business. Elizebeth knows she's giving a notorious criminal a lot of credit, but many saints were first sinners.

"Mary says the florist doesn't appear to be laundering money," Root continues, "but Mary will keep a close eye on it."

"Excellent."

"Marie's brother Rogelio is now involved in the car business."

"Cigars weren't profitable enough?"

"Maybe not. He works for a local dealer. Mostly selling to American businessmen, including mobsters."

"What could possibly go wrong?"

"Yes. Marie's family sure can't keep away from criminals. I guess it's because they are criminals."

"Or opportunists."

He laughs.

The second call is from Leila.

"The T-Men have done good work tracking Marie's scent," says Leila. "But I don't know if what we have gets you anywhere."

"Anything, no matter how seemingly inconsequential—what she orders on a menu—would be helpful."

"I don't have that, but I can tell you the dance academy is sold and the Miami house is on the market. She's rented a bungalow in Key West, and her fleet has stayed at port in the Key West Marina without movement for weeks."

"She must be lying low. I hoped the trial would shake her."

"You might have shaken her," Leila says. "You're very intimidating."

Elizebeth laughs.

"Seriously," says Leila. "Realizing it's a woman at HQ surely made Marie sit up in her chair."

"Maybe so, but as much as I want her to, I can't believe Marie Waite will go quietly into the night."

"No, me neither," says Leila. "The only other information I have is about her parents. The T-Men were curious about Angel, Marie's blond brother, who works the radio station. They've been trailing him and were able to observe Marie's parents, apparently. After some digging, they found the father is not

Mexican, as some rumors said, but hails from Spain, with French origins. The blonde mother is not Swedish. She's from Belgium. They've both been here for years, though."

Belgium.

A light bulb goes off in Elizebeth's head. Her mind starts racing through the corridors of her mind to the papers, the intercepts, and the new "unbreakable" code.

"Are you there?" asks Leila.

"Yes. Very helpful. Must go."

Elizebeth slams down the receiver and looks at Anna with wide eyes.

"Belgium," Elizebeth says.

"Pardon?"

"The country of her mother's birth. The key. Marie. She's not using Spanish. She switched to Dutch."

THIRTY-SIX

BAHAMAS

Marie

M arie didn't anticipate how good it would feel to return to where she started.

Nassau has clearly profited from America's idiocy. The harbor has been dredged, the docks are new, a growing skyline of hotels gives the island a new profile, and hundreds of fancy yachts bob happily everywhere. A bad element has increased, however, and it's the same element flooding Miami, Fort Lauderdale, and even Havana. Marie knows someone like Elizebeth Friedman or Leila Russell would consider Marie to be part of this element. Marie disagrees. She considers herself an independent operator, a lone actor, and one doing what she must to survive. She doesn't allow herself to consider how many others started the same way or how power and money make one a slave. She doesn't think of the murder and mayhem.

The ends justify the means.

In spite of knowing Cleo Lythgoe now lives in Detroit, Marie hoped her predecessor would be in Nassau, visiting, but

Cleo is nowhere to be found. The only trace of her is a drink named in her honor on the menu at the Lucerne. "The Bahama Queen" is composed of the Scotch whisky Cleo used to import, elderflower liqueur, and lemon juice. It's a woman, embodied in a cocktail. Marie feels a flash of envy. She wants a cocktail named after her, one that someone else creates, something with fire. She wants to be the only queen. At least Marie's empire spans multiple countries. She'd rather be known as the Queen of the Rumrunners than simply the Bahama Queen. Marie was hoping to tell Cleo about her final performance, the last act, the last twelve miles of her career. She thinks Cleo would approve, not that Marie needs the approval of another woman, or anyone for that matter. She knows her plan is flawless.

Marie used her old code to set up one boat—the *Isabel*—coming into Florida from Havana. The boat will be empty of booze. Using her new code, she set up her boats on the old Bahamas route, the one with bloodstained waters from Red Shannon, Jimmy Alderman, and Charlie. It's the route the codebreaker would never suspect Marie of taking. Marie will make a fool of the codebreaker.

The fleet of four boats, names camouflaged, will set out from four islands in the Bahamas. Her leader boat will depart Nassau and will be empty. The other three boats will trail hers, dropping their cargo at three separates sites along the Atlantic coast of Florida. Her bribed radioman at the windmill in Miami Beach—which miraculously survived the hurricane—will either give her the *XTAL*, for *Crystal*, if the coast is crystal clear, or the warning

Skidoo if she should keep out. If all is clear, she will dock at the marina in Coconut Grove, on the northern shore of Biscayne Bay, where her truck and a lackey will be waiting to unload the *Kid Boots*—tarp covering its name—when it comes in. The other boats will land at other points. Her clients will have their liquor by the time the sun rises, and she will have a million in cash. She will pay off her men by gifting each captain a boat of his own and a bonus. She'll keep only the *Isabel*, and once her affairs in Florida are settled, she'll take it to Cuba to start her new life with the children. She'll rename the boat *La Caridad*, and start her process of purification and reconciliation.

Freedom and independence are so close Marie can almost grasp them.

The air at the Lucerne crackles—men and women squawking over each other, drinks flowing, fights flaring and being doused just as quickly. Every patron at the bar is armed. If the fights aren't squelched, a bloodbath will ensue. The piano pounds so loudly it echoes in Marie's skull. Last night's hangover has reached its fingers into this night. Until reconciliation, she has to keep the edge off however she can. Marie downs her whisky and heads to the roof to clear her head.

The sky does not give her what she wants. The constellations are covered in blankets of clouds. The weather has been worsening all day and the seas are rough. Not one day of her life has been easy, so she wasn't expecting this to be, but she hoped.

When we are born, we cry that we are come to this great stage of fools.

Shakespeare on the mind is a comfort.

Marie closes her eyes and inhales the vanilla scent of the elderflower. She thinks she'll plant the climbing vine for Josephine's Cuba garden. She'll also plant lemon trees, lime trees, and grapefruit for Joey to pluck and eat in the warm sunshine, fragrant fruits of Eden.

Eden, she thinks. *That's what I'll name the estate.*

A foot on the stair snaps her out of her musings. She pulls a revolver out of her garter and points it at the door, where a man and woman soon appear, stumbling, drunk, and laughing. They're clearly oblivious to Marie's small shadowed form. She recoils into the shadows, staring out from behind a trellis thick with vines. When the couple reaches the balcony, the man picks a clump of flowers and slides them in the woman's hair. She reaches her arms around his neck and runs her fingers up the back of his close cut. She nibbles his neck down to his top button. He lifts her face to his and kisses her, long and tender.

Marie feels the involuntary clench of her jaw, the twist in her belly. Charlie never, ever kissed her like that. Nor did Joe. Nor has any man. Her stomach roils with jealousy. It burns like indigestion.

"Dear Robert," the woman says. "This is heaven."

"I know it."

Robert, Marie thinks. *Oh no, it's Peltz.*

"Our little Betty is growing up in heaven," the woman says.

"With only the finest things," he says. "We'll teach her to sail and fish and swim like a dolphin."

"We'll hire her the finest tutors."

"Have the most beautiful clothes made for her."

"Church her," says the woman with a grin.

"Fine," he says, with a laugh.

"Just not with that old priest. He's in the business."

"So are we."

"We're not clergy."

Peltz again laughs.

His wife settles into his side, and they look off into the distance.

"Did you see her down there?" the wife asks.

"Who?"

"Spanish Marie," she says.

Marie likes how the woman's voice hushed. It's like she's talking about a legend.

"Oh, her," Peltz says. "She looks a little worse for wear."

Marie scowls.

"I guess selling your soul to the devil will do that to you," says the wife.

Marie's temperature rises. She already felt like she wanted to crawl out of her skin. To hear this kind of appraisal is excruciating.

"Now, now. We don't know she had Charlie killed."

"Everyone knows it. Theo Waite thinks she might have had the other one, Benny, bumped off, too."

Liars! Marie screams inside her head. It's all she can do not to shoot them both.

"Nah, he was her right hand," says Peltz.

"They say she takes a new lover every week, and when she's done with them, gives 'em concrete shoes."

Peltz laughs. "They also say she's six feet tall, with blue eyes."

Marie feels like hands are choking her neck. She must escape.

"Now, Red Shannon," he says, "Alderman. I can believe she set them up."

"You better watch your back," says the wife. "I don't want you doing business with her anymore."

"Don't worry, I won't. She's too small-time to be worth my trouble anymore."

"To be clear, I don't like those gangsters you deal with either."

"Do you want to continue living in heaven?"

She sighs. "I suppose. But you promise you'll retire when we hit the target number, right?"

"I've hit that, love. Twice over. I'm afraid I'm addicted. Can you help me?"

He leans down and kisses her neck. She laughs, pulls him toward a café table, sits him down on a chair, and climbs on his lap, straddling him.

I cannot stay here and endure this, thinks Marie.

While their passion consumes them, Marie slips along the roofline toward the door. When she reaches the top stair, it takes all she has in her not to shoot them, a single bullet ending them both.

THIRTY-SEVEN

FORT LAUDERDALE

Elizebeth

I n the radio room of Base Six, all of them—including Elizebeth, Anna, Root, and Leila—are there. There's a picture of Commander Jack hanging on the wall. Elizebeth can almost feel his large, warm presence. It gives her heart an ache.

We'll get Marie, for you, Elizebeth thinks, looking at Jack's face. *We'll get them all.*

Finding out Dutch was the language used in the code set all the dominoes in motion.

While Elizebeth can speak several languages, including Spanish and German, she understands the structure and composition of many more, and has corresponding dictionaries for dozens. In deciphering, Elizebeth and William have always begun with letter frequency tables. Once the letters are counted and tallied, one can start to solve for the language. The letter *E* is the most frequent in both the Romance and the Germanic languages, so letter pairings and other hallmarks become helpful. *TH*, for example, is the most common pairing in English. Dutch is very close to English but uses more *T*s than *N*s. Dutch pairs vowels more than English does. Knowing the language allows for guessing, and one of those guesses came from her Riverbank days, where Elizebeth and William's first home was a Dutch windmill. William used to playfully call it their *windmolen*. He'd speak of the *wiel*—the wheel—and the *zeil*—the sail—and these words popped up in the intercepts.

Marie had created a formidable plan, one that involved old code, new code, two routes, a fleet of boats, and an army of trucks. Once Elizebeth and Anna mapped it all out at HQ, Root shook his head.

"I wonder if she's considered joining the military," he said. "She'd make a formidable admiral. Or general."

They laughed and immediately started planning their trip to Florida, to be there when the woman was apprehended. Root didn't initially include Anna in the trip, but Elizebeth insisted. The young woman's hard work should be rewarded. Also, Elizebeth had no desire to travel alone with her boss, a man who was not her husband. Appearances are important, and she wouldn't give fodder to the gossips in DC. She was already their target for being a woman in a man's world, and it was clear Agnes Meyer Driscoll would hate Elizebeth and William forever. The woman never tired of criticizing them for their success. Agnes and those like her would, no doubt, love to suggest that Elizebeth somehow slept her way to the top.

For this round of travel, because William has his own top-secret work trip, Aunt Edna came down for a visit and to help the nannies. This assuaged Elizebeth's guilt about leaving the children while their father was gone. They love Aunt Edna as much as their parents—sometimes, more so, it seems—and Edna has an itinerary of zoo, park, and museum visits that will keep them all happy and busy.

When Elizebeth and her team arrived at Base Six, the first thing out of Harvey's mouth was that Jimmy Alderman would be hung there, execution date to be determined.

"It will be the first hanging at a coast guard base in history," Harvey said with glee.

Elizebeth found his enthusiasm distasteful.

After that, Harvey and his crew left. They'll be aboard patrol boat *CG-249*, trailing Marie in her vessel coming in from Nassau. Hidden picket boats are positioned to follow the other vessels. They will let Marie make land, however, before she's apprehended, to give her time to start unloading the liquor. The T-men, along with Sheriff Lehman, will ensure this happens so Marie gets the full book of the law thrown at her.

This time, Elizebeth is glad not to be riding along. The joy of that has been forever stolen. She now sets sharp boundaries with the coasties and with her boss. There will be no more shared family dinners. She can't have that kind of heartbreak again. This has to be her work. Taking it personally could erode her sanity the way it has tested William's. As for Harvey, she has no love for him—and has always been wary of him, in fact. She didn't want one so quick on the draw at the helm, but she doesn't have rank, so that decision was not hers. It makes Elizebeth shudder to think of two such impulsive people—Harvey and Marie—on two sides of the law, going head-to-head. Elizebeth wants no blood shed, only to catch her enemy to get the woman on a path to a better life. And that woman is as dangerous and slippery as an eel. Elizebeth won't be able to rest until Marie is apprehended. Elizebeth feels a pang that a mother will be separated from her children for a time, but this mother has made her own bed, and now she will lie in it.

Leila's apocalyptic words come back to Elizebeth's mind.

When a civilization goes so off the rails the children in it have no hope of being brought up with decency, God takes his vengeance. God's vengeance is His justice.

Elizebeth feels a nudge at her elbow and realizes she was chewing her fingernails. Leila hands Elizebeth a lit cigarette. She inhales deeply.

"We're going to get her," says Leila. "Your plan is flawless. Your work was flawless. Both of you."

Anna beams and also takes a cigarette.

"I'm confident in the work," says Elizebeth. "It's the elements out of our control that I'm worried about. The weather, the seas, Two-Gun, the pirate radio operator..."

"He's at least under our control," says Root. "We're paying him handsomely to be a double agent. As soon as he gives Marie the *XTAL* signal from the windmill, within the hour she'll be unloading the *Kid Boots* to her truck, under the watchful, waiting eyes of the T-Men and Sheriff Lehman."

Elizebeth wishes she could be there to see the utter shock

on Marie's face when she's trapped, when she realizes Elizebeth broke down the whole operation. Those days are over, however. Elizebeth will have to wait for court tomorrow, for Marie's preliminary hearing, to meet Marie's gaze and to flash a smile of triumph.

The radio phone crackles to life, and the women and men move closer. The air is hot, smoky, and tense. There are no windows open in their top-secret war room, and Florida in March is hot as summer in DC, even in the wee hours of the morning.

"The *XTAL* signal went out," says their radioman. "Do you have a visual?"

"Affirmative," says Harvey. "She's coming in from the Atlantic. No lights on, but good moonlight."

"Can you confirm the vessel name?"

"Negative. It's too dark, and it looks like there's something covering the name. But it's her. I'd know Spanish Marie anywhere."

Elizebeth and Leila look at each other and roll their eyes.

Sure, you would, Elizebeth thinks.

She can imagine the newspaper headlines now.

HARVEY "TWO-GUN" NABS THE INFAMOUS SPANISH MARIE, TAKING DOWN HER EMPIRE.

IT'S CHECKMATE FOR THE QUEEN OF THE RUMRUNNERS.

There won't be a word about Elizebeth or Anna or Leila

until it goes to court, and that's not guaranteed even then. The codebreaker in Elizabeth is fine with anonymity, even if her ego wants recognition. At least she'll always have the deciphering high and the knowledge of what she did. That will have to be enough.

The radioman indicates the other boats are also on course and gives the T-Men the signals on their radios to keep watch from their vantages on land. They also get in a message that the *Isabel*—Marie's decoy—has been intercepted in the Straits of Florida and, as anticipated, had no contraband, so it had to be allowed to continue on course.

The minutes tick on in what feels like endless silence, and Elizabeth's cotton dress clings to her back. If only she had her pitcher of water. A fan. Anything but these damned cigarettes she can't stop smoking.

Don't these people ever get thirsty? she thinks.

Once Marie makes land, it's unlikely they'll hear anything for a while. The T-Men can't exactly narrate the arrest of a potentially violent criminal, and the coasties will be busy confiscating liquor and boats.

"She's docking," comes Harvey's voice.

Elizabeth usually stays quiet, but she can't help herself. She pushes the radioman's shoulder.

"Tell them," she says, "once they get Marie, they must not allow that woman out of their sight."

"Of course, they won't," he says.

"Tell them."

The radioman looks at Root, who nods. The radioman leans in and transmits.

"Don't let her out of your sight."

"Of course," says Harvey. "Signing off. See you on the other side."

THIRTY-EIGHT

FLORIDA COAST

Marie

Marie feels like she holds her breath the whole way back from the Bahamas, especially running the last twelve miles, not only of this job, but of her career. Getting the *XTAL* signal and seeing the looming form of the windmill and the skyline of Miami Beach gives her brief relief, but motoring into Biscayne Bay, she can't help but think of Charlie's blue, bloated, bloody, eyeless body. The thought of him decomposing under these waters consumes her like a film she can't stop playing in her mind. Is there anything left, or is it all bones? Ribs with scarry fractures from heeled shoes. A spine with a blade nick in its neck. An empty rib cage because there is no heart and never has been. A skull, watching.

Memento mori.

Marie's hands sweat on the steering wheel.

She imagines Charlie's skull staring, grinning, beating her at her own game.

No, she thinks, shaking her head. *He did not beat me. No one has.*

The prim, almost prissy face of the codebreaker comes to mind.

And she never will, thinks Marie.

Her heartbeat steadies as she gets nearer to the blackest part of the shoreline, the darkened area of Coconut Grove that is her finish line.

Never again, she thinks.

She left her watch at home—no need to make a target of herself. She doesn't need a watch to know the time to stop is past due.

Marie's eyes strain through the blackness, and soon she sees the pilings, the empty slip, the outline of her truck.

Thank God.

Marie pulls herself to her full height, arranges her face in a scowl, wipes her sweaty palms on her dress, and goes to take a quick hit from her flask. She's surprised to find it empty. She doesn't remember drinking much of it. She slips it back in the drawer and docks the boat, bumping the piling harder than she would have liked and struggling with keeping the boat steady to tie her off. Sweating, she turns off the engine. Shortly, the man in the *Kid Boots* arrives and docks. They waste no time grabbing hams of whisky to start unloading. Her man in the truck hurries to help, and they form a short assembly line from sea to land.

On Marie's second trip to the hold, a sound that strikes horror in her freezes her. A heron must have been sleeping on a piling and awakens, startled. Its ugly squawk and the brush of its wings over her hair draw an involuntary scream from her.

Unbidden, a cluster of words, her lines from *Pericles, Prince of Tyre*, rise.

Quod me alit, me extinguit.

What feeds me, extinguishes me.

With that—with the bird—she knows.

Before the spotlight of the coast guard picket boat in the bay behind her floods the area, and that awful, gleeful, familiar voice comes over the megaphone.

Before the feds' and the sheriff's cars speed to a halt and throw on their headlights, and an arsenal of guns are pointed at them, and the arrest is announced, she knows they've got her.

The codebreaker has caught the rumrunner.

How? How? How? Marie thinks.

"Marie Waite, you are under arrest."

Elizebeth Friedman broke the code. She broke the unbreakable code.

"You have violated the federal prohibition amendment."

The feds bribed the radioman at the windmill.

Outnumbered, she puts up her hands in surrender. Roughly, she's frisked. They take the revolver from one garter and a knife from the other. They handcuff her.

Harvey "Two-Gun" and his men crawl all over her boats like insects. The coasties have their own assembly line of her alcohol— her retirement, her children's future—going. It's agonizing to watch.

Not one penny. I won't get one penny from this.

While her *Kid Boots* captain is loaded in one car, Sheriff Lehman drags her toward his car and pushes down her head, forcing her inside. Her truck lackey is pushed in the other side. He's a blubbering mess. He's illegal.

He can go to hell, she thinks. *He should have realized he was being followed and tipped me off.*

"This was quite an operation," the sheriff says, driving away from the dock.

The T-Men follow, one of them driving her truck.

All my vessels, commandeered.

She's feels like she's going to be sick.

"A fleet of boats," he continues. "Multiple landing sites. Two code systems."

Please, not the Isabel, *too.*

"You're in heap of trouble, little lady."

She clenches her teeth and her fists.

Think!

Queen Margaret's words from *Henry VI* come to mind.

We will not from the helm to sit and weep, But keep our course, though the rough wind say no.

Marie mulls, she considers, she plots the whole way to the police station. This can't be it. She cannot lose. She won't allow the codebreaker or any of them to dethrone her. She will abdicate on her own terms. To do so, she must give her greatest performance ever.

By the time they arrive at the police station, she has found tears. Wells of them. Geysers. She couldn't have imagined all she had inside that needed crying out.

On the way into the station, the men falter in their step, as she knew they would. They look at each other, worried creases in their foreheads, surprise in their eyes. They were told she was a gunslinging man-killer. They weren't prepared for a desperate mother.

"My children," Marie says over and over, gazing up from long, wet lashes at the deputy who escorts her. "Poor babies. Sleeping, innocent at home. I'm all they've got. They'll be orphans. You have to let me go."

Sheriff Lehman clenches his jaw and won't make eye contact with her. Her lackeys are taken away. She figures she'll never see them again.

Good riddance.

"It was Charlie," she says. "He abused me. He got us tangled up in this life. Then he got himself killed, and we were left with nothing. He gambled everything away. All the money, gone. Nothing but debt. My parents disowned me. My business—my good, legal business—failed, because of the hurricane. My children have nothing. No father, no money. I had to do this."

They book her, take her mug shot, and escort her to a holding cell crawling with drunks and prostitutes.

"Please, release me," she begs. "Let me go home and at least make sure my children are all right. See if my parents can keep them until this is over. Here."

She pulls a wad of cash from her brassiere and pushes it in the sheriff's hands. His eyes bulge. A prostitute whistles.

"What's bail?" Marie asks.

The sheriff sends his deputy away to find out. The kid returns with wide eyes.

"For you? They said three thousand dollars."

Marie swallows. She feels the blood drain out of her. She has four thousand. It's all the cash she has in the world. It will buy her time. There's hope. She still has her jewelry. Her watch. The *Isabel*. The houses in Miami and Cuba. She'll get it all back.

She nods.

She's let out.

The clerk's eyes practically bulge out of her head seeing Marie and the cash. The clerk is matronly, gray, and wrinkled, and she wears a cross necklace. Marie thinks she might be a parishioner at Gesú Catholic Church.

"You'll get all this back in a few hours," the clerk says. "Once you show up at court. Your preliminary hearing is at nine."

The clock over the clerk's head shows it's almost four in the morning. Marie feels suddenly exhausted. She nods.

The clerk hands her a receipt, but as Marie tries to leave, the clerk's hand shoots out and grabs Marie's wrist. Marie's eyes flash with anger at her.

"There she is," the clerk says with a devilish grin.

Taken aback, Marie yanks away her arm.

The clerk rifles through her purse until she finds a cocktail napkin. It's from Nora's Cabaret. The clerk leans in and whispers to her.

"May I have your autograph?"

THIRTY-NINE

MIAMI

Elizebeth

T he ticking of the courtroom clock—hour hand just passing the nine—is all she can hear.

Elizebeth didn't sleep a wink. She, Leila, and Anna stayed up all night, keeping up with the news, only going back to hotel rooms and homes to freshen up and return to court. Elizebeth found herself taking extra time with her appearance. She didn't want to look too prim, but all her clothes were wrong. If only she wore her linen pants set or had a uniform, but neither were possible, so she settled for a cool drapey hibiscus-pink knee-length dress, with long bow ties at the neck and waist. She paid a fortune for it, but now pale-faced, with dark circles under her eyes in the glaring Florida sun, in the heat of the courtroom, she feels like a wilting flower.

A crowd gathers outside the courtroom, including newspapermen, cameras flashing. There must be a rat for news to get out this fast. Their noise seeps in through the open windows.

What a circus, Elizebeth thinks.

Five past nine.

Elizebeth's gaze meets Leila's. They don't have to say anything to know what the other is thinking.

Earlier, when the coasties and the T-Men arrived at base and relayed all that happened—including the fact that Marie had been released to see to her children's care, on three thousand dollars' bail—Elizebeth groaned.

"What?" a T-man asked.

"We'll never see her again," Elizebeth said. "I told you, don't let her out of your sight!"

"Are you bats? Three thousand dollars? You think she'd leave that on the table?"

Elizebeth *knew* Marie would leave that on the table. The woman would never let herself get beat.

"Let me guess, she batted her teary eyelashes and played the mom angle?" Elizebeth said.

"She said she was all they've got."

The men looked at each other and then down at their shoes.

Elizebeth sighed in disgust.

"There's hope," Anna said. "Maybe she'll show. That is a lot of money. And her kids need a mom. Maybe she'll finally concede defeat."

No chance, Elizebeth thought.

Ten past nine.

Elizebeth feels agony rise. She could have a tantrum, a John Ramsay–sized explosion. Red-faced, she looks from Harvey, to Root, to Leila, to Anna.

Last night Root got back in touch with the picket boat who'd intercepted and released the *Isabel*. Elizebeth was frustrated to hear the coasties had not trailed the vessel.

"Why?" they asked. "There was no liquor onboard."

Why? Elizebeth thought, biting her tongue. *Why stay one step ahead? Why think for yourself?*

The only intelligence they could offer was that the *Isabel's* course appeared charted north, instead of west. North, closer to Key Largo, to Fort Lauderdale, to Miami. North, to deposit a getaway vessel in an easily reachable marina.

Quarter past nine.

Elizebeth could cry. She could scream. Of course, she can do neither.

Elizebeth leans close to Root.

"Put out the all-call to coast guard patrols between Florida and Cuba," she says.

"You read my mind," he says. "But you know, we can do nothing outside the twelve-mile zone."

"At least we'll know."

Root leaves, Harvey and his men following.

Twenty past nine.

Elizebeth looks up at the ceiling. Her shoulders fall in defeat.

The judge clears his throat.

"It doesn't appear the defendant will show, and the docket doesn't allow for delays. Sheriff Lehman, I'll issue an arrest warrant and a search warrant for her home. Clerk, alert the papers. Mention our fugitive is likely armed and presumed dangerous."

The bang of the gavel causes them all to flinch.

The matronly clerk's eyes gleam, clearly excited by the drama. She scurries away.

Elizebeth walks over to Leila, Anna trailing.

"Can we ask the sheriff to take us to her house?" asks Elizebeth.

"I wouldn't ask," says Leila. "He can't say yes to that. But we can follow in my car."

The sheriff leaves the courtroom.

"Let's go," says Elizebeth.

———

Cameras flash. Elizebeth raises her hand to cover her eyes. She, Leila, and Anna duck through the throngs, racing toward Leila's car. On the way they pause when a policeman announces to a growing group of spectators that he's making a gutter cocktail with Spanish Marie's contraband.

Police unwrap ham after ham, passing 560 cases of whisky, gin, beer, rum, and every other conceivable kind of liquor in an assembly line. The policeman at the end uses a hammer to smash each one into the street, where a river of booze soon flows toward the sewer, crowds cheering like mad, like Puritans at a witch burning.

The women look at each other, jarred, before Elizebeth shakes her head and pushes them forward, continuing on their mission. The sheriff is nowhere to be seen.

"You know her address, right?" asks Leila.

"Of course," says Elizebeth.

Leila pulls a pocket map out from the side of her seat, but Elizebeth shakes her head and taps the top of it with her finger.

"It's all in here."

Leila laughs, and takes off, Elizebeth giving directions the whole way.

"You could try to enter the races at Daytona Beach," Elizebeth says, clutching the door handle of the roadster.

"What makes you think I haven't already?" says Leila with a wink.

By the time they arrive at Marie's house, Elizebeth is impressed by Leila's driving, but nauseated. Through the windows, the women can see the sheriff and some deputies already searching inside. The women stay in the car, watching.

While her carsickness subsides, Elizebeth takes mental pictures, surveying the house and property. The flower gardens are the only real beauty. The home is gaudy and out of place on the street of smaller, more modest dwellings. Marie might have though this castle was fit for a queen, but Elizebeth finds it garish. Strangely, it makes Elizebeth feel sorry for Marie, but only for an instant before she dismisses the emotion and remembers who she's dealing with.

One of the deputies walks outside carrying two shotguns with tags. Without a word, Leila climbs out of the car and saunters toward him.

"What's she doing?" asks Anna.

"Using her charm to get us in, no doubt," says Elizebeth.

After a few moments, the man's cheeks turn red. Leila looks over her shoulder, a grin on her face, and beckons with her head. Elizabeth and Anna hurry to exit Leila's car and walk toward the house. Sheriff Lehman stops them at the door.

"This is a crime scene," he says.

"Sheriff," says Leila. "Is there a dead body or a criminal on the premises?"

"Well, no, but we can't have a parade through the house. We're collecting evidence."

"We won't touch a thing. Special Agent Friedman has to gather intelligence for the big boys in DC."

The sheriff looks Elizabeth over from head to toe. She removes her badge from her handbag. Seeing the flash of it wakes him up, and he nods.

Inside, the atmosphere feels strange, quivery, and unsettled, like the air before a thunderstorm. The women wander to various places, noting the cloying smell of rotting leaves, like a funeral parlor. It's coming from vases and vases of flowers at various stages of life. The arrangements are pretty, but also too much. The furniture is too much. There are big expensive pieces— white and brass and emblems—everywhere. The drapes on every window are too heavy, burgundy velvet like stage curtains. There are statues on pedestals—a mixture of Christian and pagan—as if Marie couldn't decide which God to worship.

Upstairs, the drawers of every dresser and bureau are open, spilling with clothing, some empty. The beds are unmade. The children must have been awoken in a hurry. Made to pack. The air is still charged from their frantic exit. In the girl's room, a blonde-haired, blue-eyed doll lies abandoned on the floor. It gives Elizebeth an ache in her heart to see it, to think of the child's unsettled life, her lost childhood, the constant turmoil. Elizebeth feels both judgment of and pity for Marie.

She's a desperate woman, Elizebeth thinks.

Unsettled by the doll's stare, Elizebeth leaves and walks down the hallway to the master bedroom. She pauses at the door, taking it all in. There's nothing of the man who once lived here. Charles Waite has been erased, without a trace. The oversized canopy bed is made—not slept in last night—and a large mahogany jewelry cabinet, with locks, is empty. There's a smashed plastic crown on the floor and a bullet hole in the wall. As Elizebeth walks over and touches the hole, the hair on the back of her neck rises. She's being watched.

Elizebeth turns and sees it. A skull stares out at her from a center shelf in the largest closet she has ever seen. In spite of the day's heat, she feels a chill. She walks toward it. Inside, dresses and what are clearly costumes are left in various stages of disarray, some slumped one-shouldered on hangers, others in glittery piles on the floor. On a high shelf are old playbills, facing out, mostly Shakespeare. Her heart lifts at the sight of them, her mind spinning in wonder.

Of course, Marie was an actress. She still is.

On the floor, dozens of expensive pairs of shoes face out, including the most exquisite two-toned heels Elizebeth has ever seen. They're ivory on top and aquamarine snakeskin on the bottom.

Elizebeth returns her attention to the skull. There's a piece of paper with handwriting sticking out from under it. Her heart races.

A noise at the door calls her attention, and Leila and Anna stand there.

Elizebeth turns back and reaches for the note. When she reads it, she finds herself laughing, shaking her head in spite of herself.

"What is it?" asks Leila.

"It's from *Hamlet*," says Elizebeth. "'There is nothing either good or bad, but thinking makes it so.'"

She looks up at the women.

"Checkmate," says Elizebeth.

"No," says Anna.

Elizebeth and Leila turn to regard her.

"Draw," Anna says. "For this game, for now, you both won."

FORTY

CUBA

Marie

Marie drives along the Malecón in the new Cadillac 314A. It's the color of the Bahía de la Habana, and Rogelio got it for her from his dealership for a steal. The American newspapers flutter from the passenger seat, headlines like "The Bootlegger Queen's Great Escape" and "The Queen of the Rumrunners at Large" winking up at her.

When she passes the statue of Isabel de Bobadilla, Marie nods. Her own *Isabel* is now *La Caridad*. She has been remade, a new vessel. Marie thought it would please her, but she misses the *Isabel*. The gaze of the statue Isabel is stern and stays with Marie, haunting her all the way home to Eden. She parks and holds the steering wheel for a moment, steadying herself. She has to do this more and more. She feels as if she's perpetually seasick. She can always recalibrate herself, but it takes more and more time and cocktails.

Josephine and Joey burst from the garden gate, startling Marie, trailed by their new nanny, Seleste—the florist's mother—a wrinkled, cigar-smoking crone with a blind eye. Joey is afraid of her but, like Marie, Josephine has taken to the woman who feels like a guardian.

Josephine carries springs of elderflower and slides one in Marie's hair, behind her ear. The girl stares at Marie's face with her large eyes, taking her mother's temperature as she always does. Unsettled, Marie looks away and leads the children into the back garden. On the way in, Joey plucks a grapefruit and peels and eats it right there, the juice sliding all over his chin. Seleste scolds him and wipes him with a dish towel, before going back inside to finish making dinner.

Marie goes to the bar to mix herself a cocktail. Her favorite bartender at Sloppy Joe's created the drink in her name, the Spanish Marie. Rum, apple liqueur, blue curaçao, and club soda. She thinks she'll sip it and watch the sunset until she's steady. Then she'll make plans.

But she can't relax. She can't find her sea legs. A film of faces— Red Shannon, Jimmy Alderman, Charlie, the codebreaker— haunt, possess, and obsess Marie.

Should I get an exorcism? Return to confession? Will I ever be free of them?

The codebreaker stole Marie's future. If it weren't for that woman, Marie wouldn't have had to return to criminal activity. Elizebeth Friedman forced Marie into this.

Do I haunt, possess, and obsess her? Marie wonders. She hopes so.

She tries to shake the codebreaker from her mind. Marie turns her thoughts to rumrunning. It would only take one good run, when enough time is past, and Marie could retire. Then, maybe she'd be a good mother.

What is good? What is bad? She was.

They are exiles. Their freedom has been constrained. Bitterness returns. She hates Elizebeth Friedman, and Charlie, and all those who forced Marie into this. She thought she'd be happy here, but the shadows inside that have trailed her for her whole life remain. She knows now they might never be gone.

Marie makes another cocktail. She reconsiders Rogelio's proposition. He has made contacts with American mobsters, a large syndicate operating all the way to New Orleans, that could be a shield for Marie and with whom her earning potential would greatly increase. Of course, making a deal with the devil means he will collect at some point, but by the next cocktail, Marie thinks it might not be such a bad idea, after all. It could give her another play at beating the codebreaker. It could help Marie's family really get on their feet. It could get them everything they never had and always wanted. Independence.

Marie walks to the pool's edge and sees her image in the water, fluid, changeable, dancing within a thousand facets of light. She recalls the broken mirror, the dark and light versions of herself, and her longing to join the two. They still haven't merged, but maybe that's impossible. Maybe she shouldn't even desire it. Maybe being fractured allows one to live as many lives as possible, to squeeze every last drop out of the short years one has on earth.

As Marie turns her gaze to the sunset, she feels her eyes

reflect the light. She imagines them turning from black to gold, red to indigo, golden beryl to sapphire. With every breath, she lifts her posture, increasing her stature. She feels like she's on a stage, illuminated before a rapt audience. She admits to herself that she should stop fighting the role for which she was made.

Marie is queen, after all. Even if she is in exile, she knows she will again rise.

AUTHOR'S NOTE

Both women won the game.

Elizebeth nabbed Marie. Marie got away.

Marie did not stay away from the game for long, however. I could devote another book to her return to smuggling. She married again and again. She was caught by Elizebeth and the Prohibition agencies again and again. Marie's rap sheet was long, but she always managed to wiggle out of trouble at the last minute. When she returned to Miami to live, she bought a garage and was featured—grinning ear to ear—in an article about being the only female mechanic in the area.

A turning point in her life was an alcohol-fueled physical altercation with her fourth husband, Leo Fritz, where he chased her and teenaged Josephine out of the house with a gun. Marie divorced Leo soon afterward, and while she continued to be featured in the newspapers, it was in articles highlighting her talents at flower arranging, women's group party hosting, charity and church work, and her daughter's busy debutante schedule.

While no one could ever agree on Marie's family origins, her eye color or height, the number of boats in her flotilla (up to fifteen were mentioned), whether or not she had Charlie killed, or even the ages of her children (sometimes Joey is listed older than Josephine), upon Marie's death (possibly in the 1970s), the consensus was that she had become a pillar of the community.

Elizebeth had a much cleaner ascent. In 1930, because of her outstanding work, she became the first woman to head an intelligence group: Coast Guard Unit 387. After the repeal of Prohibition, her work against smugglers continued, nabbing those working in illegal drugs and human trafficking. During WWII, Elizebeth continued cryptanalysis, cracking codes of German spies attempting to access the United States via South America, helping nab female Axis spy Velvalee Dickenson, and preventing at least one Allied ship in the Pacific from being blown out of the water. Elizebeth was also called in by General William S. Donovan to create code for the OSS. She found him brash and rude.

William Friedman's star also rose. In addition to his contribution to incredible developments in radio detection finders, during WWII his team at the Signal Intelligence Service broke the Japanese's "Purple" cipher, and his work led to the creation of the National Security Agency. Unfortunately, the strain on his mental health resulted in multiple nervous breakdowns. Elizebeth was always his rock, and she never resented taking time to care for her husband. In the 1950s, they were finally able to work together again on a definitive book debunking the theory that Bacon wrote Shakespeare's plays, and they won a prize for it. After a series of heart attacks, William died in 1969. Elizebeth died in 1980, at the age of eighty-eight. They are buried at Arlington National Cemetery.

FURTHER NOTES ON CHARACTERS AND HISTORY

Shortly after Elizebeth started Unit 387, Commander Root was hit by a car and died.

Commander Jack Wilson is the only main character who is purely fictional. For simplicity of story, I created him as a composite of several men.

Harvey "Two-Gun" Parry was real, and after being transferred to a base in New York, he went to jail for murdering a horse trainer who was allegedly having an affair with his wife.

Horace Alderman was hung at Base Six in Fort Lauderdale. It was a grisly affair done by men not used to enacting capital punishment and is the only hanging ever carried out by the coast guard.

Coastguardsmen don't typically hop between vessels for various missions. I had them do so to keep the cast of characters and vessels as tight as possible.

Cassie, the Friedmans' beloved nanny, died in 1929. Carlotta eventually left, once the children were older.

Benny Waite died earlier in the timeline than occurs in this novel. I chose the date to suit my story.

Beyond Leila Russell's job and the fact that she was a pilot, I could find little about her. I used what I knew and ran with it. The same can be said about Elizebeth's assistant, Anna Wolf, and Marie's and Charlie's parents and families.

I was fascinated to learn the origins of NASCAR and Daytona racing come from Prohibition. Bootleggers had to be highly skilled drivers, at very high speeds, to outrun the law.

I am not a biographer. I write fiction. There were many missing pieces and conflicting stories, so I did my best to be faithful to what I knew and let my imagination fill in the rest. I hope this novel inspires you to read more and do your own detective work. I'm including a selected bibliography to get you started.

SELECTED BIBLIOGRAPHY

Albritton, Laura, and Jerry Wilkinson. *Hidden History of the Florida Keys*. Charleston, SC: History Press, 2018.

Casey, Barbara. *Velvalee Dickinson: The "Doll Woman" Spy*. Rockhill, SC: Strategic Media Books, 2019.

Clark, Ronald. *The Man Who Broke Purple*. Boston, MA: Little Brown, 1977.

Dorr, Linda Lindquist. *A Thousand Thirsty Beaches: Smuggling Alcohol from Cuba to the South during Prohibition*. Chapel Hill, NC: University of North Carolina Press, 2018.

Ensign, Eric S. *Intelligence in the Rum War at Sea*. Washington, DC: Joint Military Intelligence College, 2001.

Fagone, Jason. *The Woman Who Smashed Codes*. New York: Dey Street Books, 2017.

Fisher, Jerry M. *The Pacesetter: The Complete Story of Carl G. Fisher*. Altona, Manitoba, Canada: Friesen Press, 2014.

Friedman, William F. and Elizebeth S. *The Shakespearean Ciphers Examined*. Cambridge, UK: Cambridge University Press, 1957.

Greenfield, Amy Butler. *The Woman All Spies Fear.* New York: Random House Studio, 2021.

Ling, Sally J. *Run the Rum In.* Charleston, SC: History Press, 2007.

Lyle, Katie Letcher, and David Joyner. *Divine Fire: Elizebeth Smith Friedman, Cryptanalyst.* Scotts Valley, CA: CreateSpace Independent Publishing Platform, 2015.

Lythgoe, Gertrude "Cleo." *The Bahama Queen.* Mystic, CT: Flat Hammock Press, 2006.

Mowry, David P. *Listening to the Rum Runners: Radio Intelligence during Prohibition.* Fort Meade, MD: National Security Agency, 2014.

Mundy, Liza. *Code Girls: The Untold Story of the American Women Code Breakers of World War II.* New York: Hachette Books, 2017.

Smith, G. Stuart. *A Life in Code: Pioneer Cryptanalyst Elizebeth Smith Friedman.* Jefferson, NC: McFarland & Company, 2017.

Thompson, Neal. *Driving with the Devil: Southern Moonshine, Detroit Wheels, and the Birth of NASCAR.* New York: Crown Publishing, 2006.

Van de Water, Frederic F. *The Real McCoy.* Mystic, CT: Flat Hammock Press, 2007.

Willoughby, Malcolm. *Rum War at Sea.* Washington DC: Treasury Department, U.S. Government Printing Office, 1964.

READING GROUP GUIDE

1. We get Elizebeth and Marie's perspectives throughout the book. Why is it important to include them both? Who is the "hero"? Are they both heroes?

2. What are your thoughts on Prohibition? Was it ever a good idea? Were the smugglers of alcohol true Robin Hoods or just criminals?

3. Elizebeth feels extreme pressure to be the representative of her gender, seeing as she's often the only woman in her chosen field, and surrounded by men. What kind of stress does this put on a person? What allowances are the majority given that the minority are not?

4. Marie comes from a life of poverty and desperately yearns to be rich. Do you understand her motivations? Would you do anything to be rich or, in other words, to *not* be in poverty again?

5. Marie quickly gains a reputation as "Spanish Marie" with a false image of her disseminating into the public. How important is it, how others perceive you? How much control do you have over your own image?

6. There are many misconceptions about women during this time period that hurt the women in the story. The coast guard doesn't believe a woman could helm a smuggler's ship; similarly, no one believes a woman could fly a plane or work as a codebreaker. How do misconceptions and stereotypes like these affect women in the modern world?

7. There are interesting superstitions about boats, such as women and bananas being bad luck. Do you have any odd superstitions?

8. Elizebeth tries to balance being a mother, a wife, and a working woman. What advantages does she have in a supportive husband? What difficulties might contemporary women face in Elizebeth's situation?

9. Elizebeth and William help each other throughout the novel. Compare their relationship to Marie and Charlie's. What do Elizebeth and William do for each other that Marie and Charlie don't?

10.   Marie realizes at multiple points that she could simply take the money she has and leave the smuggling business. What do you think stops her?

11.   Elizebeth shares the company and friendship of many women, including Leila and Anna, while Marie reflects that she's never had good female friends. How do you think these friendships (or lack thereof) impact Elizebeth and Marie? How do Elizebeth's relationships impact her job and ability to work?

12.   In what ways do you think Elizebeth's and Marie's lives impact their children? How much influence do parents have over how their children grow up and what they grow to be?

A CONVERSATION WITH THE AUTHOR

This novel had quite a cast of characters, the smugglers being a colorful bunch. Were any of the rumrunners and their antics real, or were they mostly fiction?

I'm delighted to report that most of the rumrunners and their antics—and horrors—were real. My imagination isn't vivid enough to come up with babies on rumrunning vessels, human arms in sharks—identified via fingerprints—and radio messages for lost glass eyeballs. Truth is always stranger than fiction.

You made a return to your favorite past fictional setting: Key West, brought to life in your previous novel, *Hemingway's Girl.* What drew you back?

Aside from almost yearly trips there with my husband to our favorite haunts—the Hemingway Home and Museum, Judy Blume's bookstore: Books and Books, Mallory Square, Sloppy Joes, and seaplane rides to the Dry Tortugas—finding out the Waites' connection to Key West made returning there in this novel a no-brainer. When I realized the time period was just before my novel *Hemingway's Girl* started, I was even able to weave in my fictional protagonist Mariella Bennet and her family, the origin of Sloppy Joe's bar, and Hemingway's home before he and his second wife, Pauline, bought it. The Easter eggs are there for those who have read *Hemingway's Girl* but aren't necessary to understand if one hasn't.

Why did you choose to write the book with both Elizebeth's and Marie's perspectives? How did you decide when to switch perspectives and what to show?

This is my third novel using women protagonists as foils for each other, and it's one of my favorite structures because of the natural suspense it creates tacking between the two.

I was going to write from only Elizebeth's perspective, but I became so enthralled with Marie's story and trying to understand her that I felt she deserved her own chapters. I was surprised to find that my protagonist's arc took her to a colder place, where she learned to compartmentalize her intelligence work and detach herself in arguably necessary ways from her personal life, while my antagonist experienced a growth in empathy toward her children, especially her daughter, and movements toward personal growth, though she certainly doesn't come to fullness in this arena. That's why I kept coming back to the line about *What is good? What is bad? She was.* We are all so complicated.

What do you hope readers take away from Elizebeth and Marie's story?

I want readers to see that—for better or worse—we get what we choose, that walking the line between darkness and light is a balancing act, and that addiction to control can be deadly.

If we use our powers for good, we are capable of anything. If we use our powers for evil, we are capable of anything.

What are you working on right now?

Real women in American intelligence and war history continue to fascinate me, and I'm always astounded by both their incredible stories and the fact that so many of them still remain in the shadows. I have found another remarkable, resilient, and daring—to the point of reckless—woman from history. I can't wait to share her story with readers.

ACKNOWLEDGMENTS

I'm so fortunate to be a published writer, to have such readers, to have such love... I don't ever take it for granted, and I thank God every day for showing me these stories and for blessing me with the opportunity to share them.

To my literary agent, Kevan Lyon, thank you for helping me navigate the waters of publishing and for your guidance. You are a treasure.

To my editor, publisher, and team at Sourcebooks—Shana Drehs, Dominique Raccah, Valerie Pierce, Anna Venckus, Cristina Arreola, Molly Waxman, Diane Dannenfeldt, Jessica Thelander, Kavita Wright, the designers, and everyone—thank you all for believing in me and my books, for being my publishing partners, and for all of your hard work. I am honored and grateful.

To Ellen McCarthy—you first brought Elizebeth Smith Friedman to my attention, and you have encouraged and supported me through the Amazing Women of the Intelligence Community. You are not only a mentor, but an inspiration and a friend.

To Heather Adams, thank you for reading my work and for also telling me about the fabulous Elizebeth Smith Friedman, helping to inspire this journey.

To Melissa Davis, director of the George C. Marshall Foundation, thank you for your remote assistance with the Friedman papers and for your permission to use the quote in the epigraph from "A Cryptanalyst," *Arrow* (February 1928), Box 12, Folder 9, 531–34, ESF Collection.

To the staff of the National Archives in Washington, DC.

To Robert J. Simpson and Dr. Vincent J. Houghton at the National Cryptological Museum.

To W. David Joyner, co-author of *Divine Fire*, for granting me access to the text.

To William H. Thiesen, PhD, Atlantic Area historian, U.S. Coast Guard; Cori Convertito, PhD, curator and historian, Key West Art and Historical Society; and Chad Robuck, marine inspector, U.S. Coast Guard, for all of your CG protocol and location guidance. Any mistakes in the text are my own.

To my father, Robert Shephard, and my in-laws, Richard and Patricia Robuck, for all of your love, care, and constant enthusiasm for my work.

Finally, to my dear family—my husband, Scott, and my three sons. I love you all so much. Thank you for your support, inspiration, and enduring patience with my historic obsessions.

ABOUT THE AUTHOR

Erika Robuck is the national bestselling author of nine novels, including *Hemingway's Girl* and *The Invisible Woman*. A former teacher, Robuck was named Annapolis's 2014 Author of the Year, and she resides there with her husband and three sons.